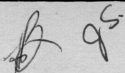

"We can't go on like this."

Even as she spoke, Shelly felt her resistance vanishing like smoke obliterated by the wind.

"I know," Justin agreed silkily. "Something's got to give. Preferably your clothing." He leaned forward, inserted a finger in the neck of her blouse and popped open a snap. The sound crackled through her like lightning.

"Justin, no." She caught his arm with one hand. With the other, she groped for the car door handle.

He captured both her hands and brought them to his mouth to carefully kiss each of her fingers. "Shelly, yes." He sounded amused, faintly mocking.

"I must go," she said weakly, but she was trapped by her needs, needs that had been fed all evening by the sight, scent and feel of him.

"I'd like to say that I wouldn't stop you if you went right now...but I'd be lying," Justin said. Then he added, more soberly, "unless you convince me that's what you really want."

"No," she said, despite herself. "I want to stay."

ABOUT THE AUTHOR

A prolific author of both contemporary and historical fiction, Shirley Larson first came to the attention of romance readers when she published as Shirley Hart. Married to her high school sweetheart and the proud mother of three, Shirley lives on a beautiful parcel of land in upstate New York.

Honor Bound

SHIRLEY LARSON

Harlequin Books

TORONTO • NEW YORK • LONDON
AMSTERDAM • PARIS • SYDNEY • HAMBURG
STOCKHOLM • ATHENS • TOKYO • MILAN

FORTY YEARS OF
Romance

Published August 1989

First printing June 1989

ISBN 0-373-70368-6

Printed in U.S.A.

CHAPTER ONE

THE FIRST CLUE Justin Corbett had that something was wrong with his father was the night he came home and found Strom sitting alone in the library with the lights off. Stromberg Corbett was a man of action, not given to solitary reflections in the dark.

Justin snapped on the lights and stared at his father, unease flickering at the edges of his mind. "Dad? What are you doing sitting here looking like you've lost your last friend?"

His father blinked and just that quickly, the blank, bleak look on his face vanished. He was once again himself—brusque, defensive. "I might ask you the same thing."

More comfortable now that Strom had assumed the familiar role of antagonist, Justin casually strolled into the room, pulling his shirt out of his trousers. Strom frowned at his son's laid-back style. Strom was dressed for bed, but his robe was velvet, the belt tied in an elegant square knot at his waist.

Shirttails flapping, Justin lifted a lean hand and pushed back a strand of golden hair from his forehead. The June night had turned hot and sticky, and he felt the need to get out of his clothes and jump into the pool. He would do that, as soon as he found out what was wrong with his father. "Let's just say the prenuptial double entrendres got a little thick. I thought Paul would enjoy himself more at his bachelor party if his big brother took off."

"How was the movie?"

Son looked at father with a bland expression that mirrored Strom's own control. Justin had learned the lesson of detachment at his father's knee. "Predictable. Very predictable."

"X-rated flicks seem juvenile to you now, do they?"

"Yeah. What are you drinking?"

Strom Corbett looked down at the glass in his hand as if he had forgotten its existence. "Bourbon. Want some?"

"No, thanks. I had my quota at the party." Justin hid his surprise. His father rarely drank alone, and his taste usually ran to a good white wine. This second bit of uncharacteristic paternal indulgence upgraded Justin's unease to apprehension.

He threw himself down into the leather chair across from his father and hooked a leg over the rounded arm. Strom was a formidable opponent, canny and determined, his skills honed by years of political maneuvering. But the past three years of Justin's life spent as the assistant district attorney in Jefferson County had taught him a trick or two.

Justin sprawled over the chair, his back as supple and relaxed as a cat's. "What are you doing sitting here alone in the dark drinking?"

"I'm not drinking. I'm ... thinking."

Justin pondered the words, his apprehension increasing. "Is it bothering you that your youngest son is getting married?"

Strom's eyes filled with a mocking exasperation Justin knew well. "Why should that bother me? At least one of my sons is giving me a chance at having some grandchildren before I die. All you produce are convictions.''

Attack and counterattack. He'd expected it. Settling in for the fight, he said, ''One of these days, I'll get married, just to surprise the hell out of you. A year later, I'll produce a squalling progeny. Maybe with luck, the little beggar can spit up on your suit.''

Strom scowled. ''Is that all you care about? Your Hart, Shaffner and Marx suit? I've surely done a hell of a bad job raising you if your values are that skewed...''

Justin's half smile clung to his lips, but his tone was cool as he said, ''I was talking about your suit, not mine. Children are a big responsibility, one I'll be ready to take on only when I meet a woman strong enough to spend the rest of her life with me.''

Mollified, Strom sat back on his chair. ''Nothing wrong with being cautious about choosing a life mate in this day and age.'' He paused. ''*Are* you being cautious? I see your picture in the paper with a new woman every month.''

''You've been in politics too long, Dad. You're exaggerating to make your point.''

''Not by much, by Zeus.''

Justin's green eyes met his father's hazel ones. ''What do you want me to do, pick one by lottery and marry her within the year?''

Strom's eyes stayed locked with Justin's. ''Would you if I asked you to?''

''No.'' Strom grunted as if he'd already known the answer. Justin favored his father with a long, examining look. ''Why don't we can the wedding talk and get to what's really bothering you.''

''What's really bothering me?'' Strom canted a disbelieving eyebrow. ''Do you care?''

The unjust accusation disturbed Justin, but he kept his face calm, his voice cool. The best weapon in his father's armory was induced guilt. "I asked, didn't I?"

Strom stared past Justin at the wall that housed the trophies of his life. "It bothers me that I'm getting old and I've accomplished so damned little."

Relieved and amused, Justin smiled. He was no longer puzzled by what was bothering his father. This was an old theme, the theme of dedication to work, service to others, a life worth living. A perfect life as set out by Stromberg Corbett, a man of many parts. It was a speech Justin heard often, usually directed at himself. It was a new experience to hear his father's verbal self-flagellation.

"What's so funny?"

In one lithe movement, Justin hoisted himself out of the chair and leisurely walked to the fireplace on the opposite side of the room from the desk. "Let's see. We have on this wall several tokens of the life that has been singularly undistinguished with lack of accomplishments. Here, under glass in a small black frame, we have your commendation from the president in gratitude for pushing his health-care bill through the House of Representatives. Below it is a plaque from the Rotary Club to you as the outstanding citizen of Glenville. On the other side, a commendation from the League of Women Voters for thirty years of public service as a congressional representative. Then we come to your Congressional Medal of Honor and your Purple Heart . . ."

"Anybody who was in the service and got a sliver in his backside got a Purple Heart," Storm growled—and flinched, as if he had been stabbed by a severe pain.

Genuinely alarmed, Justin dropped his teasing mockery and studied Strom, his green eyes traveling over his father's face. "What is it? Are you in pain?"

"Damn it to hell, it's nothing, just a little...indigestion I've been having."

"Have you seen a doctor?"

"No." At the look on Justin's face, Strom shook his head. "Don't start in on me, not tonight. I'm not that stupid. I've got an appointment with Jim Treadwell next week."

Guilt poured afresh through Justin. He'd spent little or no time with his father lately. He'd been too busy establishing his law career in Rochester. He'd thought his father was as impervious to aging as the Rock of Gibraltar. It shocked him to discover that Strom was human enough to experience pain. That his father was made of steel was a childish illusion, Justin knew, but one his father had fostered carefully.

On the infrequent occasions Justin had been with Strom lately, he hadn't really looked at him. He was looking now. He didn't like what he saw. "You'd better not fly in the air show until you get a clean bill of health from Treadwell."

Eyes as sharp as glass shot up to Justin. "I may be having heart trouble, but it hasn't affected my brain. I know better than to go up in an airplane when I'm feeling like this."

Justin's eyes darkened. "So it isn't just...indigestion."

Strom made a sound of disgust. "I have all the classic symptoms of heart disease."

"If you haven't been to a doctor, how do you know?"

"The same way I find out anything I don't know. I went to the library and got a book."

"You had time to do that but you didn't have time to go to the doctor?"

Strom scowled at his cool, logical son who stood giving him cool, logical rebuttals. "I like to know what I'm getting into before I leap in feetfirst. Besides, I wanted to wait until after the wedding. No use upsetting Paul unnecessarily."

Justin shook his head. "Unnecessarily? Suppose you have an attack in the middle of his wedding?"

"I won't."

Justin experienced a mixture of exasperation, admiration and understanding. "You'll keep from it by sheer force of will, I suppose."

"Damn right. Any man worth his salt can exercise control over his body. And he'd better, if he expects to get ahead in life." Strom examined Justin through suddenly narrowed eyes. "Have you thought any more about declaring your candidacy for district attorney?"

"No."

"Why not? Afraid of the competition?"

"No. I'm just not sure I want the job."

His father made a sound of disgust. "How long are you going to go on playing second fiddle? I thought I brought you up to want more out of life than grunting along as an assistant district attorney."

As Justin stared at his father, he mentally viewed a kaleidoscope of memories. He was five again, standing beside a whirling, brightly lit merry-go-round, crying, not wanting to go on the big noisy turning thing. His father was picking him up and putting him on it, his mother, white-faced, was watching. Afterward, when he staggered off and his rebellious stomach emptied itself on the dusty ground, his mother had talked to his father in a low, furious voice. The sound of it had made him feel better in a way he didn't understand then. Later, he did. In the few remaining years of her life, his mother had often tried to stand between her oldest child and her perfectionist husband. Sometimes she succeeded and sometimes she didn't. Justin had learned that his best was never good enough. Yet he'd never hated his father for expecting too much of him. Childlike, he'd simply thought he was inadequate. It had taken many years for him to understand that far from being inadequate, he had skills, understandings and abilities which enabled him to excel both physically and mentally. But whatever honors he had gained with his swimming or his academic prowess, it was never quite good enough. It had been many more years before he'd learned to forgive his father for expecting perfection—and himself for not delivering it.

Justin studied his father with mingled love and annoyance. The best defense with Strom was a good offensive. "When is your appointment?"

"What? Oh. Monday morning at ten o'clock."

"I'll go with you," Justin said, waiting for his father to sputter and tell him it wasn't necessary.

Strom Corbett met his son's gaze unflinchingly. "I'd appreciate that."

In his bedroom, later, Justin couldn't guess what it had cost his father to admit he needed him. He frowned, shucked off his shoes and lay down on the bed just as he was, partially clothed, battle ready. He couldn't forget his father's bleak face, his listless hands. With a feeling of foreboding, he'd left the door of his room open. Tomorrow, wedding or not, he'd have a word with Morley. Chances were Morley already knew.

He stared into the darkness, trying to empty his mind, but the lingering guilt remained. His father's condition hadn't appeared overnight. How long had Strom been having pain? And how long would this infernal weekend be before his brother's wedding was over and he could get his father to Treadwell?

Echoing memories of how he'd felt when he lost his mother flashed into his mind. He'd been nine when his lovely and apparently healthy mother had been rushed to the hospital one morning and diagnosed with cancer. A week after his tenth birthday, she'd died.

He was thirty-two now, a man. Yet the thought of losing his father was unbearable. He could—and would—see to it Strom went to the doctor, took the necessary medication, had the necessary surgery, if it was required. Medical science worked wonders these days, that is, if the patient cooperated. He would have to see to it that Strom accepted help. He would not allow his father to pigheadedly play Russian roulette with his own life.

CUMULUS CLOUDS FLOATED over Corbett Hill, tantalizing Shelly Armstrong. Those clouds meant thermals and thermals meant good soaring weather. An August sun cast a golden sheen on the green pastures of the horse country in Western New York, making it a perfect day to take the sailplane up and discover the secrets in that late summer sky. Instead, she was going to Paul Corbett's wedding.

"I know what's going through your mind," her father, Mel, said as she pulled the car onto the grass in front of the mansion where other wedding guests had parked.

"Thinking too loud again, was I?"

Mel smiled in that easy, slow way he had. "'Fraid so." Typically Mel, he leaned back and watched while she shut off the engine and took the keys from the ignition.

"All right, I'll bite. What am I thinking?"

"You're thinking it's a shame to waste those clouds."

"You're a genius, Dad." She swung an arm over the seat and flashed him a smile. He was something to smile at, dressed to the nines for his old friend Strom's son's wedding, tall, loose-limbed and as slender as he'd been forty years ago when he was a World War II pilot flying missions over Germany.

"Nobody wants you to win that competition more than I do." For a moment his eyes gleamed with the fire that thinking about flying always ignited in their blue depths. "Nobody will be prouder of you than me when you win."

When you win. Not if you win, but when you win. A quiver of nervousness touched her. These days, now that Mel was grounded because of his health, his love of flying was channeled through her with an intensity that frightened her just a little. It was hard to live up to somebody else's dream.

"I'll do my best." As she moved to get out of the car, he caught her arm. "You always have, Shelly. And I appreciate that. I also appreciate your coming here today. I know you didn't want to come."

"Nonsense, of course I wanted to come." She felt strangely self-conscious, and wanted badly to lighten the mood. If she was going to storm Corbett Hill successfully, she needed her wits about her for these next few hours.

As if he sensed her unease, Mel released her arm and said in a lighter tone, "Well, I suppose we'd better get at it, then."

Shelly smiled. Only her father would speak of a wedding as a chore to be done. "I suppose we had." She swung a long, shapely leg sheathed in nylon to the grass. For Mel's sake she'd donned standard wedding guest regalia: faux silk dress, hose and heels. But the dressy clothes felt hot and confining. She'd give a great deal to be back at Eagle Hill, listening to Pat complain about having to work on Saturday and wriggling into her flight suit in preparation for heading up for a sky sail.

Gracing the mansion door was a grapevine wreath interlaced with pink and white roses and fluttering satin ribbons, a proclamation of the festival of marriage. Shelly slipped her elbow under her father's arm to support him, she told herself. But a quiet little voice reminded her that maybe, just maybe, she needed her father's strength as much as he needed hers. Or more.

It was all still here, everything she'd wanted as a teenager and couldn't have: the house on the hill with its kingly view and Grecian pillars; the white fences; the luxurious pastures with the costly horses. She didn't envy the Corbetts their wealth. She had envied them their stability, their solidness, their—belonging. How she'd wanted to belong as they belonged.

Rites of passage. How did a woman know when she was fully grown? Did she reach maturity when she was able to recognize the difference between fantasy and reality? Her fantasy had been that someday she would belong here. The reality was that she never had—and never would.

Once Shelly had stood on the porch of Corbett Hill and hated everything she was. All she ever wanted in the world was to be like the Corbetts. Now she thought of that eager, needy young girl who came every Saturday to take flying lessons from Justin Corbett and felt nothing but a fleeting sadness. She'd had a certain vivaciousness and love of life, that teenager, even though she'd been shoved around the countryside from pillar to post from the time she was old enough to walk.

She'd been a million places and she'd never belonged in any of them. She'd spent her childhood trailing around the country after her restless father until she was sixteen. By the time Mel finally settled down on Eagle Hill, Shelly had learned that to travel cheap meant to travel light.

There wasn't a dish in their cupboard that had been there the year before. There were no grade school report cards, no photograph albums, no treasured letters from bosom buddy girlfriends. Sentimentality was excess baggage she couldn't afford. By the time they'd settled into the soaring school Mel bought, and her dreams of a stable homelife had came true, it was too late for her. She'd lived in twenty-four of the fifty states, and she'd gained a street-wise savvy, a dislike for depending on anybody but herself, and a sense of humor that hid her vulnerability. She also had a fierce pride. She'd have died before she'd ever have let anybody know how much she envied the people on Corbett Hill.

The door opened and her thoughts of the past fled. Morley looked only a fraction more wrinkled, a hair or two more gray than when she'd last seen him. The man who prided himself on his instant recall of any twice-come guest to Corbett Hill knew her immediately. With no more than a flare of the pupils in his pale blue eyes betraying his surprise, he said, "Hello, Miss Armstrong, Mr. Armstrong. Won't you come in? We are congregating in the library before the wedding. Shall I take your wrap?"

She handed her lacy white shawl to Morley with a distinct feeling that even though she was twenty-eight years old, he saw her as a little girl playing at dress up. She had avoided coming to Corbett Hill during the past ten years, even during the traditional Christmas night fêtes that her father loved. She'd come today because Mel had asked her to. And because at last, after ten years, she'd felt strong enough to resist the siren pull of Corbett Hill.

Now it seemed as if she'd never left, as if she'd just walked onto the porch, breathlessly anxious to collect Justin to get to her flying lesson, only to be nicely set down by Morley. He always had the power to intimidate her. She'd retaliated by bedeviling him. Her partner in crime had been Justin. But Justin wasn't beside her—and those days were long gone.

Morley's gaze flickered over her bare shoulders, an incredible lapse of good manners for him. She was wearing a sapphire-blue dress with swirling skirt and an elasticized neckline that she had, in an attempt to remain marginally cool, lowered to the legal limit. The puffed sleeves rode uselessly halfway between her shoulder and her elbow. Encouraged, Shelly looked into Morley's eyes, amusement in hers. Without blinking, she raised her hand to her sleeve and nudged it another inch lower on her arm.

So much for being grown up. The habit of trying to shock Morley had returned as naturally as breathing.

He didn't say a word, but the expression on his face was eloquent enough to fill Shelly with a real need to chuckle. He ducked his head in a sketchy bow and walked away, disapproval of her bare flesh etched on every muscle of his spare body. Morley had had quiet spasms the year Strom had put in the pool and bikini-clad females of all ages began appearing at the house, drawn by the charm of the Corbett brothers. Morley believed clothes were a statement of the man—or woman—inside them. A scuffed shoe revealed a black heart. Wanton clothes, or lack of them, exposed a wanton soul.

Morley wasn't the only one Shelly had rebelled against instinctively. What if she lapsed into old habits when she saw Justin?

She lifted her head and followed her father into the library, her heels clicking on the polished oak floor, reminding her not to worry, she was grown up now. And so was Justin.

Male friends her father shared with Strom Corbett pounded Mel Armstrong on the back and drew him into conversation, lapsing into fly-boy talk about the coming air show. Caught in the grip of nostalgia, she gazed around the room as the sound of their voices drifted to the edge of her consciousness.

The walnut Victorian library table held a fluted glass dish of mints and nuts, just as it always had. The teen-aged Shelly had viewed that bit of luxury as the ultimate in high-class wealth. She could hardly imagine having enough money to have sweets sitting out every day of the year. The tidbits of food had impressed her more than the rare, unaffordable Tiffany lampshade that hung above the table glowing with red, pink and blue flowers.

A few minutes later, Morley, head bowed in reverent dedication to his task, rolled back the double doors to reveal the huge living room. A bower stood at the far end, a white-latticed affair covered with white carnations and sprigs of baby's breath, an altar for the bridal couple. Her arm linked in Mel's, Shelly walked toward the back row of chairs and sat down next to her father.

When the processional began, Shelly rose with the rest of the guests and watched as Paul and two young males she didn't know lined up outside the bower, faces turned expectantly toward the bridal aisle. Justin should have been Paul's best man, but he wasn't there. She felt a flicker of disappointment. Where was he?

The rustle of lace and satin announced that the bride was coming down the aisle. At her side was Justin. He was giving the bride away. Shelly caught a fleeting glimpse of him as he went by, but one glimpse was enough to tell her that ten years of maturity had only made his attraction more potent.

Justin was a blonde the sun loved. His skin glowed a coppery bronze; in striking contrast, his hair was new-minted gold layered over strands of wheat. The last three years in the prosecuting attorney's office hadn't blunted the fine edge of his swimmer's body. He was still tall and sleek as a tiger.

During his high-school days, he'd been good enough at swim speed racing that Strom had talked of sending him to the Olympics. But when Justin graduated from high school, he'd discovered aerobatic flying and was no longer interested in spending the long hours in the water necessary for training. His father had sputtered, but in the end, he'd been eager to see Justin fly as well as he swam. Justin had, of course, justified his father's faith in him, winning competition after competition in aerobatic meets.

Did Justin swim in the Corbett Hill pool for pleasure now? She doubted it. When would he have the time? He was either in the courtroom or in his plane. Besides, she could never remember Justin doing anything simply for pleasure. His goal was ever and always to win. Even now, a restless energy burned in him like a bright flame as he handed the bride over to Paul and backed up gracefully to sit down.

When the ceremony ended, Shelly waited in line to greet the bridal couple. Paul's face was flushed. Man-like, he looked relieved that the formality of the cere-mony was over. Her turn came, and she shook Paul's hand and kissed Kim, the bride. As she pulled away, the edge of the filmy sequined veil Kim wore caught in Shel-ly's long red-gold hair.

"Allow me," a familiar voice said, and she felt Jus-tin's hand gently disentangling her from the bridal lace.

Heat rose from deep inside her. Justin's fingers had always been long, slim, incredibly sexy. She remembered them hovering over a clipboard, checking off the mistakes she'd made in an aerobatic routine, adjusting her grip on a horse's reins, pulling her arm back to get the proper angle for swimming. In those two years between her sixteenth and eighteenth birthday, he'd taught her everything—except how to forgive him for having all the things in life she wanted most.

She lifted her chin. Green eyes slammed into hers. *He looks stressed, drawn out,* she thought, disturbed. *Where's that young daredevil I used to know?*

A little frisson of shocked surprise coursed through her, as if Justin Corbett had no right to suffer burnout when she wasn't around to talk him out of it. There were deeper lines on the side of his mouth and his skin was more finely drawn across the good Corbett facial bones. Was it really his high-powered career exacting a toll? Or was there something else bothering him? It seemed impossible that Justin Corbett couldn't handle anything life threw at him. Still, believing that he was invincible might be a hangover from her youth, when she'd been certain Justin could do anything in the world there was to do.

Despite his lean, pantherish look—or because of it—the promise of pagan attraction in the boy had been fulfilled in the man. The civilized gray tuxedo with its satin lapels did nothing to dispel the primitive appeal of a body as hard and lean as his face, pared down to the essential line of muscle and bone. A swimmer's body. A man's body.

"Hello, Red. Keeping your nose clean?"

With those old familiar words, and that smile, he made her feel sixteen again and filled her with that hunger she had nearly banished from her life, that violent yearning to be something she wasn't.

Silly to let him push the old buttons. She wasn't sixteen anymore. She lifted her chin. "It's really true, isn't it? Some things never change."

"Meaning in my case it's a damn shame?" He shrugged as if physically sloughing off her gibe. He always could turn aside her jabs with his self-deprecating, so-what-the-hell-you-got-me-on-that-one humor. She'd forgotten what a curious mixture he was of pride and self-mockery. He understood why she didn't believe in his charming golden-boy persona; he didn't believe in it, either. "The Tibetans think nothing should ever change. Maybe I should go to Tibet. I must admit though...I like the scenery around here." He kept those sea-green eyes on her face but she felt exposed, conscious of the bodily differences he had cataloged in her just as she had in him. "I may be the same, but you didn't return the favor. I remember you as a scruffy, red-haired kid with a permanent splotch of oil on her nose." His eyes gleamed, watching for her reaction to his teasing.

She ignored those mischief-making eyes. "I took a bath before I came today."

"We're honored." Her eyebrows lifted at the echo of royal "we" that was Morley's favorite. He grinned, and the years fell away as if they had never happened. Somehow they'd shifted instantly into the groove they'd once shared—he teasing her unmercifully, then shifting like lightning to her side. "In more ways than one. Your presence on Corbett Hill is a stellar event. You've been a stranger for too long. Save some time for me during the reception so we can talk."

"I'll look forward to it," she answered coolly, grateful that the crush of people behind her made it necessary for her to withdraw her hand from his grasp and walk on.

"No more than I," he murmured to her back, bringing small, prickling nerves to life. She hadn't expected to walk away from Justin with the zing of a man-woman confrontation racing through her veins. She didn't like the feeling.

She was borne along with the crowd through the patio doors to the backyard pool and the pink-and-white striped tent awning set up behind the house to ward off the blazing sun. The tent flaps thumped in the west wind that was habitual on the hilltop. Next to it, the Olympic-sized swimming pool that Strom had blasted out of hill rock, to provide his talented son with a place to practice, quivered in the wind, shimmering with the promise of cooling relief. Picturing how high Morley's eyebrows would climb made the thought of jumping in fully clothed a wonderful idea.

Shelly headed for the bar that had been set up under the tent, thinking she would capture a cool drink—rope and hogtie it if she had to—and then search for Mel. She'd gotten separated from him in the receiving line.

A young man in a white jacket serving champagne spotted her looking longingly at his tray, smiled and handed her a tall flute. She drank thirstily, then turned to look for Mel. He was at the other end of the tent, his head bent toward one of his flying buddies.

There certainly must be something to the camaraderie of soldiers, Shelly thought. After years of wandering, her father had finally settled on top of a natural soaring hill thirty miles south of Strom's high place on the world. Mel had been accepted immediately into the group Strom Corbett called friends. Their center of action was an old airplane hangar outside of Glenville that Strom was trying to establish as an air museum. The group had bought one of the few B-17s left in the world and housed it at the hangar. They felt the plane was worthy of being the center of a museum.

Mel was equally enthusiastic about the project. Whenever there was a fund-raising dinner spearheaded by Strom, Mel was there beside him. This amazed Shelly, since Mel wasn't gregarious like Strom. Nor did he normally travel in the same circles as the gentleman horse breeder, wheeler-dealer Congressman Strom Corbett. Yet Shelly had unwrapped presents under the Corbett Christmas tree, drunk eggnog on New Year's Eve from the Corbetts' cut-glass punch bowl, and fought with Paul and Justin over the Easter eggs hidden on the manicured Corbett lawn.

Still remembering old times, she wandered toward her father and the ring of cronies gathered around the punch bowl. Distracted by trying to keep her high heels from catching in the lawn and balancing her champagne glass, she walked blindly into a solid wall of gray tuxedo. "Oh, excuse me—"

Lean hands reached out and grasped her bare shoulders to steady her on her high heels. She stood struggling with a sudden and surprising infusion of warmth from Justin's hands and from the sea-green eyes glinting down at her.

Time hovered. The tent flapping was the beat of her heart. Each warm finger of Justin's clasped her bare flesh with a textured weight all its own. She tasted salt in her mouth, the wind teased her hair into a thousand tiny feathers along her cheek. Entrapped in a sensate world unlike any she'd known, she tilted her chin up and tried a smile. "You must be the on-the-premises, one-man rescue squad. I must say you're doing your job well."

"We aim to please." His grin was devilish.

"Who is this 'we'? Do you have a mouse in your pocket?"

When he saw she was willing to spar, his face brightened with unholy amusement. That flashing smile told Shelly to brace herself.

He released her shoulders, stepped away, and flipping back his jacket to offer his hips for her inspection, he looked quintessentially male—and as innocent as the devil himself. "Want to run an investigation?"

He had the nerve to look hopeful. Suddenly she wanted desperately to meet and match his audacity. She tilted her chin and murmured, "You've gotten mighty sassy in your old age, Mr. Assistant District Attorney."

"As I remember, I was sassy in my young age, too. Or have you forgotten? I don't see how you could have. I went to great pains to entertain you." There was amused masculine satisfaction in every line of his face, every facet of his eyes, every line of his relaxed body.

No, she hadn't forgotten. In contrast to his relaxation, Shelly's anxiety level rose exponentially. "Just as you're doing now." She cocked her head to one side, determined to bluff her way through. "Things must be grim in the city if you're driven to flirting with me."

"I always did flirt with you. You're finally old enough to notice."

"I'm finally old enough to know better."

"Now that's a damn shame." Justin pushed back his jacket and thrust his hands in his pockets.

The sight of that flat masculine stomach swathed in a black cummerbund did something so extraordinary to her body that the only cure was escape. "I was just going over to Mel." She was about to add, "So if you'll excuse me," but he saw through her polite dismissal and thwarted her escape attempt by grasping her elbow, turning her and propelling her over the grass toward the cluster of older men. "As long as you're headed that way, speak to my father. He's very pleased that you're here."

Stromberg Corbett wore his power differently than his son, but it was no less potent. Even though his stocky body was trussed up in the tuxedo that made him look flushed and sweaty, he exuded charm and bonhomie.

"Shelly." She was enfolded in his arms and held too tightly, as if it was his last chance to show her how much she meant to him. "It's good to have you here at Corbett Hill again. You've stayed away from us too long." He held her at arm's length and smiled approvingly. "Although I must say, you've put the time to good use."

"Thank you. You're very sweet." She felt a sudden rush of love, coupled with regret that she'd let so many years go by without seeing him.

"How's the glider business going?"

She flinched at the improper term for her soaring school, but she would never correct Strom. She was far too fond of him. "Fine. Sure you won't come down and take a free lesson?"

"Naw, that baby-buggy stuff isn't for me. I want a motor under my fuselage."

"To each his own." Shelly smiled at Strom, aware of Justin hovering at her elbow. It seemed as if she could sense his mood through the surface of her skin. It had shifted subtly from the good-natured sexual teasing of a moment ago. His eyes were locked on Strom and there was tension in the way he stood holding his glass. Was he worried that his father was drinking too much? Heaven knew Strom loved a party. His idea of a good time was to spend long hours eating and drinking in the company of friends. If he was providing the food and drink, so much the better.

Strom was far too generous a host. Shelly had pleaded with her own father to watch his alcohol consumption. The doctor had warned him that in addition to taking his medication for high blood pressure, he needed to cut out the alcohol and sweets. Mel would make a real effort to eat healthy food for a few days, but then he'd get tired of salad and go back to eating what he liked.

Shelly glanced at the glass in her father's hand. It was half full, but there was no way to tell if he was nursing his first or on his third. She gazed at her father with love and exasperation in her eyes.

She turned to move away from the fliers when Justin's face caught her attention. He was staring at his father with the same exasperation and love she'd felt for Mel.

"Justin." She had to touch his sleeve to get his attention. "Is anything wrong?"

He nodded at an open space ahead of them a few paces away from the group to indicate he wanted to talk to her out of earshot. When he led the way, she followed.

At a safe distance, Justin positioned himself with his back to Strom's huddle, his gaze fixed on the horse pasture that lay beyond the house. "He's having chest pains. He had an appointment to see the doctor this week. I hope to God it won't be too late."

She laid a hand on his arm. "Justin, I'm sorry."

Justin lifted his chin, as if determined to lighten the mood. "I keep forgetting how old he is. Crazy, isn't it? You get older, but somehow you think your parents should stay the same. The thing of it is, they do. I haven't seen Dad do anything different or make any accommodation for his age in the last twenty years. Maybe that's why he's having trouble.''

''They'll find a way to help him. There're so many things they can do now—''

''Yeah. If he stands still long enough to let them do it. How's Mel? Is he watching his diet and taking his medication like he's supposed to?''

''Only when I remind him. I'm surprised you...know about Mel. He hasn't let that many people know.''

He gazed at her steadily. ''I've seen a bit more of your father in the past few years than you've seen of mine.''

Guilt nudged her again. ''I'm...sorry. I have been a stranger—''

He examined her as if she were a witness he was questioning. ''Going to remedy the situation?''

She looked away, out over the hillside. ''I really am busy with the school and all—''

Justin stopped her words with a shrug and his raised glass. ''Sure.'' Impatiently, he deposited his glass on the table and faced her. ''I always wondered what it was that drove you away.''

She lifted her chin. ''I soloed and got my license. The lessons were over. I had no reason to come anymore.''

''Is that why you stayed away at Christmastime?''

She hadn't thought anyone at Corbett Hill had missed her. Obviously Justin had. She didn't want to— wouldn't—answer him. He might be versed in the technique of coercing a witness to tell all, but Shelly wasn't going to fall prey to those richly empathetic eyes. ''I stayed away because I needed to grow up.''

''You wouldn't do that here?''

''No.''

''Why not?''

Those two words coolly challenged her. She never could resist a challenge from Justin. "It's hard to grow up when you're still wishing for the moon."

He lifted an elegant gold eyebrow. She'd surprised him. "The moon was here?"

"Always."

She expected him to laugh. Instead, he said softly almost under his breath, "So that's what it was. You were jealous. I often wondered—"

She wished she hadn't admitted the truth, couldn't imagine why she had. "Well, now that we've washed all the old family linen," she said with a bright smile, "I'll let you talk to your other guests—"

He reached out and caught her arm, then took her glass from her. That quickly, the crooked grin reappeared. "They aren't my guests, they're Paul's. Wanna go for a swim?"

"Here? Now?"

"I can't think of a better time or place. Come on."

This, too, was familiar, Justin reacting to trouble by creating more trouble and enticing her to join him, leading her on like a goat to slaughter.

She understood his need to act wild and crazy and forget, especially the need to forget that all he could do about his father's illness was wait and worry. She knew the feeling. "Justin, I can't. I don't have a suit."

"Wear what you've got on."

"Is that what you're going to do?" she asked dryly. She knew better than to think Justin would jump in the pool fully clothed in front of all and sundry. He'd always been meticulous about his clothes. Ten years ago, Justin hadn't owned a pair of jeans and he probably still didn't. His idea of casual was designer chinos with a knife-crease press. Shelly had wondered whether he was driven by his own need to look immaculate or whether Morley was the one who insisted that Justin's sartorial image was absolutely correct at all times.

Had she made a mistake questioning him? He was studying her with that speculative gleam he got when the wheels in his head were whirring away at warp speed.

She moved to edge away from him too late. He snatched up her hand and began dragging her over the grass, ignoring her high heels, the wind blowing her skirt up past her knees and her protests. "Wait. What are you doing... *Wait!*"

But her captor wasn't in a mood to wait. He steam-rolled through the crowd, as the other guests turned and watched in amazement. The two of them must be an entertaining sight, Justin tugging her along on the grass, she digging in her heels, trying and failing to hold her ground. Everybody was looking, even their fathers, which was understandable. Justin was hauling her toward the pool like a Roman with a Sabine woman in his clutches.

Shelly gave in to the inevitable, stopped fighting Justin and concentrated on simply staying upright. Justin rewarded her capitulation by flashing her a diabolically beautiful grin.

At the side of the pool, he slid to a halt. Shelly tugged at his hand trying to escape, but he kept her wrist shackled.

He stripped off one side of his tuxedo jacket, then went through a whole silent-movie comedy sight-gag routine of trying to shake his sleeve off his and her joined hands, finally releasing her, then grabbing her with his other hand and holding her still as if that was the reason he was now able to pull his jacket free. By this time he had her silly with laughter. She wouldn't have been able to run away if she'd wanted to.

For act two, he draped the jacket around her shoulders with a great show of getting it just right. While she watched with dazed submission, he frowned in mock displeasure and tossed the jacket away. She shook her head, trying to make some sense of what he was doing, helpless mirth bubbling just under the surface. The unscrupulous blackguard took advantage of her dazed state by capturing her face to face and stiff-leg walking her to the pool edge.

At the brink, he stopped. His arms manacled around her, he teetered from side to side.

The gathered crowd called encouragement. The wind caught Shelly's hair, blowing it away from her face. Keeping her wrapped in his arms, Justin examined her with mock sobriety.

She shook her head in a vain attempt to free the hair from her face. Her ability to think vanished. Confusion reigned everywhere, riot in her mind, riot in her body. She felt warm, warmer, heated, supremely conscious of masculine hardness against feminine softness. "What...are...you...doing?"

He looked down at her and his grin faded. "Remembering what it's like to be with you." That quickly he went from silly to sober. That quickly, his words kicked a knot of nerves in her stomach. In a tone far lighter then she felt, she said, "I wonder if we could try for just a little less...togetherness?"

His eyes still wore that veiled somber look. "I'd like to try for more. Have dinner with me tomorrow night."

Blue eyes flashed toward green. She examined him carefully to see if he was serious. He was.

Memories came back, memories of Justin on the prowl for the prettiest girl at the air show, Justin separating the most vivacious girl out of the gaggle of lovelies at the local hangout, Justin carelessly discarding another young woman who'd annoyed him by staying around too long, hoping. She shook her head. "I can't. I'm . . . busy."

"You've got a date?"

"Yes." She couldn't look him in the eye when she told the lie.

"Cancel it." His voice took on an implacability she didn't recognize, a technique newly learned in the courtroom, perhaps. She forced herself to look at him. "I can't."

The soberness disappeared. He closed one eye and growled like a pirate, "Say yes, or it's into the drink with you."

"Justin, don't be ridiculous—"

He feinted a fall toward the pool. She screamed and clutched at him. His grin was back.

"Say yes."

Shelly smiled; she couldn't help it. But she shook her head no. He teetered again, wobbling wildly on the edge. She scrambled to keep their collective balance. Justin helped and they were stable again. Shelly was breathless, but not really worried. She relaxed against him and smiled up into his face. "You're putting on a great show, Justin, but you're all sound and no fury. You won't risk getting your clothes wet just to get me to say yes and you know it."

The golden flash of light in his eyes warned her too late that she'd underestimated him—in more ways than one. "You had your chance to save yourself by saying a single word. You didn't say it. Now, if I were you, I'd close my mouth and keep it closed.'' Without blinking he dragged her over sideways until they both fell with a great splash into the pool.

CHAPTER TWO

JUSTIN'S LEGS TANGLED with Shelly's. Water surged into her face, ears, mouth. Together they plunged down, together they bobbed up. It was a strange sensation for Shelly, surfacing in Justin's arms. She pushed a sopping strand of hair out of her eyes. "You're an idiot."

He grinned back at her. "Smile when you say that, pardner."

The corner of her mouth lifted in an answering grin. How could she do anything else? His blond hair was dark with wetness, his face beaded with water, his eyes glittering with fiendish delight. Justin was in two of his several favorite elements: water and trouble. He also knew how to play to the crowd. To the smiling audience gathered around the edges, he shouted, "Come on in, the water's fine."

There was embarrassed laughter and a minute or two of contemplative silence. It was hot enough for people to be tempted. Justin directed his attention to the best man. "Come on, David. Show us what you're made of." David grinned, kicked off his shoes, locked a grip on his nose, and took a flying leap into the pool. Other intrepid youths followed and soon the pool was full of clothed men and women, most of them Paul and Kim's young friends.

"Am I not a leader of men?" Justin murmured triumphantly to Shelly.

"My experience with you has been as an abductor of women."

"You did come along willingly at the end."

"An obvious mistake."

Surrounded as they were by other splashing, laughing people, their path to the side of the pool was cut off. Shelly and Justin bobbed in the middle, he treading water, she doing the same. The water was blessedly cool, but her dress clung to Shelly's thighs, hindering her leg movement. Justin, in trousers, was not so restricted.

When he saw she was having trouble, his hand slipped under her arm to offer support. "Relax. Let me do the work."

She resisted.

"Now you're being an idiot. Trust me."

Trusting Justin. Long ago in an airplane she had trusted him over and over again with her life. But she'd never trusted him in a social situation. She was being foolish. He'd hardly let her down. Shelly let her body go slack in the water, putting her weight on him. "Are you sure you can hold us both up?"

Wary, she watched him, half-expecting him to tease and then release her. That's what the old Justin would have done.

He didn't. He tightened his grip, keeping her well above the water. "You're safe with me."

"Just like I was a minute ago?"

"I warned you what would happen if you said no. Is the answer still no?"

"Yes."

A fleeting look of annoyance crossed his face. He lost his coordination and then nearly went under. Looking disturbed by his lapse and tired of his prank, he shook his head. "I'd better get you over to the side—"

"Before I get wet?"

Looking relieved, he laughed. So did she.

Justin splashed his way to the concrete border and watched as Shelly reached for it. Only when she was safely anchored did he curl his lean fingers around the rim. Facing her, a slight frown creasing his brow, he raised his other hand to her cheek. "Are you okay?"

She shook her head helplessly, not wanting to feel the things his gentle touch was making her feel. "I'm fine."

"Did I ruin your dress?" His fingers reestablished contact with her face, rubbing lightly over her cheekbone.

"It's washable." She slicked her hair back and tried to analyze the expression in those green eyes, shielded so effectively by his golden spiky lashes. She remembered him bullying her when he thought she wasn't paying attention to her flying. She remembered him chastising her for being too tense while she worked the rudder and stick of the aerobatic trainer. She remembered him teasing her about her red hair. She couldn't remember him ever being protective of her.

Justin dangled in the water, feeling strangely exhilarated, more alive than he had in months, younger than he had in years. Seeing Shelly again had freed him from chains he hadn't known he was dragging: the constant barrage of court cases; the feeling of frustration watching guilty men he'd spent hours of his time trying to convict go free; the worry about his father. After months of celibacy caused by his schedule and his lack of interest, he was thinking about—and wanting—a woman.

Not just any woman. A red-haired spitfire who could ward off men with one-liners and do aerobatics with the best of pilots. He'd spent a lot of time with Shelly teaching her to fly, two years, if he remembered correctly. And never once during that time had he thought of her as a woman he'd want to take to bed. Which was a hell of a good thing. She'd been a kid then, a skinny, vulnerable kid. It did cross his mind once or twice that she'd give some man a run for his money. He never dreamed he might be the man.

Touching her wet skin was like... He couldn't think of what it was like. All he knew was that it felt good. Too damn good. She wasn't a girl anymore, she was a woman. A woman he wanted.

To Shelly, the look in Justin's eyes was odd, as if he gazed inward at a waking dream. The glide of his finger along her cheek moved in slow motion over her cheekbone and slowly, slowly, down to her chin, taking inventory. Her skin was cool from the water, but under his touch, her nerves blazed to life. In a minute that wet fingertip would drift off her chin down to her throat and neck...

"Justin, I'm going to get out now."

As if her voice had wakened him, his eyes cleared. The dreaming look vanished and the devil gleam reappeared. "Want some help?"

Her eyes flashed in warning. "No." It was time for an end to the fun and games. She turned her back to him and prepared to lift herself out of the pool. His hand cupped her bottom with a familiar ease that sent a shiver of sexual anticipation through her.

The man was a menace. Safely seated on the side of the pool, uncomfortably aware of her clinging clothes, Shelly pushed her hair back in a futile attempt to recover her poise. She was annoyed, of course she was. Then why, in that instant of having him touch her bottom with the casual intimacy of a lover, did she want it to be so?

He looked like a naughty boy who enjoyed the crime too much to care about the punishment. "Definitely not a kid anymore. Very much a woman. At least, that's how it looked from here."

"Do you get your power of keen observation from twenty-twenty vision or that criminal mind?"

"It's an innate skill. Comes naturally to Corbett men." His eyes shone with mischief. "It's in their genes."

That she believed. Though why he was making passes at her, she didn't know. She must be a sight. While he looked—edible. His hair was sleeked back from a face that was bare, hard-boned, classically symmetrical. His formal tucked shirt was soaked and clinging to his broad shoulders, making their width more impressive on top of his narrow, cummerbund-wrapped waist.

Justin liked seeing Shelly like this, wet, good-natured, sitting at the poolside with her feet dangling in the water like a kid. Yes indeed, he certainly did like seeing her wet. She had a shapely throat, nice arms, and small high breasts, each feminine mound separate and clearly visible under the clinging fabric. To say nothing of her legs. Long, long legs, beautifully shaped, progressing up to curving hips that would fit under a man's hand smooth as silk when he brought them under his body.

On the other side of the still-rippling pool Morley stood frowning, sending out disapproval in waves. Beside him Strom tried—and failed—to echo his expression.

Strom launched the attack. "What in the name of all that's holy are you doing, son?"

Chilled, Justin chastised himself for being a fool. For an instant, he'd forgotten everything but Shelly. He'd carried her into the water with him without once thinking about the effect his horseplay would have on his father. "Cooling off."

"So is everyone else, thanks to you."

Strom sounded torn between annoyance and amusement, but he wasn't breathless or ill. Justin relaxed a little. Cheekily, he looked around at the chaos he'd created. "They don't seem to mind."

"Well, I do. Get out of there and get some dry clothes on. You, too, Shelly."

"That might be a little difficult," she murmured.

The accused hoisted himself out of the pool and plopped down beside her, splashing water, looking relaxed as a cat. "The difficult, Congressman Corbett does immediately. The impossible takes a little longer."

Shelly sneaked a look at Mel. Unlike Strom, he was surveying the impromptu pool party with a smile on his lips and a twinkle in his eye. Cheered by her father's expression, she surrendered to the forces of fate and enjoyed the coolness a little longer by letting her nylon-clad feet dangle back in the water.

Justin touched her knee, sending a little chill snaking up through her. "Look at Morley. He looks as if he's smelling something bad. Did you lose your shoes in the pool?"

She made a great show of offended dignity. "For your information, my feet do not smell." Shelly lifted a foot out of the water and wiggled her nylon-clad toe.

"You did lose your shoes."

"In the interest of self-preservation, I kicked them off. Too bad, too. They're the only ones I have that match this dress."

Without warning, Justin arched over the pool edge and jackknifed in.

Nothing's changed. The man still has lightning reflexes.

He surfaced, holding one of her high-heeled pumps in his hand. "Hang on to this one while I get the other."

While she emptied water out of the shoe he'd retrieved, he popped up with the second one.

"I'll help you put them on." He bobbed upright in the water effortlessly, as if a liquid medium were his natural environment. Looking at him, Shelly thought tuxedo shirts ballooned with water might just catch on as a swim wear, if Justin were the model for them.

"This close to the pool? I might get them wet."

Grinning at her nonsense, Justin teased her by holding her shoe just out of reach.

"Prince Charming. How kind of you to swim across the ocean to bring me my slipper."

With great ceremony, he presented it to her. "Princess Charming. How kind of you to sit by the sea and wait for me to present you this gift . . . and with it, my heart."

She reached for the shoe. He held on to it, his hands meeting hers, her eyes meeting his.

For one quiet, electric moment, the laughing crowd in the pool behind them faded away. Nothing existed except the feel of his hand on hers, and the deep darkness of his eyes.

Her voice carefully light to break the mood, she said, "I'll take the shoe, but you'd better keep your heart. You might need it."

He released the shoe into her keeping but went on staring at her, his lashes spiky with water, his eyes a shade greener than the pool, his hands sculling to keep him afloat.

Suddenly afraid, she said, "Are you okay? What . . . is it?"

He shook his head as if shrugging off a spell. "Nothing."

He was lying and he knew it. He wasn't okay. How was he going to hide the evidence of her effect on him when he climbed out of the water in his soaked pants? She was doing strange things to him, and it wasn't because she looked so delectable. Why wasn't she angry about his dunking her? Why wasn't she worrying about her hair and her makeup? Any other woman would have been livid. He'd read somewhere the brain was the real sex organ. His had gone into overdrive. She was too damned...cheerful. He wanted to be a part of that tolerant cheerfulness. He wanted to be a part of her.

But dammit—suppose she didn't care what she looked like with him because there was another man in her life? Chances are there was. She was exquisitely feminine, so how could she not have a man?

He was hit with a sudden fierce sense of injustice. She shouldn't be with another man. She should be with him.

The sudden darkening of Justin's eyes brought thoughts, secrets, longings to her mind Shelly didn't want to have. She scrambled to her feet, her wet dress clinging, her mind asking what she thought it was she was doing. Answer: escaping...surviving. "This has been fun. You certainly know how to show a lady a good time."

"Shelly. Wait a minute." Feeling suddenly panicky and not knowing why, forgetting his wet clothes and the state of his body, Justin levered himself out of the pool, water sluicing from him in streams.

Shelly turned. The man was on his feet, dripping water from his sleeves, his pants, his hair and looking completely unaware of it. She hadn't known he could be so utterly unself-conscious about his appearance. Like a lighthouse beam, his gaze focused on her.

"Strom wants you to have supper with us."

She'd expected an invitation to stay after the reception and she'd prepared a polite refusal. She found she wasn't quite as ready to give it as she'd thought. "I couldn't do that. I . . . have other plans."

"I have a sure-fire way to make you say yes."

"No, really, I can't. I've got to get out of this wet dress and—"

"If you'll eat supper with us, I'll tell Morley he has to dry your shoes in his oven."

His grin was as outrageous as his bribe. She wanted desperately to laugh. The smile curled the edges of her mouth upward. "You've learned to fight dirty in the courtroom."

"Evidently." His eyes flickered over her. "In more ways than one. I've already got you thinking about stripping."

That patently sexual look and lazy, spine-tingling drawl were hard to treat with detached calm, but she did her best. "What makes you think I'd change my plans just to get even with Morley?"

"I know you pretty well."

"Knew."

"Uh-uh. Know. You haven't changed as much as I thought you had. I used to trust you with my life. I see I still can." All the sexual teasing was gone. He meant every word he said. And when serious, the man was potent. "Will you stay for dinner? Mel is staying. You don't really have other plans, do you?"

She gave him full marks for perception. "I planned to have other plans. They just didn't . . . happen. Really, I should go."

"No, you shouldn't."

Shelly shook her head in a gesture of mock exasperation and moved forward as if to brush past him. He had trapped her at the edge of the swimming pool and he wasn't giving an inch. "What's the matter, Red? You used to have more courage than anyone I knew. Have you lost it in your old age? Are you afraid to stay?"

Her head came up. Her eyes glittering, she kicked out of her wet shoes and handed them to him. "Tell Morley to bake them for a half hour on low."

His sudden grin wolfish, he took the shoes. "'Atta girl. I knew you could do it." Whistling, he pivoted and with her shoes dangling from his fingers, walked toward the house.

She'd been had. Neatly, expertly, in the same way he'd egged her on while he was teaching her stunt flying, he'd made her do exactly what he wanted her to do. She gazed after him, wondering why ten years hadn't changed that.

One by one the guests crawled out of the pool, spread themselves out on the loungers to dry in the sun and wind, drink more champagne and eat more snacks. The bride and groom escaped amid confetti throwing and laughter into a white limousine and were whisked away. Like old wine, the party fizzled. A few die-hard guests hung on, but soon they, too, climbed in their cars and departed and the house on the hill resumed its mantle of customary dignified quiet.

As Shelly slipped into the chair next to Mel at the informal table Morley had laid in the breakfast room, her dress and hair dried, her makeup replaced, she relaxed in the placid atmosphere.

The quiet didn't last long. They sat around an oval banquette, she and Mel with their backs to the wall, Justin and Strom in chairs on the other side of the table.

When Morley came in to serve Justin the scalloped chicken livers he had prepared as an appetite teaser, Justin gave him an elaborately innocent, puzzled look and asked, "I say, Morley, is this the concoction that's been making that . . . unusual odor?"

Without batting an eye, Morley answered, "I believe it's Miss Armstrong's shoes you're smelling, sir." Stiffly offended, he marched through the kitchen door.

Shelly bit her lip in a desperate attempt not to laugh. Strom cleared his throat. "If he leaves, I'll know who to blame, son."

"He won't leave. It's taken him twenty years to organize us, but he has us nicely trained now. He wouldn't have the strength to start all over again on some other family of uncivilized savages—"

The door swung open, admitting Morley, his hands laden with dishes of cucumber salad, potato salad and chicken salad bristling with slivered almonds. He set out the dishes and said to Strom, "I took the liberty of preparing a light lunch for the evening meal, sir, since refreshments were served at the reception. Fresh fruit will be following. Would you care for anything else?"

"No, this is fine, fine."

Morley returned to the swinging door, paused for a moment and then turned back. "And you're quite right, Master Justin. After twenty years with you, I couldn't possibly start over again with another family, especially if they were in the same crude state of half civilization that you and Master Paul were enjoying when I came. As I recall, you had to be taught to eat your mashed potatoes with a fork instead of a spoon." He smiled with dry pleasure at getting a bit of his own back. "You did say a half hour on Miss Armstrong's shoes? They should be...done now. Would you be needing them right away, Miss?"

Aware that if she laughed at the mock-cowed look on Justin's face, she would spoil everything, Shelly fought to keep the amusement out of her voice as she answered, "No, thank you, Morley. Just set them out on the floor to cool. I'll collect them later."

Satisfied he'd met the enemy honorably and acquitted himself well, Morley pivoted and disappeared through the swinging door.

Justin flicked a glance at Shelly. His fake-chastened expression slipped from his face like a mask. He grinned at her, and she grinned back.

Strom raised an eyebrow and cast Mel the long-suffering look of a fellow parent. "What have you two been up to with Morley?"

"Nothing, Dad."

"Don't lie to me, Son. I can always tell when you're lying."

Justin met his father's gaze, his posture relaxed, his face open. "I must be a real whiz of a lawyer. Can't even slip one little white lie past my father. So much for the poker face I'm supposed to have in court."

"Just be glad your jurors don't know you as well as I do."

The golden head bowed. "I'm eternally thankful for the small favors of fate."

Strom himself turned prosecuting attorney. "Shelly, what did happen out there? I didn't see anything till you and my son—and most of our guests—were in the pool."

Conscious of Justin's eyes on her, Shelly tried to look composed. "Your son was trying his hand at blackmail. I didn't succumb so he . . . dunked me."

"She's not telling it right. I was much more of a gentleman than that, Dad. I went in with her."

"Oh, that makes it much better," Strom said dryly.

Getting into the spirit of things, Shelly added, "If that wasn't bad enough, he bribed me to stay for dinner by promising to make Morley dry my shoes in his oven."

"It appears you've had a good day's work, son." Strom abandoned his judicial stance, looked pleased, smiled fondly at Justin and then at Shelly. Leaning over to slap Mel on the shoulder, he said, "Well, this is more like it. Seems like old times, with you and Shelly both here, and our two offspring pitting their wits against Morley." He sat back, his eyes narrowing, his gaze traveling from Shelly's faintly flushed face to Justin's bland expression.

Justin knew that look. Thoughts were clicking away inside Strom's head that boded ill for somebody, and unless he missed his guess, which he usually didn't when it came to his father, the somebody was him. Justin stared at Strom. What was his wily old fox of a politician father plotting now?

Morley returned to pour the white wine his father liked. Over his lifted glass, Strom gazed at Shelly, looking as innocent as Santa Claus. Then he smiled angelically and drank his wine. Mel followed his example, draining his glass.

Shelly frowned. "Dad, you know you aren't supposed to drink when you're taking that blood-pressure medication."

"Then I'll skip the medication." At Shelly's startled look, Mel raised his hand. "Stop treating me like an invalid or you're going to turn me into one. One night won't hurt me."

She opened her mouth to protest and closed it. It would upset her father even more if she made a scene in front of his closest friend. Flushing, she lifted her wineglass. Across the table, Justin raised his glass in a silent toast to her. *Fathers are a royal pain, aren't they?* His eyes met hers in silent sympathy, his lips curled into a rueful smile. His support warmed her, eased the tension as she drank the tart wine.

Strom fingered his glass, his eyes on Mel. "Not like the old days, eh? Remember when we used to drink all night and have nothing more serious than a headache in the morning?" He sighed. "Now you're taking medicine and they're talking doctor's appointments to me. Hell to get old, right, Mel?"

"The alternative isn't that great, either," Mel said dryly. "Some of our wartime buddies didn't have a chance to get old."

Strom's eyes gleamed. "You're right about that. Let's drink a toast to their memory...and to all the gallant fighting men we've known."

When they had drunk the toast, Justin's eyes caught Shelly's. "I smell a strong hint of reminiscence in the air. How about leaving these two to their fun and coming out for a walk with me?"

"By all means," Strom said effusively. "Don't let us old duffers keep you young people inside. It's a beautiful summer night. Go out, enjoy it. No need to hurry back in. You are staying the night, Shelly."

"I hadn't planned—"

"Nonsense. Your father agrees with me that it's foolish for you to drive back tonight and then return tomorrow for him. I'll tell Morley to get Adelaide's room ready for you and lay out a shirt of Justin's for you to sleep in." He spoke as if the decision was already made.

"Congressman, you've got more than a bit of steam-roller in you."

Caught, Strom switched from authoritative command to effusive concern without batting an eyelash. "It's much better for everyone if you stay. You're snug and safe here, I won't worry about you being out on the road alone at night, Justin won't worry and Mel will sleep a lot easier, too, right, Mel?"

Her father played the traitor and went over to the enemy without hesitation. "I would feel better if you didn't drive home alone, honey."

"Mr. Stromberg Corbett," said Shelly, as she and Justin went outside, "looks like Santa Claus and thinks like Napoleon."

"I'm not sure your father is any better."

"You're probably right. After all, he's had all these years to watch and learn from your father."

Justin laughed, and Shelly enjoyed the sound ringing through the blessed coolness of the night air. They had automatically taken the trail that led to the stable, Justin on the outside, Shelly next to the white fence that enclosed the paddock.

"It's good to see our fathers together again," Justin said. "They're good for each other. Keeps the lying down to an acceptable level."

Shelly smiled in amused agreement.

"If you stop and think about it, their friendship is pretty amazing. Even while you two were in your restless mode, Dad kept track of you with a map and pins. Blue pins were where you'd been, history, red pin for where you were currently."

Shelly lifted an eyebrow. She hadn't known that. "Like a battle campaign?"

"I guess." Justin stopped walking and leaned his arms on the fence.

"Looks like neither he nor Strom will be flying in the air show next month."

She nodded. "I guess not. I know Dad doesn't like being grounded, but he hasn't said too much. I try to keep him busy at the school."

Keeping his voice carefully casual, he asked, "How are things going there?"

Her face was expressionless. "We're doing fine."

Justin wondered about that. They'd bought the soaring school and the bluff on a shoestring and paid what he thought was an exorbitant price for the package. Their outgo had to be high and their income low.

But it wasn't an evening to think of practical matters. The sky behind them was rose and gold, and streaky clouds over their heads trailed banners of delicate pink. The crickets chirped complacently, sure of themselves and the summer warmth. The cool breeze flickered across his skin like a soothing balm.

One of his horses, a sleek brown Morgan with characteristic dark mane and tail, came to the fence and whickered low in her throat.

Thankful for the diversion, Shelly held out her hand to the horse. While Justin watched, the mare nibbled velvety lips over Shelly's fingers. "She's a beauty. What's her name?"

"Misty. Do you ever ride anymore?"

"No."

"Why not?"

Shelly withdrew her hand from the horse's nose and turned to look at him, her mouth lifting in a dry smile. "No time . . . and no money."

He ignored the tiny jab. "Pity. As I remember, you had an excellent . . . seat."

She turned away from him, stretching to touch the horse again, liking the feel of the short-haired, prickly skin, the smooth nostrils and the way communing with the mare took her thoughts away from Justin. She heard the caw of a crow, felt the horse shift from one leg to another. If she ignored Justin's attempt to flirt with her, he'd soon give it up.

There was a rustle of cloth and suddenly Justin was behind her, trapping her with his hands locked on the railing on each side of her, her back to his chest. How foolish she'd been to think a cool shoulder would stop this man. "Justin—"

The whispered protest was barely out of her mouth when he brushed his lips over the cool, bare shoulder she'd turned to him.

Her skin tingled in response, heating. She couldn't let him do this to her, launch a sneak attack from the rear and demolish her resistance with one touch of his clever mouth on her bare skin. She twisted around and put her palm flat against his chest to keep him from leaning toward her mouth.

He allowed her to keep him at a distance, but his face was dark and determined, with an intent that made a quiver of restless anticipation trickle up her spine. "We've been building up to this all day and you know it," Justin said in a voice that was all soft seduction and promise. "Don't disappoint me by making the token protest."

He captured her hands—hard, male, insistent, silently asking for surrender. She stiffened her wrists and held her ground. "This isn't a token protest. It's a real one." Her eyes locked with his.

"You came into my arms willingly enough at the pool."

"There were people around then."

That quickly, his patience snapped. "Well, hang on a minute. Maybe I can flag a car off the road and drag the driver up here to watch me kiss you."

All heated male anger and mocking determination unleashed, he let go of the railing and turned away as if he meant to carry out his hare-brained threat. She supposed he had a right to be angry. She hadn't discouraged him. But she hadn't encouraged him, either.

He'd actually gone a couple of steps by the time she reached him, caught his shirt and pulled him around to face her. "Did anyone ever tell you you're a spoiled brat?"

"Only you." Slowly, mockingly, his gaze roved over her face and down to her hands. "As far as I'm concerned, you can call me anything you like as long as you grab me at the same time."

Deliberately she controlled her breathing and pulled her fingers away from his shirt.

"Such a bundle of contradictory impulses. Interesting," he murmured.

"Some of us aren't quite as single-minded and ambitious as others—" The flare of darkness in his eyes made her stop her attack. She hadn't meant to hurt him, didn't want to hurt him, hadn't thought it possible to hurt him. He was more vulnerable than she'd ever dreamed Justin Corbett could be. Yet she couldn't let him kiss her. The primitive need to survive told her she had to resist him. For he had the power to destroy her.

Somewhere in the back of Justin's mind, ironic laughter echoed. He'd known many women in his life, scheming women, beautiful women, rich women, ambitious women. He'd heard any number of different words come tumbling from their lips, words that pleaded and cajoled and invited him into their lives. He had never, in all those years, stood in the dark wanting to kiss a woman so badly his body ached with it and been told no. He didn't like it much. He didn't like it at all.

He stood absorbing the look of her, pale skin with the bloom of color underneath, tangled flame-red hair, a vulnerable softness in her face, as if she were torn. Yes, she was having second thoughts. Her mouth was softening and her eyes were dark with regret. All she needed was a little push in the right direction. He was more than willing to give her that. He lowered his head.

She dodged his seeking mouth, her hands going to their familiar place on his chest to push him away. "No."

He let his body weight rest on her palms, confident that if he kept the pressure on, her resistance would collapse. But when her blue eyes flashed up to his, her pale face held a depth of anger he'd badly underestimated.

"You're offended because I'm trying to kiss you?" He looked astounded.

"I'm offended because you think you can reach out and take whatever you want without a thought for my feelings or plans or life—"

"One kiss doesn't lead to a lifetime commitment."

Her eyes locked with his. In the deep blue-purple silence of a night falling into darkness, she said softly, very softly, "The defense rests."

"Neat. Very neat. Hoist on my own petard. Shot down by my own admission of guilt. The courtroom is missing a great talent in you." His tone was light, determinedly casual. So was the arm he threw over her shoulder. "Come on, you'd better get back to the house. You're getting cold."

She'd won. So why didn't she feel better? Why did this dose of never-retreat-in-the-face-of-defeat, don't-let-the-enemy-see-you-hurting Corbett pride make her feel as if she wanted to hide her face in his chest and cling to him until his hurt went away?

And he was hurt. She could feel it, taste it, smell it.

If he'd been angry, if he'd stalked off and left her there in the cool dark, she could have tolerated it better. The friendly, impersonal touch of his hand hurt more than harsh words.

Of course, wanting desperately to be as smooth and sophisticated as he, she snagged her heel in the rough turf and stumbled. Justin snatched her up by her elbow, steadying her. As soon as he felt her regain her balance, he released her. She wanted to have the ground open up and swallow her. The spicy scent of his cologne wafted to her nose, indicting and condemning her. He was a man, not a robot. He had feelings. She had no right to hurt him.

Nor did she have the right to pass judgment on him. He hadn't lived a free and easy life-style, he'd always striven for some impossible goal, usually one set by his father. She'd seen him meet and surpass those goals. She'd also seen him compensate for the sacrifice by stalking—and getting—the prettiest girl, the one specimen needed to match the most perfect requirements.

She wasn't perfect. She stumbled when she should be graceful, enthused when she should be cool, inflicted hurt when she should be kind.

The house was quiet as Justin guided Shelly up through the side entrance that led into the kitchen. How long had they been out there talking, skirting the edge of disaster? His hand on her back, Justin murmured something and directed her past the library. The door was closed but there were low male rumblings coming from the room. Mel and Strom, talking.

Wordlessly Justin steered her toward the stairs. "I know the way,"? she whispered, but he shook his head.

As crisply efficient as a hotel concierge, he flipped on the light in the room that had belonged to his mother. It was decorated in soft shades of rose and lavender, and the faint scent of Morley's meticulous housekeeping lingered in the air. She'd never known Adelaide. But even so, she missed her, perhaps because she'd lost her own mother when she was a baby. It was another bond she'd had with Justin. He'd known she'd suffered a loss, too. Once he'd brought her up here to see his mother's things, which Strom had kept sacrosanct. She'd known it was Justin's excuse for revisiting his mother's room without losing face. Shelly had willingly let him use her, knowing too well that grinding rasp of irreparable loss.

"I think you'll find everything you need here. Morley's laid my shirt out on the bed for you."

She hated having him talk to her in that cool, detached tone. She hated looking into Justin's eyes and seeing a shade of green ice. He might wipe his emotions from his face, but the backlash of control shimmered dangerously in those green depths.

"Thank you . . . for bringing me up."

"Thank you for putting me down." He turned his back to her and headed for the door.

"Justin . . ."

He paused in the doorway and turned deliberately, his face bland, waiting.

"I'm . . . sorry."

Something indescribable flitted across his face, an emotion that made her breath catch in her throat. He looked like a primitive man trying to decide whether to risk his life and go after the prey, or walk away from the sustenance his life's blood demanded. The look vanished, leaving the old, cold mask in its place. "Don't be. You were right to nip it in the bud. I'm glad one of us has good sense. Sleep well, Shelly." Quietly, with a lithe grace all his own, he went out and closed the door, leaving Shelly to struggle with a guilty ache that he'd taken her gibe with more grace than she'd given it.

In the darkness, undressed and wearing Justin's shirt, her nerves still stretched and vibrating with regret, Shelly sprawled crosswise on the bed, her thighs bare, her toes seeking the cover of the sheet. The window was open. A breeze wafted across her thighs, tantalizing her flesh as Justin's mouth on her shoulder had.

Disturbed, swallowing hard, she shut her eyes. Now the images of Justin danced on her lids, his face alive with devilry, dark with sexual intent, icy with self-control. She'd done the right thing, of course she had, for both himself and her. She'd been sensible all her life, sensible about leaving school friends year after year, sensible about the love affair she'd recently broken off, sensible about who she was and what she was. She was Shelly Armstrong, the daughter of a rolling stone who gathered neither moss nor money nor influence, a woman who'd had years and years to learn to apply cool common sense to emotional relationships. To care too much meant suffering too much pain when her father moved on and the friendship died a lingering death of a few exchanged letters. Yes, she'd learned the lesson of detached good sense and she'd learned it well.

She rolled over, burying her face in the pillow to erase the thought of how lonely it was to be sensible.

She could not—must not—think what being with Justin would be like. Physically he was perfect, all any woman could ever want. And if those brief touches of his mouth were any indication, his expertise as a lover matched his physical perfection. She would never be able to look at him and see her ersatz big brother again.

She'd made a mistake breaking her ten-year ban on visits to Corbett Hill. She wouldn't have, if she'd known a physical attraction of such power could spring up between Justin and herself so quickly. It was as if it had always been there, latent, needing only the catalyst of their mutual presence to spring to life. She rolled over on her back and stared up at the ceiling, wondering how soon she could get her father to leave in the morning—and when she might reasonably expect to fall asleep tonight.

CHAPTER THREE

COOLLY, JUSTIN STOOD in his room, stripped off his clothes and hung them in his closet. He wrapped a towel around his nude body, strolled down the stairs, went through the double doors to the pool, let his towel drop and dove in. Pacing himself, he began to swim. He thought best when he was moving. And he needed a drink.

Dammit, the woman was a menace. She should be collected off the street and stored in a lead-lined container. She laughs like an angel, feels like a dream, and thinks like a computer.

All right, so she's got me pegged. I don't want commitment, never have. A good time, yes. A few laughs, yes. Is that a crime? I've never met a woman I wanted to spend the rest of my life with. If I did meet her, I'd want to make damn sure the loving was worth the pain when it ended.

With Shelly, it would be.

Pull, breathe, pull, breathe. If there's anything you want in this life, son, go after it.

"Without a thought for my feelings or plans or life—"

A needle of guilt pricked him. He didn't want to hurt Shelly, or disrupt her plans or her life. He just wanted to take her to bed, to feel her legs and arms tangle with his, feel her body yield to his. She wasn't a teenager any-

more, she was a woman. A damn fine looking woman,
with damn fine legs and damn fine breasts. He wanted to
touch those legs, those breasts. He wanted to touch all of
her.

The frustration riding him hard, Justin increased the
speed of his stroke. For the first time in his life, he
wanted something he couldn't get by sheer hard work and
determination. He wanted to win back Shelly's regard
and good will, something only the gods could give him.
He didn't like leaving his fate in the hands of that capricious bunch. If he remembered correctly, they were given
to indulging in human faults, like jealousy and revenge.
He needed a steadier helping hand.

*"If you want a helping hand, look on the end of your
arm."*

Funny how his father's homilies came back to him
when he swam. Maybe because his father had stood at the
edge of the pool and shouted them at him while he
worked out. The body has a memory, too, Justin
thought. The feel of Shelly flashed into his mind, her
tension as he stood with her at the side of the pool, her
relaxation just before he'd gone in with her.

She'd guessed wrong about his willingness to dunk her,
but afterward she hadn't complained. His sweet little Red
had crawled out of the pool and sat on the edge swinging her legs and unconsciously captivating him with every
word, every glance.

His body warmed, hardened. If he kept thinking of
her, he was sure as hell defeating the purpose of the cool
water and exercise. Yes, the body had a memory—and a
life and will of its own. If he wanted a helping hand he
would look on the end of his arm. But he might look on
the end of his father's arm, too. Strom owed him one.

IN THE LIBRARY Strom was holding the wine bottle up to Mel. "Want another one while your watchdog isn't looking?"

Mel's mouth curled in a smile. "She means well."

"The wheel of fortune, eh? We look after the kids when they're little and they end up looking after us when we get old."

"You're not old. And neither am I. A little frayed, maybe, a little used, but not old." Deliberately, Mel pulled a cigarette from his pocket and tapped it on the pack.

Strom smiled, but his eyes were guarded. "I thought you were supposed to give up those things."

"You indulge in your sins," Mel said, nodding toward Strom's glass, "I'll indulge in mine." He sat back in the chair, his face blissful after his first puff, his gaze on Strom watchful. "Unless you plan on taking over for Shelly?"

"Maybe I should." Strom fingered his wineglass, staring into the clear liquid. It was good to be here with Mel, good to put the ghosts at bay with fine wine and the company of the one man in the world who knew him for what he was and still called him friend. "How's her young man?"

"Gone."

"She isn't seeing him anymore?"

Mel blew a ring of smoke toward the ceiling. "No, thank heaven."

"Didn't care for him much, did you?"

"He ate tofu."

"A certain sign of profligacy." Strom smiled at his joke, so did Mel. "So he's out of the picture. Doesn't look like either of us is ever going to have any grandchildren."

"You're closer to it than I am. You've got one married."

"They aren't going to have children for a while. At least that's what they say. And if they do have kids, I won't see them much." Strom grimaced. "Gone for a honeymoon in Hawaii, and then going straight to his new job in Toledo. I didn't want Paul to take that job in Ohio, but he thought it was what he wanted. I don't like having them move five hundred miles away, but what could I do about it?"

"Not much. Kids these days have to do things their own way."

"To tell you the truth, I'm not in a hurry for Paul to reproduce. He's young yet. On the other hand . . . there's my oldest. Past thirty and making enough money on the investments he inherited from his grandfather to support a wife and several children." The heavy lids came down in an instinctive shielding of his eyes. His friends on Capital Hill would have recognized that look as Strom Corbett's "working" face. "I detected some . . . undercurrents at the dinner table between my son and your girl."

Mel had known Strom too long to be fooled. "Don't make the mistake of thinking she's a girl. She's a grown woman, old friend, with a mind of her own. If you have any ideas of pushing her in Justin's direction, forget it. They flew together for two years and nothing happened—"

"She was a kid then. As for mine, Justin was twenty years old and knew so damned much there was no telling him anything. Now he's older, smart enough to listen to me once in a while, and your girl is at an age to be thinking about babies."

"I learned long ago that Shelly's her own person, Strom. You'd be wise to think the same."

"You won't help me try a spot of working the bill through committee?"

"Absolutely not."

"Well at least promise me you won't veto it if it gets laid on your desk."

"Of course I'm not against it. My godson's a fine young man, but—"

"Good. Let me get some of the details worked out and we'll talk about it again."

THE WOMAN WITH a mind of her own lay in bed listening to the velvet swish of the water being stroked by a swimmer's arms. Adelaide's room overlooked the pool as did the two other bedrooms at the back of the house. The room Mel would stay in had the front view of the valley.

She'd lain there for an hour and she wasn't in the least bit sleepy. Her heart throbbed with tension. Wasn't the man ever going to give up and come to bed?

Her skin burned. She wanted to go to the window, to cool off her body. Wrong. She wanted to go to the window to look at Justin.

Why shouldn't she? He wouldn't see her, he was in the water, she was upstairs. It was dark, he would be wearing a swim suit.

But as Shelly approached the window, she could see that it wasn't dark and the patio-pool lights were on. And when she looked down, Justin wasn't in the water, he was just climbing out. He wasn't wearing a swim suit.

Justin didn't believe in ghosts or telepathic thought transference. Yet he felt, thought, *knew* when he crawled out of the pool and wiped the water out of his eyes that

Shelly was watching him. He knew and didn't know what to do about it. Should he pretend he didn't know? Turn around and wave at her?

Too intelligent to kick away an opportunity when one was presented, Justin rubbed his face in the towel and let his mind sift through the possibilities. Perhaps the gods weren't as capricious as he'd thought. They'd set the stage but it was up to him to play the part. He only hoped he could play it well.

From her place behind the curtain, Shelly watched Justin lean over to bury his face in his towel. His back was an endless curve of spine sheened with water and a tight male rear with a dark line of division between the two muscled cheeks. Long legs, water sluicing down their golden furred length.

She felt restless, excited, guilty. She should turn away. She shouldn't be standing there like a peeping Tom intruding on his privacy. It was disgraceful, it really was. Her heart throbbed with guilty excitement, but she went on watching him.

He bent over, scrubbing down his legs with the towel. Muscles stretched sleekly to torsion, the pale skin over his buttocks glistened with water. He was hard and male and muscled, infinitely desirable. Her breasts swelled with aching want, her loins tingled. She felt the golden rush of desire, and the empty ache that followed. She clutched the curtain tighter and told herself to go back to bed.

Justin had done many things in the courtroom for effect. He'd never done anything this deliberately daring. Still, if he was a man worthy of the gift the gods had given him, he couldn't lose his nerve in the time of testing. Slowly he swiveled to face the window. With a graceful ease that was unconscious, he raised the towel and began to whipsaw it over his back.

Shelly felt her breath stop in her throat. The golden light of the patio flickered over his bronzed body with its paler girdle below the belt, its sleek line of essential muscle. His shoulders looked even broader than they did when he was clothed. His belly was flat. Bravely, she let her eyes drift lower. His hips undulated gently with the movement of the towel. Below the board hard surface of his abdomen, nestled in dark gold curls, was all the evidence of his gender gently set in motion.

She felt odd, looking at him nude. Aroused, yes. Awed, yes. But more than that, she felt . . . possessive. It was as if she had known all her life what he looked like, known how golden dark his damp chest hair was, how muscled and powerful his thighs were, how uncompromisingly male he was. In the deep well of her unconscious, she already knew his body—and recognized him as her mate.

Feeling like a man who'd gone temporarily insane, Justin wrapped his towel around his hips. Now that it was too late, he was having second thoughts, and third and fourth ones. What kind of a damn fool was he? What made him think Shelly would want him any more after seeing him nude? She hadn't wanted him at all and she'd told him so, in a way that made him believe she meant it. He was crazy to try and tantalize her with his body. Women's minds didn't work that way. Women liked flowers, candy, candlelight, moonlight. Women liked to be wooed, not titillated. Muttering to himself that he had as much intelligence as a donkey's hind end, he strolled into the house and headed toward the library, thinking he needed a large dose of male company.

The rumblings were lower now, refined by the wine the men had been drinking. They'd been at it for nearly three

hours, and that helped Justin feel better about interrupting them.

When Justin rapped his knuckles on the panel and then
pushed open the door, the lights seemed too bright in the
library, and he seemed to be too undressed. Strom still
wore his formal tucked shirt, but he'd shed his tie and
undone a couple of the studs. he lounged behind the
desk, the wine bottle and glass in front of him. Under
Mel's crewcut graying hair, his tie hung around his
throat, and the jacket of his navy suit was slung over the
wing of the fireside chair he sat in. Beside him was an
ashtray full of cigarette butts. The window was open to
the cool country air, but a faint hint of smoke lingered.
Beyond the fluttering curtain, crickets chirped.

Neither man seemed to regard Justin's entrance into
their lair as an intrusion. Both looked happy to see him.

"Ah, son. Have a good swim?" His father's eyes
flickered over him, and there was approval in them for
Justin's tall, muscled form.

"Excellent, father." The faint mockery in Justin's
voice was for himself.

"Good, good." Strom rubbed his hands together in
anticipation. "Join us, son, join us. Sit down. Can I get
you a drink?"

"No, thanks." Justin was relieved to see his father was
feeling well and evidently suffering no pain in the aftermath of the wedding and his own unceremonious leap
into the pool with Shelly. He should have known better
than to think the wedding would be stressful for Strom.
The man thrived on crowds. Justin liked people, but he
wasn't the crowd lover that his father was.

Justin pushed the end of the overlarge beach towel a
little deeper into the wrap. He worked it around his hips
and lowered himself into the leather chair that was his

favorite and could take the dampness. He turned his head to look at the other man in the room, the man who always seemed to fit in the shadow of his father. "How are you, Mel?"

"Sitting up and taking nourishment," Mel said with his usual dry humor.

Justin's lips curved. "I'm glad to hear it." Why was it Mel could make him feel better just by being there? There was something solid about him, something a man could trust. Little wonder that Strom had cultivated the friendship of this man for nearly forty years. Strange, once he'd resented their closeness. Now he envied his father.

The corners of Mel's mouth moved, tucking back a smile. Justin directed his gaze back to Strom. There was something going on here that he didn't understand, but he had a feeling it concerned him. He'd strolled headlong into the lion's den.

"What mischief are you two plotting?"

Mel looked amused, his father mock-offended. Strom was the first to protest. The guiltiest usually were, thought Justin.

"We're too old to be thinking about mischief. Right, Mel?"

Mel's smile was his answer. The man was the complete antithesis of his father, quiet, soft-spoken, self-contained. In all the years he had known him, Justin had never seen Mel lose his temper. Red got her hair and her fire from her mother, a woman Justin had never known.

"You two won't live long enough to be too old for mischief," said Justin.

Mel chuckled, his eyes on Strom.

Justin too, examined his father. "Hard to believe you're the same man who sat in this room last night and groused about your lack of accomplishment."

Strom's scowl was instant. "Stow it. Mel's not interested in my troubles."

"You've got troubles, Strom?" His tone was gentle, but his eyebrow lifted. Once set on the track, Mel was immovable.

Strom fiddled with his glass. He was self-conscious, oddly ill at ease. His manner seemed strange to Justin. He'd never known Strom to hide anything from Mel, never known him to be self-conscious in Mel's presence. Reluctantly, Strom said, "There are times lately...getting older... I think about what happened and I wonder if it isn't time to—" Strom's eyes flickered to the wall beyond Justin's shoulder, the wall where his awards, acclamations and his Medal of Honor hung.

A mixture of emotions flitted across Mel's face, discomfort, displeasure, fear. "No use pondering the past. That's over and done with." Mel's voice was flat, final. He turned to Justin. "I think you ought to know—your father's out to set a trap for my daughter."

Strom fixed him with a stern, chiding gaze. "For a man who doesn't say much you can sure spill the beans when you want to."

"Justin has a right to know," Mel said, sitting back in the chair, looking relaxed again and at ease with himself and the world.

Carefully Justin regarded Strom. "Isn't she a little young for you?"

Strom shook his head, grimacing at Justin's attempt at humor. "Not for me, you idiot. I want her for you."

Justin ignored Strom's sputtering and turned to Mel. "You approve of this?"

"My daughter has a mind of her own. She's not likely to be pushed around, even by an old warhorse like your dad with the whiff of battle in his nose and the bit between his teeth."

Justin considered his options and decided the gods had indeed been busy tonight. Why should he reject their second gift? The trouble was, if his father did anything too overt, he'd send Shelly running like the wind in the opposite direction. To Mel he said, "What does he plan to use for bait?"

"You . . . and a Decathlon airplane."

"Not necessarily in that order," Justin said drily.

Mel chuckled and agreed, "Not necessarily in that order."

Justin was aware that Strom had been watching his exchange with Mel with narrowed eyes. Obviously he'd already mapped out a campaign to Mel. "You're willing to go along with this?"

Mel regarded the younger man steadily, his blue eyes unguarded. "The question is . . . are you willing?"

To Justin, it seemed as if there must be a thousand motives swirling around in the room. His father's motive was easy enough to figure out: he wanted grandchildren. Justin's own motives were a little more . . . basic.

What were Mel's motives? His daughter wasn't a young innocent anymore. Justin supposed there was a certain point when a father accepted that his daughter was a woman who made her own decisions about her sex life. Still, he felt ill at ease, his skin chilled and exposed above his towel, out of his league in a way he hadn't felt in a long time. It was Mel more than Strom that bothered him. Justin knew what Strom had to gain. What did Mel have to gain? A moneyed son-in-law? Justin didn't think so. There wasn't an avaricious bone in Mel's body.

Conducting an affair with Shelly in full view of both their fathers had its disadvantages. It also had its advantages. Shelly in his bed, without paternal censure. Shelly, walking beside him, freely, openly, his to look at and touch whenever the urge arose. He could already see her walking beside him down a path, her face illuminated in the glow of the setting sun. Then he thought of the vulnerable but determined look on her face as they'd stood together beside the fence while the sun slowly sank to meet the earth, and his dream bubble burst.

"Gentlemen, as much as I approve of your . . . battle plan I'm afraid the question is academic. I already asked the lady out to dinner. She said no."

Had Justin thought he'd take the wind from Strom's sails with his admission of failure? He was wrong. Strom had a great, grinning, I-told-you-so expression on his face. "Well, if you fumbled the ball, you'd better let me try."

Justin shot a look at Mel to gauge his reaction. The older man looked cool, unmoved, a slight smile pulling the corners of his mouth up. To him, Justin said, "Are you sure you approve of this?"

"More to the point, will Shelly approve of you?" Mel calmly tossed the ball back in Justin's court.

"Probably not." Justin's voice was neutral.

"Are you going to let that stop you?" Mel's tone matched Justin's own.

That was enough encouragement for Justin. He turned back to his father. "What's the plan?"

"SLEEP WELL?" Justin murmured to the tousled, slightly sleep-dazed looking Shelly as he slid into the banquette next to her. In the bright morning sun, her hair shone like fire. Her face was pale, washed clean of makeup, beautiful. She was sipping orange juice, dressed in a different shirt of his than the one she'd slept in and some khaki shorts he'd had a hundred years ago. Morley must have gone digging in the attic. He had to admit the cuffed edges looked better on her slim thighs than they ever had when he wore them.

"Very well. And you?" She wanted to hit him. The man looked fresh out of *Gentlemen's Quarterly*, immaculately turned out in white pants and white shoes, a tan shirt that enhanced the color of his green eyes, his hair still shower damp. She felt like an extra from an African bush movie.

"I slept quite a bit better after my swim."

"Oh, were you swimming? I didn't know."

Silently, Morley served him a glass of orange juice. Justin held it up, using it as a tool for drama, the way he might have a water glass in the courtroom. "Didn't you? You should have. Your window was open. You should have heard me splashing away out there...unless you dropped off to sleep right away."

The devil knew she'd been watching him. "I...must have." She flushed, but didn't look away.

"That's a good trick, lying with a straight face. Do you do it frequently?"

Morley went back into the kitchen and her capitulation was instant and graceful. "How did you know I was...watching you?" Her voice was low, controlled.

"I'm not sure. I think I...felt you with me." He caught her eyes, held them with his. "I should apologize."

Looking at her the way he was, genuinely concerned for her feelings, soberly gentle with that old-world courtesy he could occasionally affect, she'd forgive him anything. "No need. I was as guilty as you." She lifted her chin and smiled. "I have to admit that I . . . enjoyed the view."

"Score one for honesty," he murmured.

"I'm usually honest." She toyed with her silverware. "What did you do after you came out of the pool?" At the quizzical lift of his brow, she shrugged. "I was concerned. You didn't come upstairs and I went back to check the pool to see if you'd drowned."

"Worried . . . or hoping?" He grinned lazily.

"Don't be an idiot. I was worried, of course."

"I haven't drowned . . . yet." He controlled her eyes with his, searching for their secrets, letting her see that he meant exactly what she suspected he meant. "I have a feeling it's only a matter of time."

She moved restlessly. She couldn't let him follow up on the advantage he'd gained last night which, despite all his charming contrition, he obviously meant to do.

He said, "I've a proposition for you."

Her eyes flashed to his face.

"Not that kind . . . unless after last night you've changed your mind."

"You're shameless." She shook her head, but she was smiling.

Encouraged, Justin launched the attack. "Dad has a new Decathlon. He wants you to take it up and check it out for him."

She dropped her eyes but not before he saw the blaze of interest—and envy. He baited the trap with more succulent lure. "If you like the way it handles, he wants you to fly it in the air show."

Shelly shook her head. She wasn't an idiot, there were strings attached, there had to be. She just didn't know who had attached them or what kind of strings they were. Who had instigated the scheme to put her into a Corbett plane—Justin, his father, or her father? Mel didn't say much . . . but he thought Justin was the closest thing to perfect a young man could be and he'd been unhappy about her ten-year hiatus from Corbett Hill. "No, I—"

"It's all gassed up and waiting at the hangar."

"I don't have my flight suit here."

"You seem to do all right with my clothes. I can probably dig up a smaller suit you could wear."

"I . . . couldn't."

Justin leaned back against the banquette, knowing he'd won. She wouldn't make it an easy victory. But she would surrender. At the thought of Shelly surrendering, his body warmed, stirred. Carelessly he lifted a shoulder. "You're probably wise. It is a plot, you know. Dad hatched it as an enticement to get you involved with me."

He leaned back on the banquette, one arm spread lazily over the top of the seat, his face composed, his body easy, totally uninvolved with the bombshell he'd dropped.

"You aren't serious."

"I wouldn't joke about my father's attempt to procure me a woman."

She considered him. He seemed cool and poised, unconcerned. Yet his shirt lay open exposing his throat and she could see the pulse beating there. Justin was a fine athlete with a slow pulse, but the blood throbbed under the surface a shade too fast to be called *slow*. He might look as if he didn't care, but he did. Justin was very proud—and very male.

With just the right whisper of a sultry drawl, she said, "If what I saw last night is any indication, you don't need any help from your father in . . . procuring women."

He smiled, too slowly, too deliberately. This was a game, and she was out of her depth. "Stop dodging the question. Are you going to take the congressman up on his offer?''

She could feel her heart beating, feel the need, the ache, the want to say yes. "Not until I understand what the offer is.''

"You take the plane up, I take you out to dinner.''

"That's it, that's all there is to it, one flight for one dinner?''

"You've got it.''

She hesitated. It seemed too easy, too pat.

"Scared, Red?'' he taunted gently.

Her chin came up and her blue eyes sparkled with spirit. "How soon can you find that flight suit?''

AN INCREDIBLE JUNE SKY. A three-knot wind. Lazy wisps of cirrus clouds. A gorgeous day.

Blond hair blowing in the breeze. A tall lean form striding across the field in his flight suit. Tanned hands sliding in easy coordination with his legs. A gorgeous man.

Twin Decathlon planes stood beside each other, the one Justin would be flying and the one Strom had bought for his own use. Shelly walked over the dry grass, her borrowed flight suit rustling with each step, the grass-hoppers bouncing in panicked flight in front of her. She felt as if a few of them had bounded into her stomach.

It was silly to be nervous. She'd flown partners with Justin many times. They would be rusty at first, she supposed. They would have to give each other room, until they picked up the timing again. They had always had good timing, as if they were two parts of the same whole. In the air.

"Preflight check done? Parachute fastened?''

She nodded. At an age when other young men had been careening around corners in their cars, Justin had been making her repack her chute to make sure it would deploy. He was a stickler for safety.

"See you up there, then."

She smiled. "See you."

In the air Shelly worked stick and rudder to do a banking turn to the left, then to the right. The plane handled like a finely tuned horse, lots of muscle power at her command, ready to respond instantly. Flying in a machine like this, on a day like this, was like having a long, sexual high. She was filled with an incredible feeling of power and lightness. She could do anything. The world was hers.

A beautiful world it was, patches of green and brown laid out in a crazy-quilt pattern which made no sense except as a pleasure to the eye.

Gratitude. Her heart filled with it. *Thanks, Strom, for thinking of letting me fly your plane, no matter what your motive was. Thanks, Justin, for teaching me to fly. Thanks, God, for making this world for me to fly in.*

She was feeling the euphoria, Justin knew. He felt it, too. Crazy how he had forgotten what it felt like to fly with her. To slip into the air beside her and lift into that first loop, to know that her skill equaled his own and that she was doing what he did and feeling what he felt was like nothing he had ever known before or since.

As effortlessly as that, they began the old routine. Together, like two gliding seagulls, they circled up in perfect unison, side by side. At the top, the weightlessness of a negative G. Justin, as he'd learned to do, as he'd taught Shelly to do, tightened his abdominal muscles. It was an old pilot's trick, a necessary one. It prevented the blood from falling away from the brain and pooling in his abdominal cavity when he dropped to the bottom of the loop and the four positive Gs hit him.

Shelly came down with him, as if tied to his wingtip with a string. He did a programmed climb to gain back height and speed, Shelly beside him. A cross-over spin, following Shelly. An Immelmann turn. And finally, the Hammerhead. He aimed the airplane like a sword piercing the sky, straight up at full power 145 miles per hour. Just before he lost airspeed, he applied left full rudder... knowing that Shelly was doing the same.

Shelly. Suppose she made a mistake? Suppose she turned too late, throttled too soon? It was too late to change his mind. He turned tail for head and dropped into the dive, recovering just above the fifteen-hundred-foot minimum.

He lifted up and leveled off and found himself trembling. He'd done that dive a million times and he'd known the danger, but only as a high, as a good-to-be-alive surge of adrenaline. This time, as he hung there in the sky on the turnover, the thought bloomed in his mind that he was endangering Shelly needlessly. He was a fool to put her through such paces in a plane she'd never known before.

He spotted her in his peripheral vision. Shelly was right beside him, safe, level, in the air.

Justin's throat loosened, his shoulders relaxed. She'd done her Hammerhead as perfectly as he, but in the backlash of his agonizing, he knew an intense need to shake the living daylights out of her. She should know better. *He* should know better. They weren't kids anymore, too dumb to realize the dangers. If anything had happened to injure her... he couldn't live with that.

He let his breath out in a long, slow sigh. He hadn't felt this anxious about her when he was instructing her. It was a disturbing thought, one he didn't have time to examine. For Shelly had slipped behind him and was firing at him in a dogfight simulation.

According to plan, he dropped and came up behind her to tail her relentlessly, shadowing each sudden, sickening drop, each bobbing lift, till they reached the point where she was to dive under and come up behind him.

He decided he wasn't going to let her elude him as planned in the routine. He readied himself to follow her sudden drop, but suddenly—she was gone.

She'd read his mind, the little fox, and she'd slipped into the drop before she was supposed to. He knew without turning to check that she was on his tail.

He used every ounce of his concentration, all his cunning, all the wily, clever moves in his repertoire, dipping, bobbing, weaving in an erratic course in an attempt to shake her loose. She stuck like glue. There was no longer any routine, there was simply Justin and Shelly pitting their wits against each other.

He tried every trick he knew, but his sideways slides, his sudden drops were shadowed with maddening tenacity by hers. He looped and she followed. He spun and she followed. He turned and she followed. The lady witch was reading his mind.

Shelly felt the euphoria bubbling inside her. She was in tune with the sky, the sun, the earth, the plane—and Justin. Whatever he did, she did. He couldn't escape her. If their game had been in earnest, Justin would have been spiraling to the earth by now, his plane on fire.

Justin liked a good contest, but he was no fool. Working in the courtroom taught him that when defeat is inevitable, it's best to bring the battle to a quick end. He waggled his wings at her to concede his loss, circled around to come in for a landing—and found Shelly zooming headlong at him.

It was the old stunt, the way they used to end their routine, the suicidal, headlong flight at each other like two guided missiles on collision course. Justin gritted his teeth. They hadn't discussed this, hadn't prepared for it. His first instinct was to pull his plane up and away from the deadly game of chicken.

A sudden, sickening realization hit him. He couldn't. He didn't know which way—or when—she was going to break away. If he didn't want to run the risk of slamming into her, he'd have to wait for her to make the first move.

But she wasn't moving. Damn the woman! He had exactly five seconds to decide what to do. Mumbling a curse, he jerked back the stick and swung to the left, praying, praying, praying he'd made the right decision. The searing sound of the wind told him he'd flown clear.

His heart hammered. He tasted brass on his tongue. He'd been afraid, mind-blowing, nerve-shattering afraid. Suppose he'd made a mistake and slammed into her, killed her?

Cold with fury, Justin brought the plane down, taxied to a stop and unbuckled the restraining belts. She'd broken every rule in the book and he'd tell her so. He'd rip her to shreds for endangering her life so recklessly.

He shrugged out of his parachute and climbed out of the plane. Shelly was on the ground before him, her face flushed, her blue eyes sparkling, her red hair blowing free and wild.

Justin took one look at the vivid animation on her face and heard himself saying in a mild tone, ''Proud of yourself?''

"Yes, actually." She shimmered like a Christmas tree ornament, all light and brilliance.

"You were taking a lot for granted up there. Suppose my timing was off or I'd forgotten which way to turn and slammed into you?"

She lifted a delicious, red-gold eyebrow. "You sound like you've got a toothache. Are you angry?"

"I'm working on it."

She laid her hand on his arm, and he could feel the shimmering incandescence of her. "I knew you'd remember how we did it before. You're the big-city lawyer with the phenomenal memory."

He stared at her, wondering whether that stirring of nerves was from anger or sexual excitement. "Right now, I'm forgetting what the penalty is for murder."

"I knew exactly what I was doing up there and so did you."

He wondered about that. He felt as if he hadn't known what he was doing since the moment he reached out and untangled Shelly's hair from his sister-in-law's bridal veil.

Perky as a sprite, she asked, "Ready for that cup of coffee?"

He was readier to wring her neck. "What were you trying to prove up there?"

That brought her down to earth. Shelly's smile vanished. "Nothing. Not a darn thing, except that your father's airplane flies like a dream." At his disbelieving look, she made a gesture with her hand. "All right, maybe I was trying to show you that things have changed since I was your pupil, that I can fly with you as an equal now—"

"Is that what you were showing me...that we're equals? Somehow I felt...outranked."

"Are you...upset?"

"My ego will survive, if that's what you're worried about."

"Your ego is the last thing of yours I'd worry about damaging, Mr. Corbett."

"Are there other things of mine you would worry about damaging?"

His voice was smooth as silk and twice as sensuous. "Oh, stop trying to make me self-conscious!" she said angrily.

"I'm not trying to make you self-conscious. I'm trying to make you conscious of me." Holding his helmet in one hand, Justin let the other drop to his side and reach for hers. His fingers were warm, evocative. She struggled not to react. She couldn't reveal how well he was succeeding in his efforts to intrude on her senses.

"You do remember the second part of the bargain?"

"I have a pretty good memory myself, counselor. I'll be looking forward to eating dinner at your expense." The touch of his fingers wrapped around hers disturbed her. She had to make sure he understood a shared meal didn't mean she'd changed her mind. She had to keep things as light and undemanding as they were now. "I'll even get dressed as the occasion demands, in my best bib and tucker."

There was a teasing, needling mockery in her eyes he didn't understand. He felt a need to retaliate. "What makes you think you'll need your best bib and tucker? I might take you to Hamburger Heaven."

Her lips lifted. "You? In Hamburger Heaven? Impossible. I know exactly where we'll go. You'll take me to The Inn on the Hill where they serve oysters on the half shell, pheasant under glass, and the waiter brings the bill in a leather-bound book."

He felt exposed, ridiculously transparent, as bombed out of the sky as he had been a moment ago. The Inn was exactly where he'd been thinking about taking her. "Lady, you'll get what you deserve. It's Hamburger Heaven for you."

She laughed. She was back on high again, a devilish angel, full of herself and her accomplishment, still soaring on the adrenaline of her dare-devil flight.

"Don't be ridiculous. You wouldn't be caught dead in that place. And you'd look ridiculous, too. They wouldn't let you in. It's a denim haven as well as a hamburger heaven and you don't own a pair of jeans."

Stung, Justin stood stock-still, his eyes fastened on her face. She was teasing, but he had a feeling her teasing was deadly serious. "What's so bad about not owning a pair of jeans?"

His eyes held hers. She realized suddenly they'd ventured into a mine field. One false step and the world would explode. "I don't think I can explain it to you in the time we have at our disposal."

He grabbed her arm with a violence that had her eyes flashing and a flush blooming under her cheeks. She didn't like being manhandled. She especially didn't like being manhandled by him.

But Justin wasn't in a mood to consider her preferences. "Don't fob me off with that ridiculous cliché."

Tense, she gazed at him in stunned silence. She wanted him to remove his hand from her arm and that look from his eyes. She reached into her mind for coolness, for logic. "There's nothing wrong with not owning a pair of jeans, especially for your life-style. Not a thing. I'm not questioning your masculinity." A pause, then like a battling kitten cornered but determined to hold her own, she added, "I could hardly do that after last night. Now would you be so kind as to let me go?"

"Not until you tell me why you think denim pants are so damned necessary in a man's wardrobe."

She tried to twist away, he held her fast. Angry now, disturbed by what she was feeling, the excitement she always felt when he touched her laced with the guilt for the hurt she knew she'd already inflicted even without answering the question to his satisfaction, Shelly said, "Just forget it."

"No." Implacable, proud, he tightened his grip on her. "I want the truth from you," he said through his teeth, "and I don't care if we have to stand here all day to get it."

She should have known better than to take on the assistant district attorney. "All right. You want the truth, here it is. Your lack of denim pants is just one more thing that marks you as 'perfect' and sets you apart from the rest of the world."

Justin didn't move a muscle. His face might have been carved of stone. "I'm not perfect."

"No, you aren't, but you were brought up to think you were by a martinet manservant obsessed with keeping you immaculate and an ambitious father obsessed with seeing you excel." She took a breath, steadying herself for the coup de grace. "You don't live on the same humdrum level as the rest of us."

In the echoing silence that followed, life and vitality drained from Justin's face. "And I thought you could only shoot me down from inside a plane."

"You wanted to know what I thought." She twisted her arm, asking for release.

He let go of her. "I should know better than to ask the witness a leading question."

She shoved an unruly lock of red hair out of her eyes. "We'd better forget about dinner."

Justin went on staring at her, as if he were seeing her for the first time in his life. "No. You made the bargain, and you'll keep it."

Vexed, Shelly stared at him, waiting for him to change his mind. He gazed back at her, his face impassive. Muttering a word about the stubborn pride of the male population in general and one man in particular, she started the trek across the grassy runway toward Justin's car.

CHAPTER FOUR

THERE WASN'T ENOUGH MONEY in the county budget for Justin Corbett to have a secretary of his own. He shared Jenny Sims with his boss and two other assistant district attorneys out of the sixty A.D.A.s employed by the county. Jenny was young, only nineteen years of age with long brown hair and brown eyes to match. She'd gone for a year's secretarial training and taken the job six weeks ago. Her normal expression was that of a frightened doe, but today she came out of Justin Corbett's office looking like a puzzled, frightened doe.

Mrs. Davis, the receptionist, a motherly woman of fifty-plus years who tried to keep the tension level on the third floor of the county courthouse somewhere below the intolerable level, eyed Jenny as she stood outside Justin's closed door.

"Is something wrong, dear?"

Brown eyes like beacons turned to Carolyn. "I think Mr. Corbett is sick," Jenny confided breathlessly in a tone that reminded Carolyn Davis of Marilyn Monroe.

"Does he look ill?"

"No, he just acts sick." Those brown-doe eyes flashed up to Carolyn. "First he took the file I handed him from Mr. Harrison's office, the one on Thomas Kemp, and dumped it out on his desk. When I said he should be careful, he said he was tired of being careful. Then he pulled some books out of his bookcase and just sort of threw them on top of the file. And then he looked up and asked me if I didn't ever wear anything besides a dress, didn't I have a pair of jeans. Mrs. Davis, you told me the day I was hired I couldn't wear jeans here at the courthouse."

"Yes, I know. Mr. Corbett knows it, too."

"Then what did he mean?"

"I don't know, I'm sure. I'll speak to him if you like."

"I don't think you'd better. When I left, he was up on a chair looking for dust on top of his bookshelf almost as if he wanted to find it and muttering something about 'not so damned perfect as all that.' Excuse the language, Mrs. Davis."

The imitation of Justin's tone was wonderfully authentic, all the more surprising coming from the feminine Jenny. Carolyn managed to maintain her sober, interested expression and suppress the smile that threatened to surface. "That's all right, Jenny. You're allowed some latitude when you're quoting directly." Amused, Carolyn watched Jenny look back at Justin's office door, shake her head and sink into her desk chair across the aisle as if seeking sanctuary.

Carolyn had worked in the Justice Department for twenty years and she prided herself on knowing when to mind her own business. Still, the temptation to look in on the immaculate Mr. Corbett and see if he really was buried in papers and looking for dust was too intriguing to resist. She had a batch of phone messages that had collected over the morning for him while he was with Jenny. Normally she would have given them to the young woman to deliver and stayed by the phone.

The heck with the phone. Let it ring. She collected the yellow slips into a pile, carried them to Justin's door and knocked. "Justin. Messages."

A clatter like a book hitting the floor and a muttered curse were her answers. *Curiouser and curiouser,* Carolyn thought. Justin Corbett was never angry in the office, never swore with such vehemence. Secure in her position as the oldest employee and the true office boss, she pushed open the door.

Justin looked very...unusual. His tie was pulled down from its place just under his Adam's apple. His hair was mussed, his jacket hanging half-on and half-off the back of his chair. He stood behind the desk, keeping her at bay.

Carolyn leaned against the doorway and folded her arms. "Well, you came down off the chair, I see."

Justin only scowled and glared uncomprehendingly at her.

"You created this chaos just since ten o'clock this morning? My friend, you need a vacation."

Those famous, probing eyes cut her. A young punk Justin had prosecuted once said he'd rather be knifed than hit with those eyes. Carolyn agreed. "Are you all right?" she asked.

"I'm fine."

"I can tell. Still planning on having lunch with Canfield?"

"I suppose." He looked vague, distracted, totally unconcerned about his upcoming lunch with the politician who had the power to make him the next district attorney.

Carolyn looked around the cubbyhole office that Justin usually kept in apple-pie order. "Is he coming up here to meet you?"

"No. We're getting together at the restaurant."

"Good thing," Carolyn murmured. "Well, if you need any help, let me know."

"Carolyn."

She turned, something in his tone making her heart twist. She'd always had a warm spot in her heart for Justin. "Yes?"

"Do you own a pair of jeans?"

She smiled. "Who doesn't? Green ones, blue ones, purple ones . . . I even have a pair with rhinestones on the back pockets. My oldest son gave them to me last Christmas. Why do you ask?"

"I . . . no reason."

Carolyn cast a jaundiced eye around the room and then over Justin. "Are you sure you don't need any help?"

Justin shook his head.

"Well, do us both a favor and comb your hair before you keep your lunch date, hmm? We don't want it bandied about that we're a bunch of riff-raff up here." Smiling, Carolyn leaned on the doorknob and swung the door closed. It was only when she got back to the desk she discovered the messages she'd meant to give Justin were still in her hand.

IT WAS A GLORIOUS FRIDAY on Eagle Hill, the kind when the sun turned everything to green and gold, with thermals to make a sailplane pilot grin from ear to ear. Shelly wasn't smiling. She was waiting on top of the hill with a student for the last ride in her Dierderhoff sailplane, looking up the tail of the Super Cub and finding it hard to keep her attention focused where it should be, on her teaching. The lady in the rear cockpit was the fourth "mouse" she'd taken up that day and the greenest. Fatigue dulled Shelly's mind, making her drop her guard. As they had last night, thoughts of Justin intruded. Guilty thoughts.

Why had she made such a silly issue over his not wearing jeans? So what if he didn't live like the rest of the world? What business was it of hers?

Derek, her teenage helper and man-about-the-premises, hoisted the wingtip off the ground, bringing the sailplane level. The tow plane started, and they were in motion, rolling down the runway, Derek running alongside. The sailplane lifted and they were airborne behind the still-grounded plane.

Shelly came awake to her responsibilities. Those few minutes of takeoff were tricky and required her attention, especially with her student at the controls. "Remember to keep the stick forward a little," she told Ruth. "That lets you sink and takes the drag off the tow plane so it can take off."

Her student, a thirty-five-year-old woman named Ruth Haslitt, obeyed, but she was nervous and her hand was tense on the stick. Shelly knew from the woman's previous lessons it did no good to ask her to relax. She sighed, thinking how hard most people made things for themselves. There was minimal danger in sailplane flight as long as you knew what you were doing and didn't take a foolish chance. But people had the idea that a lack of motor was less safe, not more so. Then she reminded herself that most people hadn't been strapped into the seat of a plane when they were two years old by a diehard World War II pilot like she had.

"Stay above him. Try not to overcontrol. When the tow-plane turns, you point your nose at his outer wingtip to keep the rope taut."

The towplane lifted off the ground and they were up, flying in tandem. One circle to gain altitude, then another. Shelly told Ruth when to slack off on the tow rope and pull the release. She did so, and they were up, free.

The teacher forced her hand to rest lightly on the stick and let the student retain control. Calmly Shelly kept her eyes on the variometer, the rate-of-climb indicator that gave a human being the sensitivity of a swallow toward lift. The markings were in German, *Steigt* for lift and *Stinkt* for drop. The needle flopped over to *Steigt*, telling Shelly what a great day it was for soaring. Beyond the snub-nosed canopy, their shadow skimmed the meadow, sleek, long-winged, a bird like no other bird. Sailplane flight was unbroken by the roar of a motor, but it had a symphony all its own of whistles, pops and bleats created by the wind raking past the plane. That wind was her companion. Usually it meant peace of mind. Not today. Nor any other day. All week long, the replay of the things she'd said to Justin kept going around in her head, like a tape loop that had no end.

... brought up by a martinet manservant ... ambitious father ... you don't live ... where the rest of the world lives ... including me.

That was the most damaging thing of all. She'd set herself apart from Justin irrevocably.

Justin didn't deserve that from her. He'd given her lessons in aerobatic flying and provided the plane, at no cost to her. All she'd had to do was show up. It had never occurred to the teenage Shelly that a twenty-year-old man might have things he wanted to do on a Saturday morning other than teach a stripling girl to fly.

He'd been a hard taskmaster. At times she'd hated him. But she'd learned. The way Justin had looked the day she'd soloed flashed into her mind. Pride. He'd been proud of her—and happy for her.

And now when she was old enough to understand his altruistic giving of himself and his time, she'd repaid him by telling him exactly what she thought of him and his life-style.

Guilt poured over her in waves. She felt nearly ill with a stomach-clenching nervousness that told her she'd done something that could never be undone. How could she have been so unfeeling?

She could have put him off with a light, easy answer, a lie. It hadn't been necessary to hit him coldly in the face with the truth about her opinion of him. No, she wouldn't have been able to lie either, not really. She'd never been able to tell Justin a fib, not even a little white social one. He knew her too well. One day she'd gone out to the field feeling rotten the way women often did, and he'd taken one look at her and asked her what was wrong. She couldn't tell him of course, so she lied and said she was fine. He'd cast a derisive look over her face, dragged her by the arm back to his car, driven her to a restaurant, and ordered up tea and aspirin. While she drank the tea, he chatted with her as if they were there for no other reason than to pass the time of day. He'd never mentioned that day again and neither had she.

"I thought you could only shoot me down from inside a plane."

He'd been nothing but kind to her. Why had she been so cruel to him?

Because she was afraid.

Of what?

Of herself. Of the restless wanting she hadn't known was inside her until Justin looked at her, talked to her, touched her, a fiery need capable of burning away the control she'd cultivated so carefully. She'd taught herself never to need anyone. Justin was the one who could set her ablaze and transform her into a phoenix reborn, a woman who rose from the ashes of passion needing him more than she needed flying, or independence, or sanity.

Senseless, all this protracted worrying. It was over. She'd half expected him to call during the week and make a token effort at arranging the dinner she owed him, but when he hadn't, she knew she wouldn't hear from him again. Justin was a winner who didn't like to lose.

It was all for the best that she wasn't going to see him again, of course. She was relieved. He was an added complication in her life she didn't need. If for an instant, she had allowed herself to glimpse a foolish dream and pretend it might come true, well, she was human, after all.

A lift followed by a drop of the plane signaled that Ruth had missed a thermal. The woman wanted desperately to learn to soar, but her tension interfered with what might have been a natural feel for the sport. Ruth was afraid to trust herself.

That was the trouble with trying to teach a human being to soar. You could give them the rules, but in the end, soaring was an art. A sailplane pilot had to think like an artist, to relax and let go of the fear, and trust the creative leap between knowledge and intuition.

Suddenly she thought, life is like that. You have to let go of the fear and trust creativity to tell you how to soar highest and longest. But it was hard, too hard to trust, too hard to let go. She had learned, through experience, to play it safe.

She could fly but she couldn't soar.

Suddenly, Shelly's philosophical musings gave way to basic survival instinct. "Circle around and see if you catch another thermal closer to the cliff," Shelly shouted at Ruth.

"I'm getting dizzy," Ruth yelled back.

First things first—keep Ruth from throwing up in the cockpit. "I'll take the stick and we'll go down."

"Hey, how come you didn't stay up longer? Today was all *Steigt* and not much *Stinkt*, eh?" Patricia Hennings, Shelly's tow pilot, came to join her where Shelly stood in the shadow of the sailplane watching Ruth pick her way across the rippling sheen of blowing grass toward her automobile.

Shelly nodded at Ruth. "That's why."

Pat turned her head to follow Shelly's gaze. "Not feeling too good, is she?"

"I wanted to take her home. She insisted she'd be all right once she's in the car."

"And you were thinking she's crazy. But you're a little crazy, too. You think she's safer up there," Pat pointed at the sky, "than out there." A slender finger stabbed toward the road that led down off the top of the hill.

"We all have our little...blind spots." Without warning, Justin popped into her mind. He was her blind spot.

Pat shot her a quizzical glance. She was too shrewd, this six-foot-tall woman with a heart to match. During the two years Pat had piloted for Shelly, their relationship had gone far beyond employee and employer.

"Too bad your mouse got queasy. It sure is a gorgeous day for soaring. You want to go back up? I've got enough fuel for another tow."

"No, thanks." Shelly ran a hand through her flame-red hair and squinted into the sun.

"You must be sick, too."

"No, I'm not sick, I'm just not into it today."

Patricia's eyebrows climbed. "You not into soaring? That's a first. What's the matter? Man trouble?"

Shelly's blue eyes flashed. "Why do you say that?"

"Hit a nerve, did I? Whenever a woman gets a look on her face like you got, it's man trouble."

Shelly stared into the distance. They stood on a grassy hill, a flat-topped cliff with a jagged, glacier-eaten edge that fell away to a sheer drop of three hundred and fifty feet, making it one of the best soaring spots in the world. "He's not trouble. He's . . . an old friend."

Pat nodded sagely. "They're the worst kind."

More than a little afraid Pat was right, Shelly stuck her hands in her pockets and headed for the shack where they sold tickets for Sunday rides and drank coffee. Pat fell into step behind her, waiting for more revelations about this mysterious man who'd entered Shelly's life, a man who had the power to put a look on Shelly's face she'd never once worn during a two-year relationship with the health-food addict.

At the shack, Shelly turned and faced Pat. "Did you ever do something you were sure was right at the time and after it was over, know it was terribly wrong?"

"Yeah. I married my husband." Shelly smiled at that. So did Pat. "You couldn't have made a mistake that bad."

"Maybe I did."

Pat's gaze went over Shelly's shoulder to the grassy track that provided an entrance to the primitive parking lot. "Well, well well. What have we here?"

A sleek beige convertible in a brand of car so well known only the initials identified it swooped into the parking lot and turned neatly to rest its nose against the rickety rail fence. The elegant car looked out of place in the ratty air field, just as the man climbing out of the car looked out place in his three-piece suit, a city slicker come to bargain with the country mouse. The wind rushed to do homage, to rearrange Justin's blond hair, lift his suit jacket away from his lean hips.

She was wrong about his looking as if he didn't belong. Unmindful of his sleek hair's sudden unruliness and the flapping of his jacket, Justin strode toward them with the ease of a man who is at home in his body, supremely matched to the elemental beauty of land and sky. He was as primitive as the earth—and as full of life and passion.

"So he's what's making you look like boiled cabbage," Pat murmured. "Come to think of it, I'd look like boiled cabbage for him, too, if I thought it would make him notice me."

Justin came closer, his eyes only on Shelly.

"Hi," she said, wanting desperately to smooth the uncertainty away from his face.

"Hi." The arrogance was there under his easy manner, but it was muted by the ride of his eyes over her, searching for welcome or rejection.

She tried to keep both out of her expression and show him only a friendly curiosity. "What are you doing out here on a Friday afternoon?"

"I happened to be in the neighborhood," he lied lightly, but the truth burned in his eyes for her to see. Courage. Justin had the courage she lacked to let her read the truth in his face. "I talked to Mel in the hangar. He said you should be just about finishing up. I'm not interrupting anything, am I?" A glance at Pat acknowledged her presence.

"No. No, we were just about ready to call it a day." Shelly shoved a hand through her hair, thinking she must look cute with her old orange sweatshirt, her hair blowing to the four winds, and her jeans thin from too many washings. "My student got sick. I knew how she felt. I remember the first time you took me through a Cuban eight.''

"You had a pretty strong stomach."

"I needed it to fly with you." Casually, she linked her arm in his and introduced him to Pat. Intelligent woman that she was, Pat murmured, "Nice to meet you," and looked as if she meant it.

"You look tired," Shelly said. "Can I get you a cup of coffee? I think there might be a little left in the shack."

The woman was going to drive him crazy. Justin hadn't known what to expect, except that it wouldn't be easy. He'd been braced for a fight, was sure he would get one, almost needed one after a week of trying to figure out what to do and when to do it. But when the invitation came to Brad's party, he made his decision. He forced himself to wait until Friday to drive down to see her, when he had the time to concentrate fully on her. By the time he worked up his courage to climb in the car and drive the distance, he'd convinced himself he was in for a tough fight just to get her to speak to him. When she threaded her arm through his and offered him coffee, she knocked him off balance.

"Much as I'd like to join you," Pat's voice was dry, showing she'd noticed she hadn't been invited, "I'd better be on my way home. Tony will be chomping at the bit to go out for his fish fry."

"Oh, Pat." Shelly raked a hand through her hair again, wondering what was the matter with her. "Please, do stay and have some coffee. Tony won't mind waiting—"

Pat smiled sheepishly. "No, I'm afraid he will mind. I'll catch you another day. Have a nice night." She made a fast exit, striding away to leave Shelly standing much too close to Justin.

With Pat's protective presence gone, Shelly wanted to remove her arm and step away, but she wasn't sure how to do it without looking like a fool.

"How about that coffee?" she said brightly. She started to move forward, he stayed where he was. Their entwined arms and his hard body stopped her. "So this is where you hang out." His eyes swept the blacktop runway, the grassy field, the disreputable little shack that was supported by shaky corner studs and God's own grace, the hangar where the other tow plane was housed and toward which Derek was rolling the sailplane.

"This is it." She felt oddly nervous, like a mother with a child on display who was behaving badly. Seeing things through Justin's eyes, the shack looked disgraceful, the hangar World War II vintage. Which it was. "Is that why you came, to see where I 'hang out'?"

"No. Who's the stud?"

He felt her flinch at the explicit term, but at that exact moment, he didn't care. He hadn't pictured Shelly working day in and day out with a dude who resembled Don Johnson.

"Derek is a high school boy who works here in exchange for soaring lessons."

"Pretty big for a 'boy.'"

"Derek needs to be big to do all the work he does around here. Is that why you came, to run a check on my employees? Am I breaking some county ordinance?"

He scowled at that, his brows coming down. "Don't be ridiculous. I came to take you into the city shopping."

"Shopping?" Shelly stared at him blankly. "What do you need—" At the look on his face, she knew.

"I thought the jeans expert ought to at least have the courtesy to help me find a pair," he drawled.

"Justin, I didn't mean—"

"Oh, yes, you did," he said. "And you were right. I need a pair of denim pants for a party I've been invited to. I want you to help me look for them."

"I don't think—"

He didn't move, didn't say a word. He simply looked at her, his eyes darkly green, eloquent with a number of things, all of them disturbing: mockery, challenge, vulnerability. She measured that vulnerability and knew it was the most dangerous of all those lurking emotions. She mustn't give in to his silent plea for mercy.

"I should change clothes—"

"Why do you need to change clothes?"

"I'm not exactly dressed for the city. . . ." It was a feeble straw to clutch at, and she knew it. It broke and let her down.

"You look fine. Come on. You can comb your hair and put on lipstick or whatever you think you have to do on the way in." This time he tugged and she moved with him.

The tension eased out of him like water flowing downhill. He recovered control of his features quickly, but not before she saw and knew what he was feeling. For in a kind of madcap insanity, she felt the same way: vastly relieved. As if he'd planned it all along, he caught her elbow to help her walk over the grass.

It felt good to win one, Justin thought with a deep pleasure that warmed him through and through. Damn good. "All right if we catch something at a drive-in window of a fast-food place on the way up? You haven't eaten, have you?"

"That sounds fine." He put her into the car and when he slid in beside her, she said, "I'm supposed to comb my hair while I'm riding in a convertible?"

"I'll put the top up." He reached forward, but she put her hand on his arm.

"No, don't. It's such a beautiful afternoon. I can comb it when I get there."

He drove carefully over the grassy track that led to the bottom of the hill. Once he was out on the main road, she said, "How's Strom?"

"He went for the angiogram Wednesday. He came through the test well, but the doctors are still conferring. How about Mel?"

"He seems okay."

Justin reached over and clasped her hand. Slowly, he dragged her to his side. "I can hear you better if you're closer."

Insanity. This was sheer insanity. She'd had such good intentions. Now she looked down at their entwined hands resting on her jeaned thigh, his arm clothed in the expensive pin-stripe cloth of his made-to-order suit, and she knew she'd lost her mind. Or just simply . . . lost.

JUSTIN DISCOVERED SHOPPING with Shelly was like being with some woman he didn't know, had never seen before. Her hair mussed from the wind, her cheeks bright from the ride in his car, she had the enthusiasm and energy of a steam engine.

"Look at those golden chrysanthemums. Aren't they gorgeous? They weren't here last month. Oh, look in this window. They're getting the Halloween things out. I've always loved spooks and ghosts in white sheets and costumes."

"You're a demented woman," Justin said, but he smiled indulgently and, grasping her elbow, steered her into the store.

"But we came to buy you jeans—"

"There's plenty of time." He liked to see her face, as radiant as a kid's. She noticed and exulted in everything, the dainty Hummel figurines, the grotesque vampire faces decorating a helium balloon, the ceramic ghosts perched on red maple leaves. She hummed along with the old ballad that was playing over the speaker, blissful in her contemplation of the Halloween cast of characters.

Ingenuously she lifted a witch and probed the inside of her skirt for a price tag. "Fourteen dollars and ninety-eight cents. That's a lot to pay for a witch, even if she does have the scariest face this side of Boris Karloff."

"Let me buy it for you."

"No." Her cheeks filled with color and she set the witch down and wandered on to examine a beautifully carved wooden decoy. Frustrated, Justin jammed his hands in his pants pockets and wondered if he would ever understand women in general, and this woman in particular. She was an especially obstinate card-carrying member of the species—and he was beginning to like her more and more.

It was when they had gone the complete circuit of the store and were back in front of the Halloween display again that Justin began to get a glimmer of what was going on. Shelly looked at everything, treasured everything—but coveted nothing. All things passed freely from her fingers.

Justin smoothed a thumb over the black skirt of the witch. "Why don't you buy it? You can afford it."

She flashed him an amused look. "Of course I can't afford it. I squander my money on nonessentials like food and gas and Pat's salary. Besides, I can't clutter my life with knick-knacks and possessions and—"

"Lovers?"

The moment he said the word, Justin wanted to take it back.

"We'd better try to find you those pants," Shelly said quietly, as color rushed to her face.

Turning, she marched out of the store and felt him catch up to her. She wasn't looking at him, but the way he'd examined her—with one eyebrow wryly raised while he drawled the one word in mocking politeness—danced inside her brain, permanently etched there. She deserved it, she supposed. She'd called him a spoiled brat. That gave him the right to zero in on her shortcomings. But in all her twenty-eight years, she'd never met a man who took her measure so accurately.

She told herself it didn't matter what Justin thought of her, but the sheen had gone off the day. She led him into a jeans store that had the garments folded and stacked in cubbyholes from floor to ceiling. Shelly carefully avoided his eyes while the young woman asked Justin what type of jeans he wanted—straight-leg, boot-cut, unwashed, washed, pleated, stone-dyed, or designer?

Justin didn't care how many kinds of jeans there were. He stared at Shelly, willing her to look at him and forgive him just a little. She wouldn't meet his eyes. She stood, transfixed by a spot past his shoulder, the animation gone from her face, her mouth sober. He felt a twist of nerves, an unfamiliar sensation of regret. How long were they going to go on like this, so vulnerable and so taut with wanting they felt compelled to hurt each other? She wanted him as much as he wanted her, he knew she did. If he could just make her admit it. . . .

He didn't want another round of estrangement to come from the shopping trip. He'd had enough of sleepless nights and wondering what to do. He'd meant to get closer to her this time, not farther away. He'd meant to ease through the afternoon and evening and finally draw her into his arms and kiss her. If they went on like this, by the time he drove her back home, she wouldn't be speaking to him.

"Excuse me."

The unmistakable authority in Justin's voice made the salesclerk stop talking and stare at him.

"Do you have a dressing room?"

"Yes, in the back...did you see a pair you want to try on?"

"Yes, I have something I want to try."

"Well, if you'll point them out to me——" The clerk was talking to the wall. Justin had grabbed Shelly's hand and was towing her after him down the crowded aisle.

The dressing room had a door cut away at the top and bottom. Justin pushed Shelly in, came in after her, and slammed the door shut.

"What are you ... doing?"

He looked down at the woman he'd kidnapped and his lips curled in satisfaction. The mannequin look was gone. She was incredulous, surprised and ... excited. She said, "Everyone will think we're crazy——"

"Hush." He tilted her face up to his. Her blue eyes shone with glittery anticipation, an anticipation that sparked in his own gut like heat lightning. He lowered his head, sought and found her mouth.

An explosion of feeling rocketed through Shelly. He was water in the desert, food after starvation. Sweet heated maleness pressed against her, taking not asking, but giving, too.

"Shelly. Shelly..."

Her name was a gasp of deep, profound satisfaction. "This feels good," he breathed against her face. "So...very...good—"

He took her mouth again, his hand cupping her chin, his fingers warm, evocative. With a flick of his tongue, he asked her to open to him. On a shudder of pleasure, she obeyed. He flooded her with sensate pleasure, sated her with moistness and heat. Behind her, his hands sought and found the wonderfully sensitive spot in the middle of her back, and with a subtle adjustment, he brought her hips into the cradle of his. Just that quickly, despite the clothes they wore, he claimed her body. Willingly she gave him possession. Her mouth was his, her body was his, his to do with what he would, to enjoy, to savor, to explore. And explore her mouth he was, his tongue seeking the velvety darkness of her cheek, devilishly dancing, inciting to riot, while his hands tracked the curve of denim-swathed hip and buttock.

He took her with his hands, with his mind, with his heart. He made her his for all time, for always.

No. It couldn't be. It was a terrible mistake to let him kiss her, make love to her. He couldn't belong to her, nor she to him. She pushed at him asking for release. Reluctantly he lifted his mouth from hers.

"Justin, we can't . . . do this."

"Why not?"

She was breathing again, thinking again, herself again. "Because they'll call the mall security and have us thrown out on our ears. Think how that would sound in the papers, 'Assistant district attorney arrested for accosting woman in dressing room.'"

He cast a shrewd glance over her face, his long fingers on her throat, the heel of his hand resting in the hollow. "Was I . . . accosting you?"

She met his eyes bravely, but she couldn't utter the lie. She shook her head. "No, of course you weren't. I'm as guilty and eager as you. But that won't make good copy.

You're vulnerable, Justin." *And so am I.* "Please. Let's get out of here."

He liked her most of all like this, her eyes alive with truth and arousal. Her willingness to be honest with him fired his blood as much as the press of her soft body against his. But he didn't want her to be uncomfortable. She deserved better than that. She deserved to be taken home and taken to bed and given a long, leisurely loving that would exhaust them both. He eased away from her a little. "But I haven't finished my shopping." His eyes flickered over her flushed face, her sparkling eyes. "Although I must say the selection in this store is . . . delectable."

"You're going back out there and buy something after what you just did?"

He leaned away from her, an eyebrow raised, a smile on that erotic mouth, quintessential Corbett. "Sure. Want to come watch?"

Careful. She'd been careful most her life. With Justin, she felt ready to be wild and reckless. "Why not?"

As jaunty as a tasseled horse, all the tiredness and tension gone from his face, Justin sauntered back up the aisle with his hand twisted behind him to hold Shelly's. "Excuse me, miss. Do you have a pair of jeans that are stone-washed, pleated and designer?"

The young woman eyed him warily, not quite sure of his sanity. When he'd taken his girlfriend down the aisle and disappeared with her into the dressing room, she hadn't known quite what to do. She'd been relieved to see the lunatic coming back up the aisle. Still, crazy or not, if the man wanted to spend money, she'd oblige him. She struggled to appear unmoved by his antics. "Yes, sir. A shipment of Fazio jeans just came in a few days ago. What size do you wear?"

"Thirty-two waist, thirty-six long."

The salesclerk's eyes flickered over Justin in obvious admiration. She liked hunks even if they were crazy. "Yes, sir. I think we still have a pair in that size." She climbed up on the ladder and pulled a mottled pair of denims down from a cubbyhole to hand to Justin. "Would you like to try these on?"

"No. Those dressing rooms are too crowded, especially since my girlfriend here follows me everywhere. She won't let me out of her sight. I'll try them on at home where I can hold her off with my whip and chair."

The woman's eyebrows climbed and Shelly favored him with a darkly warning glower. Justin flashed the full force of his green eyes and his brilliant smile at the salesclerk, and that young woman's wariness changed to dazed awe.

"If you'll wrap them?" he reminded her gently.

"Uh . . . yes, sir, of course." She was bedazzled, bewitched, bewildered. And more than ready to accept a quick, easy sale.

"That'll be forty-eight dollars, sir."

"Forty-eight dollars?" Justin's eyebrows climbed in soaring flight. He turned to Shelly. "You didn't tell me I'd have to mortgage the farm to buy these."

She patted him on the shoulder, enjoying his reaction. "You picked the best, most expensive ones in the store. What did you expect? Anyway, don't worry, those pants will last forever."

"For that price, they'd better," Justin mumbled.

When the salesclerk had taken his money and handed him the package, he said, "Oh, miss. I just wanted you to know. Your dressing room fits very well." With her wide eyes on him, he turned to catch Shelly's hand and stroll casually out of the store.

"You're incorrigible," she said to him when they emerged from the mall and headed toward his car.

"But I have a good time. It's gotten late. Want anything to eat or drink before we start back?"

Shelly shook her head. She felt as dazed as the salesclerk had looked. She wouldn't be able to put anything in her stomach for several hours.

She felt even more removed from reality when she climbed into the convertible. From the other side of the car, Justin tossed the package with his jeans in the back and slid under the wheel as casually as if he hadn't kissed the life out of her in a store dressing room. He put the top up, insisting it would be more comfortable in the cool darkness. She thought he must know best, but when the canvas unfolded and came down over their heads, it enclosed her in a dark cocoon with him. His presence on the seat beside her fueled the memory of his mouth and his body on hers and started her nerves tingling all over again.

Out on the highway with the city behind them, a misty moon gilded the sky, casting light and shadow on the road ahead and on Justin's profile.

He seemed determined to ignore her. They drove through the silver-sheened darkness for nearly a half hour without speaking, the music on the radio the only sound in the car. No, not the only sound. Occasionally Justin whistled through his teeth, an aimless tune that had nothing to do with the recorded music. He kept his hands firmly on the wheel and away from her. The tingling excitement melted away. She felt isolated and very alone.

Captain's Corners, the village where Shelly and Mel lived, was too small to be called a town. The location's only advantage was that of being situated three miles south of Eagle Hill.

Captain's Corners didn't bustle much during the week. By ten-thirty at night, it was a veritable ghost town. Outside her house, the porch light glowed, a pool of light splashed against the door. Her car was gone.

"Mel must have decided to drive over and see your father after all," she said, her voice sounding too loud, too hearty.

"So it seems." Justin cut the motor and leaned back, one arm thrown over the seat, his fingers nearly touching her shoulder.

"I'd ask you in for coffee, but you're probably anxious to get home—"

"Come here."

Her chin lifted, her eyes flew to his face.

"Come here," he repeated softly, as if he were gentling down a colt.

"You can't talk to me as if I were some primitive woman you own—"

"Stop talking nonsense and come here."

His tone was cool with authority, but it didn't matter. She'd been given permission to do what she'd been aching to do since he climbed into the car beside her. She slid over to him, her jeans sighing softly against the leather upholstery.

"Put your arms around my neck."

"No—"

"For once in your life, Red, reach out and take what you want."

In that soft darkness, she stared into the shadowed planes and hollows of his face, unable to see his eyes but feeling their intensity. Then a moan escaped her throat, a cry of mingled relief and distress and she leaned against him, taking the strength and sustenance she needed, wrapping her arms around his neck. His breathing caught, quickened. Cheered by that tiny lapse of self-control, Shelly laid her forehead against his cheek, feeling as if she were riding a thermal lifting her up, up, up.

Justin let out a long sigh of relief. He acted on hunches in the courtroom more times than Hanley thought he should, but he was seldom wrong. He hadn't been wrong about Shelly. She did want him. So much that she ached with it, just as he did. He'd been right to hold off on the long drive home, right to wait until he could put the responsibility for making the first move squarely in her hands, where it belonged.

"Come onto my lap, love. Let me...hold you." He slid the seat back and tilted the steering wheel, preparing a place for her. Her heart pounding, she felt his hands catch her waist and turn her, lifting her up and into his lap. She had released her hold on him to allow the change, but once she was resettled, she slipped her arms around his neck again. "Ah, that's it, love." He snuggled her against him, his hand cupping the back of her head to tuck her into the hollow of his shoulder. She was warm and supple against him and he felt oddly complete. "I didn't know it could feel this good just to hold a woman."

"I didn't know it could feel this good just to be held."

She sat curved into his body, his hard thighs under her, strangely content. He stroked her back with sweet, caring gentleness. She sighed and relaxed deeper into sheer contentment.

"I teased you unmercifully tonight, didn't I, sweetheart?"

"Yes, you did."

"Do you forgive me?"

She lay against him, listening to the beat of his heart, knowing there was nothing to forgive. He inserted his hand under her chin, lifting her face to the moonlight. "Do you forgive me?" He sounded genuinely concerned.

"No." He frowned and she lifted her hand to caress his cheek. "There's nothing to forgive. You've always been outrageous and I've always...admired that about you." Her lips curved in a smile. "I like a 'Damn the torpedos and full speed ahead' man."

"I like...you," he said and brushed her lips with his. He stayed to nibble lightly and then pulled away, his mouth twisted. "Soft, sweet woman. I like you too much."

"That's not possible."

"Oh, yes, it is," he said with heartfelt fervency, his hand dropping to the bottom of her sweatshirt and sliding underneath the ribbed edge. She expected him to sweep upwards and find her breast. Instead, his hand lowered. The snap of her jeans gave and he was inside, rubbing his fingers over her abdomen, lighting her skin with tiny tongues of flame.

"Justin—"

The zipper rasped downward under the pressure of his hand. He made a soft sound of approval. "I can see jeans have definite advantages I wasn't aware of."

Her contentment vanished. He was setting her on fire with his teasing rubbing of her belly, the long fingers brushing the top of her bikinis.

"Justin, please don't...spoil this."

"I have no intention of spoiling—" he reached lower, savoring her arousal "—anything."

"Jus—"

He kissed the protest from her mouth, his tongue discovering secret places, his fingers discovering secret places.

The sudden plunge from sweet relaxation to intimacy was pure Justin, victory ensured by a bold surprise attack and an audacious claiming of the prize. Damn the torpedos and full speed ahead with a vengeance. "Justin, please—"

It wasn't a protest, and he knew it, although he murmured a love word to her in conciliation.

Insidious, his possession of her. Relentless, his sweet, deep, heated caressing that stroked to the heart of her. Heat rose within her, a heavy dizzying, drugging heat that sapped her will to protest, and left behind only a pleasure so acute it bordered on ecstasy. She sought his mouth with hers, a crazy seeking of moisture from the source of the fire that burned her.

He accepted her kiss and her tongue with an easy grace that destroyed her. It was as if he had waited all his life to be kissed by her. She dragged her mouth away from his, searching for one last remnant of common sense. There was none, nothing left in her but a thousand sparkles of light emanating from Justin's touch. "Oh, please don't," she breathed, but she clutched the collar of his shirt and knew a traitorous longing for him to ignore her breathless protest. He smiled, the curve of his lips an erotic pleasure to the eye and went on plying his soft, sweet music. He knew her too well.

"Just . . . relax."

Filled with an unwillingness to move that told her she lacked the will to push him away and an acute need to take the pleasure that rolled over her in drowning waves, she lay back in his arms.

Time ceased. There was only the warmth of his breath on her cheek, and the sound of his breathing and hers, mingling together in a symphony of sighs.

She writhed, opening to him. "Yes," he murmured, "yes, like that, love. Let it happen, love. Just . . . let it happen."

His voice, husky with his own arousal, murmuring into her ear, exhorting her to release the tiny bit of control she retained, pushed her over the edge. The pleasure flared out of control, consuming her, bringing her to shuddering release.

In the darkness, Justin held her, feeling the pulse of her climax, and knowing that he had never been filled with such a strange mixture of frustration and satisfaction. His own body was hot with need, but it was muted, eased by her enjoyment. It was strangely satisfying, more erotic and intimate than he had ever dreamed it could be, to sit in the dark and hold her, while she clutched his collar with fingers warmed with sexual arousal and buried her face in his shoulder in a desperate attempt to mute her ragged breathing.

As she quieted, and sanity replaced ecstasy, her grip on his shirt loosened but her head stayed where it was, pressed against him. He allowed himself the luxury of smoothing his hand over her head and down the long tangled strands of her flame-red hair.

For a long, breath-held time, she lay in his arms unmoving. When at last she raised her head, she still wore the flush his loving had brought to her cheeks and throat. He gazed at her flushed face, at the tangled depth of her hair, at the gleaming white triangle of flesh below her waist still exposed by the open placket of her jeans, and his own throat closed. She was erotically feminine, infinitely desirable, softly moist and ready for him. And he wouldn't—couldn't—take advantage of her. Not now. Not when she was so vulnerable.

Feigning a lightness he didn't feel, he ran the zipper up. "You'll have to snap it. It's easier with two hands."

Like a child, she bent to the task, her hair falling over her cheek. When she finished, she sat up straighter and held herself away from him.

"Shelly. We're not children anymore. We're adults, a man and a woman with adult needs—"

She raised her head to look at him. "Is this your polite way of telling me it's your turn?"

He resisted the urge to fling her off his lap. "When I get closest to the bone...that's when you really hit out at me. Am I very close to the bone, Shelly? Is it hard to admit you're a human woman with human desires just like the rest of the human race?"

"I don't like...the way you make me feel."

He said an earthy word succinctly conveying his opinion of the truth of that.

"No, you misunderstand. I don't like feeling...out of control."

He went very still. "You mean you're not in the habit of just relaxing and letting it happen?"

"Not...like that."

He didn't move, didn't speak. She swiveled off his lap and slid to the other side of the car. He had to clench his hands to keep from dragging her back.

"I...knew this would happen," she said, her voice low and nearly breaking. She stared out into the darkness. "That was why I didn't want to...encourage you."

He wanted to lash out at her, but he knew he couldn't. His own sexual frustration was riding him hard, but that certainly wasn't her fault. He was the bloody fool who'd started the whole thing. A sixth sense buried under the anger and the frustration told him to hold back. The game wasn't over yet.

He faced to the front, gave the key a savage twist and started the engine. Over the motor's quietly expensive hum, he said, "I'm picking you up for the dinner you owe me next Saturday at three. We're going on a hayride. Wear something casual."

She twisted around to look at him, and even in the darkness he could see the disbelief on her face. "You can't be serious."

"I've never been more so."

"We can't see each other again. We'll . . . destroy each other."

"If you aren't ready to go when I come for you, I'll spread it from one end of Captain's Corners to the other that your father may have flown twelve bombing missions over Germany but you don't have the courage to keep a dinner engagement with me. Think you can live with that?"

CHAPTER FIVE

ON THAT SAME EVENING Mel raised a glass to Strom. The lights in the library were low, the men sat relaxed in chairs in front of the fireplace. It was too hot for a fire, but their chairs were turned as if a blaze crackled in the firebox.

"My daughter is out with your son tonight, did you know?" Mel said casually.

"No, I didn't." Strom beamed with pleasure.

Mel fingered his glass and stared past Strom. "That's something we hadn't thought would happen."

"Maybe you didn't . . . but I always had hopes."

Mel smiled. "You've put up with the Armstrongs for a lot of years. What if you have to put up with us for the rest of your life?"

"Nothing could please me more. Think of it. Our blood united in our grandchildren."

"Don't count your grandchildren before they're hatched," Mel said drily.

"I'd just be happy if I had the possibility of counting grandchildren. My boys haven't been as fast off the mark as I'd like. Especially that oldest one. Dances away from marriage like a buck deer."

"Shelly doesn't seem to be too eager, either."

Strom glanced down at his glass. "Guess we haven't been such good examples for them." His eyes lifted to Mel. "Ever think of getting married again?"

"No. You?"

Strom's cheeks reddened. "I've thought of it. Plenty of women in Washington. Convinced myself I was in love with one or two. But I . . . can't seem to follow through with a wedding ceremony."

"Like father, like son," Mel murmured.

Strom scowled, then laughed. "I suppose you're right." He glanced at Mel. "Still miss your Madge?"

"Every day of my life. You?"

Strom set his glass carefully on the table. "This probably doesn't come as any surprise to you, but Adelaide and I never had the relationship you and Madge had. I used to envy you like hell. Everyone told the two of us how right we were for each other. Funny how right you can be . . . and still not . . . feel anything."

Mel studied Strom's face while he considered the words. "Justin know how you felt?"

"No. Neither of the boys do. They believe their mother was a wonderful woman who loved them, and that was the truth. She loved them far more than she did me. I think we did a reasonable job of hiding our . . . estrangement from each other." His mouth twisted. "Washington gave us plenty of practice." Strom raised his glass in a mocking salute. "We're getting old, Mel. The game's nearly over."

"Speak for yourself, Congressman."

Strom glanced at Mel, his gaze quizzical. "You're sixty-five years old, my friend. You've done and seen a hell of a lot of things. You've lived through World War II and action in Korea. You've knocked around Alaska, California, Idaho, Wyoming. Hell, it was you who researched that parks bill for me, living out there. You performed a great service to your country that year. And you've raised a wonderful daughter. You've lived a life to be proud of."

"Do me a favor and don't deliver my eulogy yet."

Strom surveyed his friend, thinking he'd never met a man who could be as coolly unmoved by words as Mel. Armstrong wasn't a man to care what others thought of him. He did what he thought was right and let others thing what they liked. He was his own man. A man to be admired. For more reasons than one.

Strom broke eye contact with Mel, his eyes going to the fireplace wall where the symbols of his achievement hung. "If that should happen, if you go and I'm still here, I want you to know I'm going to tell the world the truth about—"

"Now that would be a damn fool thing to do and you know it." Mel set his glass on the table with a little click, in an uncharacteristic show of emotion. Praise hadn't got a rise out of him. The turn of conversation had. "We made an agreement."

"Funny. When I was younger, it seemed like a good idea. The older I get the more I hate living with a lie."

"Don't tell me you're getting sentimental in your old age."

"Not sentimental, just . . . practical. I don't want any excess baggage when it's my turn to go."

"Then talk to God about it, not me."

Strom turned to Mel. "Maybe I need to talk to you."

"There's nothing to say."

"Yes, there is. There's the truth . . . the debt I owe you—"

Aroused, Mel's voice turned softer, quieter, deadlier. "If you want to talk about the truth, then let's talk about what I owe you. My life, my daughter's life. The debt is as heavy on one side as the other and if we talk about the one we must talk about the other. You're breaking the rules, Congressman. The rules were we would never speak of it again.''

''But damn it, man, I need to talk about it.''

''Why?'' Mel's eyes were frosty. ''Why talk now after all these years? Because you need my absolution? My approval? You don't need my approval. You never did.''

Strom's eyes dropped. He hadn't needed Mel's approval when he was twenty-one. He'd been careless then, thinking the world was his oyster and he had an eternity to pluck and savor the pearls: wine, women, the friendship of a man. But now he was older, wiser, and the nonessential things in his life had fallen by the wayside. Nothing was as durable, as long-lasting, or as priceless to him as his regard for Mel. For of all the men in his life, Mel Armstrong had the greatest opportunity to destroy him. In forty years, he'd never acted on it.

But while that long-ago mistake of Strom's fused them together in a secret fire, it also acted as a barrier between them. By refusing to acknowledge Strom's debt to him, Mel maintained that distance, a condition on their friendship. Mel didn't want Strom to give too much—or ask too much. Mel needed the illusion of independence, while he, Strom, needed the illusion of total loyalty. ''Don't you ever wish that you—''

''No. I like things the way they are.'' Mel's eyes locked with Strom's. ''And I want you to leave them that way. If you are my friend, you'll respect my wishes. I don't want to live in a damned hornet's nest. And that's what you'll stir up if you open that can of worms. The stench would carry clear to Washington and you'd lose your next election sure as hell. Use your head, man. In your position, you can't afford trouble.''

''No,'' said Strom, his eyes old with regret, ''I can't afford trouble.''

THROUGHOUT THE WEEK Shelly examined the skies, wishing for rain, snow, flood, earthquake, or some other natural holocaust that would prevent the world from rolling around to the weekend. There was none. Every day was a gift from Mother Nature, a drifting, hot, lazy, late-summer reprieve.

Shelly tried to maintain a cool, calm face, but she wasn't sleeping well, and her appetite suffered. Justin had trapped her well and truly and she knew it. There was no way she could back out of her agreement with him. That wasn't what bothered her. What bothered her was the deep, hidden knowledge that she ached to see him again, needed desperately to see him again, was counting on seeing him again.

How could she reconcile her need for him and her need for independence? How could she make him see that he of all people could never be the man in her life? There was no way to make him understand without hurting him. She'd hurt him so much already, she couldn't go on meeting him in the fiery furnace of her need for him— and his need for her. They would both be burned. Yet her nights were filled with a restless ache to reexperience the ecstasy Justin had given her. Especially when she lay in bed and an errant night breeze feathered over her body...

Her father was a live-and-let-live man, but as they went through the ritual of their days, breakfast with the paper, a hurried lunch when Shelly dashed home from Eagle Hill, and a late leisurely dinner that Mel prepared, it was apparent to Shelly that he was eyeing her and wondering. But he said nothing, until, inexorably, Friday rolled around. That night Mel sat at the dinner table with Shelly, looked over at his exhausted, on-edge daughter, and asked casually, "Going out this evening?"

"No." Shelly got out of her chair and carried her plate over to the sink. "You cooked, I'll clean up, okay?"

"Hey. If you think I'm gonna argue with that, you're mistaken."

Shelly turned and braced herself against the sink. "Did you take your medicine today?"

"Are you my keeper?"

"Answer the question, Dad."

"Yes, I took my medicine. Satisfied?"

Shelly turned around to the sink and bowed her head. She hated acting as his guardian. But she knew if she didn't, he wouldn't take the hated medicine at all. More collected, she pivoted back to face him. "I'm sorry. It's just that I don't want to lose you."

"Nobody's going to lose me." He sat back in his chair, calm as a glassy sea. "Hell, the way everybody talks around here, you'd think I had one foot in the grave." He swung a leg over his chair in the easy, lithe way he had and carried his plate to the sink.

"Hey. I said I'd clean up," Shelly protested.

"Is there any law that says I can't help?"

Shelly returned to the table to collect the glasses and the food dishes. They'd had spaghetti, the sauce a special recipe of Mel's. "No, of course not." She glanced at Mel's tall, lean body, thinking it was ironic the man had high blood pressure when he appeared to have the constitution of a horse. Other than a few lines in his face, he didn't look much older than he had when she was a teenager. He still kept his hair in a regulation World War II crewcut and he wore the khaki-colored work clothes that resembled an army uniform. Sometimes she wondered if he wasn't locked permanently in that time frame, playing his records of the Andrews Sisters and the Glen Miller band, acting as if he was still a young man of twenty-one. She knew that's why he resisted taking his medicine. Mel was an intelligent man, but he just couldn't accept the fact that his body, the body that had stood him in such good stead for so long, needed medication in order to function normally. At every opportunity he denied the reality of his condition.

He worried her. If he skipped his medicine too many times, he could have a stroke. The doctor said he didn't think it was likely, that Mel could keep things under control by watching his salt intake and taking his medication. Therein lay the rub.

"Who else has been talking to you about your health besides me, Dad?"

He looked at her quizzically. She had something that was eating her alive inside, but she still didn't miss a thing. "Strom was delivering my eulogy the other night." At flash of distress in her eyes, Mel cursed himself for being so honest with her. "It wasn't like that, babe. He was just telling me all the things I'd done with my life. Trying to butter me up."

Shelly relaxed and smiled. "Why was he flattering you? Going to put the touch on you for some campaign funds?"

Mel's eyes darkened and he stiffened, as if he were in pain. He turned away from Shelly and went back to the table to carry the butter and the left-over slices of garlic bread the two steps to the counter. "I wouldn't have enough excess cash to give him two cents and you know it."

She stood very still, feeling the old frustration, the old anxieties. Her father never shared his worries with her. He always seemed to expect her to know what he was feeling without his telling her. "No, I didn't know that, Dad. You keep your finances under pretty tight wraps."

Carefully, not looking at him, Shelly ran the hot water into the dishpan and added soap. "I thought we were doing pretty well."

"We're meeting our expenses," he said gruffly. "You don't have to worry."

"Maybe you should let me keep the books—"

"No! If I can't fly, I can at least do the accounting."

And that will be the end of it, Shelly thought, scrubbing a plate, feeling the rise of irritation. *So much for women's lib.* Still, she understood how he felt. Being grounded had been a low blow for him. It had necessitated her hiring Pat on a full-time basis. Mel hadn't said anything but he'd been very quiet that first week in May when he'd gotten the word that he wouldn't be able to fly until his condition stabilized and he no longer needed medication. The air show was scheduled for the first weekend in October and this would be the first time in twenty years that Mel wouldn't be flying in it.

"How is Strom doing? Have they made any decision about surgery?"

"They want to do a bypass on him but since his situation isn't critical, they're going to wait until after Christmas to perform the surgery."

Christmas. By then Justin would probably be a memory in her life. Would she be on easy enough terms with the Corbetts to visit Strom in the hospital? Filled with an aching emptiness, she scrubbed the plate with unnecessary vigor. Somehow, even though a breakup with Justin was inevitable, she would have to maintain a relationship with Strom. For Mel's sake. And her own.

THE NEXT DAY, SATURDAY, on the day of his date with Shelly, Justin Corbett slid into Corbett Hill house through the side entrance. He hadn't planned to sneak into the house like a thief, but he was running late and if he could sidle up the stairs, rummage in his old room and get his riding boots without being forced to give Morley or his father an explanation about his Western garb or where he was going, he could be out of there that much faster. If he got delayed, by the time he headed over to Captain's Corners to pick up Shelly, then drove half-way back to the city to Brad's country home, he'd be more than fashionably late. In fact, he might miss the hayride altogether. And he didn't want to do that. He wanted to see Shelly perched on a hay wagon with a dozen other people, watch her red hair blow in the breeze, see her laugh. Most of all, he wanted to see her eat her words about his taking her to a fancy French restaurant.

He managed to make it up to his room undetected. Breath held, he moved quietly in deference to Morley's sharp ears, collecting his boots and his father's hat. As he descended the stairs he breathed a sigh of relief, but he relaxed too soon. That damn creaky seventh step betrayed him.

Morley came hustling through the swinging door as if he expected to catch a burglar red-handed, a frown on his face. "Justin. I didn't hear you drive in."

"Hi, Morley, how's it going? Nice to see you." Justin flashed a smile at the obdurate man and backed toward the front entryway.

Morley cast a jaundiced eye over Justin's red-checked shirt, his blue flowered bandana and came to rest in the area of his hips. His mouth curled derisively at the sight of Justin's jeans. "I presume you're going to a costume party."

"A Western hayride. You know, quaint old American custom. Everybody dresses up like a cowboy and rides behind horses on a nice, double sprung wagon and pretends they're roughing it.''

Morley's eyebrows climbed toward the ceiling. "I see.''

"I just came by for my riding boots." Jauntily defiant, he kicked a foot out for Morley's inspection. "And Dad's old Stetson." He lifted the hand that held the hat he'd pilfered from Strom's bedroom. Strom had bought the hat to wear campaigning the first year he'd run for office. He hadn't, to Justin's knowledge, had it on since.

Morley surveyed Justin's Western gear with the expression he usually reserved for finding a mouse in the barn. Justin had used it once in court to convey his disdain for a defendant. He had the technique down rather well. It involved wrinkling the nose as if smelling something bad and pulling the mouth down at both corners. "You aren't leaving without greeting your father, are you?"

"No, of course not." Resigning himself to his fate, Justin asked, "Where is he?"

"Out in the pool."

Filled with concern for his father, Justin frowned, his need to stand firm in the face of Morley's displeasure forgotten. "Did the doctor say it was all right for him to swim?"

"As long as he didn't overexert himself and experience pain. Shall I tell him you're here?"

Justin's mouth tightened in irritation. "No, that won't be necessary. I said I'd speak to him and I will."

Justin strode through the dining room and out onto the porch that led to the patio and pool. His father was stroking through the water with slow, methodical slices of his arms.

"Looking good, champ."

Strom lifted his head, swirling water out of his eyes and hair in order to focus. When he saw Justin, he smiled with pleasure, ducked his head to swim to the side of the pool and pulled himself over the edge. Justin picked up the towel from the lounger and carried it to him.

Strom scrubbed his face with it and wrapped it around his neck. He cast a look of sheer disbelief at his son. "Roy Rogers, as I live and breathe. What brings you home today, son?"

"Larceny. I'm stealing your hat. Do you mind?"

"Not at all, not at all. You look like a refugee from an old Western movie."

"Thanks... I think."

"Where are you headed for this last roundup?"

"Brad Conning's. He's got a place in the country outside of the city about fifteen miles. He's throwing a Western party this afternoon complete with a hayride. He's hired somebody with Belgian horses to pull the wagon. It's a beautiful team, so Brad says."

The rambling dissertation about horses didn't deflect that narrowed look in Strom's eyes for a minute. "Taking anybody with you?"

Justin met his father's gaze head on. "Just Shelly."

"Just Shelly," Strom repeated, his face wreathed with satisfaction.

"Don't get your hopes up, Dad. We aren't involved. We're just... friends."

"Remember when I said you shouldn't try to lie to me, son?"

"Yeah, I remember."

"I like her."

"I know you do, Dad." Justin had had enough of pussyfooting. He decided to take the bull by the horns.

"Are you telling me you'd like to have her as a daughter-in-law?"

"I'm telling you that if you married her, I'd be a very happy man."

"Right now, the possibilities of my marrying Shelly Armstrong are less than nonexistent."

"But you are going out with her."

"Give it up, Dad."

Strom stared at his son. Justin made an impatient gesture. "Just . . . give it up."

"What is it you want me to give up?" Strom's voice was deadly quiet.

"I want you to give up pushing me."

"I wasn't aware that I was pushing you."

"Sure you are. You want me to marry, you've known Shelly all your life, you think presto, bingo, here's the perfect solution to your problem so you start lobbying for it. Good old Justin doesn't know what's good for him, I'd better take care of him." Justin lifted his chin. "I'm thirty-two years old, Dad. I'm old enough to take care of myself."

Strom scowled, twisted his head and stared out over the pool.

"The irony of this whole thing is," Justin drawled, "you'd hate it like hell if I knuckled under to you every time you said boo. You'd tell me you raised a spineless fool. You can't have it both ways. You either have to accept that I have a mind of my own or we'll be at each other's throats for the rest of our lives. You ought to go down on your knees and thank your lucky stars I'm strong enough to fight you. If I weren't, I would have been a parasite."

Strom swiveled his head back to Justin, his scowl deepening. "The hell you would. I wouldn't have let you.

I've made you what you are—'' At the expression on Justin's face, Strom stopped speaking.

"Exactly," said Justin softly. "You've made me what I am, carved me out of the stone of your will. Now it's time to let me see what I can do on my own."

A breeze rippled the water of the pool and wafted over Strom's moist skin. His father was chilled, Justin could see the rise of goose bumps on his arms. "What do you want from me?" Strom asked.

Your love. "How about a little benign neglect? Isn't that what you give a bill going through the house that you're neither for nor against? Try it on me."

"You're my son."

"But I'm not a little boy anymore. I'm an adult," Justin said gently. "When you were thirty-two, you'd already been through one war and were fighting in another. As I recall, your father didn't want you to go to Korea. But you went."

"I was drafted—"

"You could have gotten out of it. Grandpa told me so. He may have been angry at the time, but he was also proud. Give me a chance to earn your respect on my own terms the same way you earned your father's."

Strom said nothing, merely sat there staring across the pool with his chilled skin.

Justin hunched his shoulders. He'd thought the way to make his father see the truth was to point up Strom's relationship with his own father. It hadn't worked. If anything Strom seemed further withdrawn. Was there a way to make Strom see that they could be close even if Justin was independent? That it could be just as satisfying after having been father and son, to be friends? "You'd better go inside and get something warm on. I've got to go, Dad, I'm late."

"Yes, of course." Strom came out of his reverie and dropped his chin. He seemed more like himself, but he still didn't look at Justin. "Is it all right if I tell you to have a good time and give Shelly a kiss for me—or would you consider that unwanted interference?"

Yes, Strom had returned to normal. He meant to have the last word. Justin tamped down his impatience and reached for tolerance. "I'll take it under consideration, Dad. Especially the kiss. Go in and get some clothes on before you catch cold."

Strom swiveled his head to look at Justin, triumph in his face. "I'm an adult. I can take care of myself."

Justin smiled the slow, charming smile that destroyed witnesses, men and women alike. "Touché, Dad. You win. Again." The son sketched a salute to his father. "Now come on inside before I tell Morley on you."

Strom shuddered with mock-exaggerated dread. "Not that. Anything but that," he said, which proved that a brave man can have an Achilles heel—and a sense of humor about his weakness. Justin was smiling as he helped his father to his feet and guided him into the house. And so was Strom.

THE APPOINTED TIME Shelly was to be ready for Justin clicked by on the kitchen clock. So did three-thirty. And three forty-five. And four o'clock, the time Justin had told her the party began. Shelly paced the floor, half the time envisioning a terrible accident in which Justin was lying on the road hurt or dying, and the other half thinking he'd be lucky if she didn't kill him when he got there.

At four-fifteen, Justin's convertible glided up in front of the house and Justin swung agilely out.

Caught in that special combination of fear and fury over a loved one's lateness, Shelly pushed open the door and ran down the walk toward him. "Where have you been? I've been worried sick about you—"

At the sudden darkening of his eyes and the lift of his mouth, she knew how badly she'd betrayed herself.

"Were you?" he asked softly.

She shook her head and stepped back, turning around, her ostensible purpose to lead him up the walk, her real goal to hide her face from him. He'd already seen too much of the churn of emotions he'd caused in her: anger, fear, relief.

He followed her through the door. When she kept her back to him and moved to collect her purse and shawl from her bedroom, he caught her arm and brought her around to face him. "I'm sorry I'm late. I made the mistake of stopping off at home, and Strom was in the mood to chat. I couldn't get away. Forgive me?" He flashed her that superheated smile that had the power to take her breath away. Had she thought his appeal would be diluted in Western clothes? Wrong, wrong. In his checked shirt tucked in across his flat stomach and stone-washed denim hugging muscled thighs that rose endlessly to his waist, he was masculinity in its most potent form.

The urge to kill vanished, replaced by other, more basic urges. The urge to smell, to taste, to touch. With those urges came the memory of how it felt to lie in his arms and feel her femininity mined, brought to the surface and refined to pure, primitive femaleness. She struggled to look calm and cool and in control. "I can understand how you wouldn't want to be rude to your father."

It occurred to him that for the first time in his life, he didn't have to explain his relationship with Strom to the woman he was seeing. It felt like a load off his shoulders, a wonderful luxury he could get very used to enjoying.

There were other luxuries he could get used to. Like looking at her. Her plaid shirt, her neckerchief, her long, slim jeans skirt and her boots owed their origin to masculine clothes, but on Shelly they looked as essentially feminine as ruffled lace. There was only one thing about her appearance he didn't like. She'd pulled her hair back into a leather thong, giving herself a cowgirl ponytail. The hairdo did accent her cute, perky nose, but it hid the wild beauty of her red mane. "Did I remember to say you look delectable? You do." He leaned forward to brush her cheek with his mouth as casually as if she were his wife. "Except for this."

In one swift move, Justin took out the pick, jammed the thong in his pocket and took his hands to ruffle the sides of her hair, bringing it out in tousled, flaming glory. While Shelly stared at him in shock, he stepped back to survey his work, his mouth curved with satisfaction. "Yes, that's much better."

How easily he destroyed all her good intentions to be cool but friendly. Her head tingled from his high-handed destruction of her coiffure, her body tingled from his easy assumption that he could touch her in any way the mood struck him. She'd expected, after the way they'd parted a week ago, to feel awkward with him, and she was more than willing to keep her distance. Justin, whether by impulse or design, allowed no awkwardness. He was a man who trod where angels feared to go. And he wasn't even aware of how attractive his audaciousness made him. Maybe it was a good thing for the female of the species that he'd never worn jeans before. Some besotted woman might have attacked him in the street.

Shelly reached for control. "Did anyone ever tell you you've got a lot of nerve?"

He grinned. "Yeah, it's come up a few times. Fairly recently, as a matter of fact. Shall we go?"

He put her in under the wheel on his side of the car and with a hand on her arm, kept her in the middle of the seat. She was caught in what seemed to be her accustomed spot just under his elbow.

Out on the road, the countryside whizzed by at an alarming rate while Justin gave her a thumbnail history of the people she would meet. Her hair, released from the fetters she'd thought would keep it tamed during her ride in his convertible, swirled around her face, giving her a view of the trees and the blue sky through red-gold strands. She was beginning to recognize the way she felt, the way she always seemed to feel when she was with Justin—young, free of responsibility, able to look at the world without thinking of what must be done next.

"—and Gregson, watch out for him. He's pure practical joker and he's got it in for me."

"What did you do to him?"

He shot her a quick look, smiled, then switched his gaze back to the road. "Gregson is a cop. It had to do with entrapment."

"A blonde?" she asked dryly.

Justin shook his head, his smile sheepish. "Brunette. He liked dark-haired girls...being a plebeian who doesn't have my superb taste in women."

"Which is?"

"Red-headed and feisty." Justin cast her a sidelong glance again, his smile pure sin. "With a touch of cowardice."

"What?" She turned to him, one hand holding back her hair. "How can you call me a coward?"

"Easy." His eyes were on the road, his profile pure nonchalance. "You want to touch me, but you're afraid to do it."

She flared to stinging life, and without thinking, laid her palm on his thigh, the denim abrasive against her sensitive skin, the hard muscle beneath well defined.

"Not such a coward after all," he murmured and she saw then how neatly she'd fallen into his trap.

But it wasn't till a minute or so later that she discovered how two-edged the trap was. Her palm registered every shift and flex of Justin's leg muscles as he drove the car. This carefully circumscribed touching made her want more.

She should take her hand away, she knew she should. But her foolish pride made her keep it where it was. By the time they arrived at the party, her face was as flushed and wind-kissed as her hair from both external and internal turbulence.

Brad Conning's house was tucked back from the road, bordered on one side by old suburbia and on the other by new. The place had once been a farm, but when the city encroached, the farmhouse had been renovated and Brad had bought it. The young city lawyer, with his abiding interest in horses, had painted the barn a shiny white and turned the pasture into a paddock. A horse grazed there, a mottled gray with a dark tail and a proud way of carrying his head.

"Brad's got ten acres of land with the house. We call him the Land Baron at the office," Justin said, helping her out of the car. "He's lived in the city all his life. Now he's like a kid with a shiny new toy. He keeps turning it to the light to see what different fun he can have with it." Justin clasped her hand with casual familiarity and led her around to the back of the house. There, in a shaded

grove of trees, the party was in full swing. On a red-
wood patio, round tables groaned under plates of hors
d'oeuvres, sheltered by umbrellas. A huge square metal
cooker emitted fragrant smoke from the roasting pork.
Men and women stood and sat about, drinking and talking. Justin stepped forward, his hand towing Shelly
along. People looked at them with curiosity.

He made the introductions, and though she had
trained herself to be skilled at remembering names, Shelly
found it hard to keep them all straight. A few people were
easy to remember: Hanley, the district attorney, whose
picture she'd seen in the paper; and Mrs. Davis, who like
Hanley was older than most of the crowd. A young
woman, Jenny, was introduced as the secretarial assistant in Justin's office. The girl was gorgeous with her doe
eyes and her Western togs, a suede vest that showed off
her tiny waist to perfection, a classic white blouse, and a
fringed brown skirt that brushed the top of her boots.
Her smile was heart-stopping. And quite unreservedly
aimed at Justin. Justin seemed unaware that his young
secretary had a crush on him, or that the young man escorting Jenny had stepped forward and put a proprietary arm around her waist.

Justin's eye was on his hostess. Barbara Conning had
a cherub propped on her hip, a boy who had the chunky
look of a year-old baby who hadn't yet learned to walk.
Without hesitation, Justin reached for the child.

"Here, give me that big lug while you get acquainted
with Shelly. What's your good-for-nothing husband
doing, anyway?"

"Watching the pig roast. And drinking hard cider."

Justin raised one elegant eyebrow. "You better watch
him."

"Watch him drink it? That's about all I can do. You know Brad."

"Yeah, I know Brad. I also know his son." Justin patted the boy's diapered rear end. "You've been a busy little fellow in the last few minutes, haven't you?"

"Oh, here, let me take him," Barbara said, reaching for her offspring. "I knew he needed changing but I saw you come, and I wanted to meet your Shelly."

Justin elbowed Barbara away from her child and shook his head. The boy looked curiously at Justin and stabbed a chubby hand into Justin's hair. "I'll take him inside and do the dirty work. Being an A.D.A., I'm good at that. Besides, he's attached to me." Justin tried to pluck the boy's hand from his hair and failed.

Barbara laughed. "If you think I'm going to argue with you, you're crazy." While Justin sauntered away with the child in his arms, Barbara linked hers in Shelly's. "That man is getting positively paternal. He ought to have children of his own. I thought only women were hit by the nesting instinct when they turned thirty, but maybe men feel it, too. From the look on your face, I'd say you're surprised. You'd probably be even more surprised to hear that Justin often sits with our kids so we can escape the little dears for a few hours and go to the movies. That's our oldest, over there by her dad. She didn't see Justin or she would have been over here like a shot. She's just five, but she's a normal female. She adores Justin." Barely stopping for breath, Barbara turned to her, her eyes innocent. "What about you? Are you a normal female?"

Shelly met Barbara's gaze steadily. "I've known Justin for years," she said lightly. "We're just good friends."

"And pigs fly," Barbara drawled, but she was smiling. That quickly, Shelly knew she'd been vetted and accepted. What fierce loyalty Barbara must feel toward Justin. As casually as if she hadn't just asked a highly personal question, Barbara switched from inquisitor to hostess, inquired what she'd like to drink and poured both of them a glass of white wine. "So, tell me about yourself. I know you've known Justin since you were both kids, and that you're a pilot."

"He's . . . talked about me to you?"

Barbara's eyes were guarded. "He's mentioned you occasionally. He said he was bringing you here because you lost a bet. That piqued my curiosity. I wanted to see the woman who had to be *coerced* into going out with Justin Corbett." Barbara looked down at her glass, then up at Shelly. "Quite frankly, I was afraid you'd be . . . impossible. Just arrogant enough and conceited enough to throw Justin Corbett for a loss because you didn't really care enough about him to . . . care for him. I'm relieved to see you aren't like that at all."

"You really . . . like him, don't you?" Shelly said.

Barbara sobered. "There was a case a few years ago . . . it involved a black man and a white cop. Brad handled the prosecution of the cop. He took a lot of flack when the cop was acquitted. The police said the case should never have come to trial in the first place, the black community was unhappy with the not-guilty verdict. Brad couldn't have won no matter how he handled it. So he handled it the way he thought best, with honesty and courage. Justin backed him up all the way, listened to him grouse about the way things were going when the case was in court, and gave out statements to the press afterward praising Brad's courage. The statements didn't change anybody's mind, but they made

Brad feel better. He didn't feel so isolated and alone. They're in a tough spot, the A.D.A.s. No matter what they do, they're going to make somebody mad. Has Justin talked to you at all about that aspect of his work?''

"No, he hasn't."

"Well, he's been handed a firecracker of a case—his turn, I guess. I can't tell you anything about it, of course, but if I were you, I'd keep my eye on the papers. It'll be coming out soon. I . . ." Barbara glanced past Shelly's shoulder, lifted her glass to Shelly and said in a utterly different, bright tone, "I'm so glad you could come. I hope you like the roast. It should be good . . . if my husband knows what he's doing well enough to watch it . . . ah there you are, Justin. Everything under control?''

"Temporarily." A breeze ruffled his blond hair, released now from the determined grip of the child. Justin stood with the boy in his arms, utterly at ease.

"Here, let me take him so you can introduce Shelly to the rest of the gang. I'd better go and see if my husband is turning the pig into bacon." Barbara lifted the gurgling boy out of Justin's arms and marched away with him.

"So." Justin folded his arms and leaned back against the corner of the house. "What do you think of Barbara?''

"I think she reminds me of a hurricane."

Justin laughed, threw his arm over her shoulder and said, "You'll get used to her."

CHAPTER SIX

STUFFED FULL OF ROAST PORK, dressing, hot German potato salad, fruit salad and apple pie, Shelly cuddled in the sheltering curve of Justin's arm and watched the bonfire burn. Brad had built a big blaze in the center of the yard, well away from the trees, and Barbara had brought out blankets for them to sit in a circle a safe distance away and watch the flames. The night was balmy, with the breeze playing through the trees in soft sighs.

The haywagon and the horses had long since departed. The guests, most of them suburban and city dwellers, had played at being country dudes throughout the afternoon. It had been a wonderful ride on a wagon with two rows of facing seats. Roy Rogers and the Sons of the Pioneers serenaded them from a battery powered radio tucked under the driver's bench while the Belgian horses, two handsome four-year-olds, paraded slowly and sedately up one street and down another. Shelly had sat next to Justin and found the ride relaxing, even though Brad, seated on her other side, had drunk enough cider to make him boldly toss his arm over Justin's where it lay on her shoulders and ask her if "this overgrown Yuppie" was treating her right.

Later on, at supper, Brad had sat down next to her. By that time, his eyes were glazed and he was feeling no pain. The topic of discussion was movies, and he wanted her to name the film that had won the Academy Award two years ago. When she admitted she couldn't remember, he exhorted her to try. She must remember, he said. While Justin smiled, Brad continued to half-badger, half-tease her. Shelly suspected Brad wouldn't remember any of it the next day. In desperation, Barbara had tucked her children in bed and turned her attention to her husband.

At the moment, Brad was subdued, sprawled on his back, his head in Barbara's lap. The talking drifted into singing. The fire burned lower, the singing modulated into silence. People began to get to their feet and recite their thank you's, nice to meet you's and good-byes.

"Ready to go?" Justin murmured into Shelly's ear. She nodded, thinking she wasn't ready to go at all. She felt as if she could sit curled into Justin forever, her mind and body relaxed by the primitive pleasure of fire gazing. It seemed as if Barbara and Brad had created a little oasis of time where no worries encroached.

In the car Shelly went on cuddling next to Justin as he seemed to want her to do. He made her so warm and comfortable that she dozed most of the way back to Captain's Corners.

When he stopped the car in front of her house, Shelly roused and tried to bring herself back to wakefulness. "You have nice friends," she said to his dark shadow in a cool, impersonal tone meant to show him she wanted no repetition of the other night. "Thank you for a lovely evening."

He didn't reach for her. In the dark, in the silence, he sat perfectly still, the magnetic force he created holding her fast. She wanted to go—and couldn't. It seemed as if she could hear him breathing—feel him breathing. The sane, sensible speech she'd prepared about it being better for both of them if they didn't see each other again vanished from her brain like smoke obliterated by the wind. In the dark, warm silence, nothing but the truth would do. "We can't go on like this."

"I know. Something's got to give. Preferably your shirt." He leaned forward, inserted a finger in the neck of her blouse and popped the first snap open. The sound cracked through her nerves like lightning.

"Justin, no." She caught his arm with one hand. With the other, she groped for the car door handle.

He captured both her hands and brought them to his mouth to carefully kiss each of her fingers. "Shelly, yes." He sounded amused, faintly mocking.

"I must go." But she didn't pull her hands away from his warm grasp. She hung suspended there, trapped by her needs, needs that had been fed all evening by the sight, scent and feel of Justin, his golden head next to the dark head of the child's, his indulgent smile at Barbara, his warm body curled around Shelly's while they watched the fire.

"I'd like to say I wouldn't stop you if you went right now . . . but I'd be lying," Justin said. Then, more soberly, "Unless you really want to go."

She wanted desperately to say yes, she had to go. "No," she said, her chin coming up as she told the truth. "I want . . . to stay with you." Her eyes on his face, she trembled with anticipation.

"No cowardice at all, none to be found in a single, lovely bone in her body." He held her close for a moment, cherishing her.

"Justin, I—"

"Relax, sweet. Put yourself in my hands. You're safe with me." He paused, putting a finger under her chin to tilt her face to his. "You do believe that, don't you?"

"Yes," she whispered, knowing it was half truth and half lie. She was physically safe with him, but her heart was in dire jeopardy of being captured. She didn't love him yet . . . but many more nights like this and he would own her, body, heart, soul. She was playing with fire, staying to taste the sweetness one more time. How long could she dance near the flames and come out unscathed?

Justin moved away from her, the jacket he wore rustling in the silence. As if he sensed her fears, he said soothingly, "Trust me, love. Just . . . trust me."

She had trusted him many times with her life. To trust him with her heart was a thousand times more dangerous. But even while she thought that, he leaned toward her, the light playing around his curved mouth. Tucked so close to him that she could feel the warmth of his breath, her nerves stinging with anticipation, she could only watch as he lowered his head. While the sheen of the faint light gilded his golden hair, his lips grazed the top of her breast, exploring her bare flesh in the opening he'd created for himself. Stunned by her own complicity and the sudden rush of sexual arousal, she stifled a groan of pleasure. He muttered a satisfied word, as if she'd pleased him. Then he murmured against her skin, "Tell me what Barbara said to you."

"What?" She couldn't think, couldn't breathe. She felt frozen—and hot where his mouth touched.

Another snap gave. He moved his mouth lower to the mound of flesh above her bra. "What did Barbara tell you about me while I was gone?"

Her wits, at least a few of them, returned. "Counselor, your interrogation methods should be investigated by the American Civil Liberties Union."

Justin chuckled, his breath warm on her skin, his mouth engaged in its relentless tracking of her bare flesh. She lifted her hand and found it doing nothing more defensive than cupping the back of his head. He murmured a sound as if approving of her touch and smoothed her shirt and her bra strap away from her shoulder in one expert motion. Only a thin sheath of silk remained clinging to her nipple.

Her sleepiness vanished. She was quivering quicksilver, alive with awareness of him: his body weight pressing lightly against her, his warm mouth on the fragile, close-to-the-bone skin of her shoulder, the urgent grip of his hand on her waist holding her in place for his onslaught. The heated ache began, that familiar deep burning within her engendered by Justin's touch.

His lips wandered lower, his tongue testing the edge of her bra. "Tell me," he commanded.

"She told me you were a good friend to Brad," she said in a breathless whisper that filled the silence like a shout.

It took only a small nudge of his tongue to send the silk covering sliding down and away from the peaked crest. "Is that all?"

"She thinks you're developing a paternal instinct."

That brought his head up. "What?"

"She suspects you of having fatherhood leanings."

"The woman's crazed," he said, but he was smiling.

The cool air wafted over her tongue-wet breast. She shivered, and at once he cupped his hand over her, enveloping her in his warmth.

She fought to subdue the second, more insistent rise of sexual excitement racing through her heart, her blood, her brain. Yet to tear his hand away from her body would be to tear away heaven. It felt so right. Justin had stolen a part of her heart a week ago when they sat in this dark car, and now he was taking more. She was helpless to stop him. She wanted to give him all, everything . . .

Justin absorbed the scent and feel of her, his heart pounding with want and need. How unutterably sweet her cool, soft flesh was but how much that small taste made him burn to see, touch, taste all of her. She raised huge eyes to him, eyes so dark with sexual arousal that he wanted to drown in them. She was his perfect complement, softness to his hardness, sweetness to his cynicism, femaleness to his maleness.

"Do you think she's right about my getting paternal?"

"I . . . don't know. I would never have suspected you to be so good with children. I thought you were too—"

"Self-absorbed?"

His palm circled, abrading her nipple. Her body twisted in a sharp stinging pleasure. She found it difficult to keep her mind on their conversation. "I think a better word would be . . . driven."

"So you learned something about me tonight."

"Yes, I—"

"And I learned something about you."

"What did you learn . . . about me?" She breathed in sharply. His caressing had turned insistent, erotic in frank, primitive possession.

"I learned it doesn't make any difference whether you're eating, or laughing, or trying to be tactful with a man who's had too much to drink, you still make me want you like hell." In a sudden quick motion he pulled her bra and shirt up covering her bareness, shocking her. "And I'm getting damned tired of trying to make love to you in a parked car like a teenager." He bent his head, applying himself to the task of refastening her snaps. She sat in frozen silence, her body unable to adjust to the sudden deprivation. As if he, too, felt the void, he brushed his mouth over her lips. While she struggled with a surge of emotion, need, shock, disappointment, he sat back, his breath coming fast and hard. It was only then that she realized he was paying the cost for arousing her and not seeking satisfaction himself. His hand strayed behind her, caught a lock of her hair. Not looking at her, he said, "Will you come to the city next weekend and stay with me?" Before she could speak, he turned to her and focused all the power of his intense concentration on her. "Don't fob me off with some nonsense about my ambition. If you're going to refuse, have the courtesy to be honest about why I don't appeal to you."

"I can't come, Justin."

"Why not?" he asked in a cool, measured tone that chilled her.

She wanted, needed to shock him out of his cynical mood. "I'm afraid . . . I'll fall in love with you."

He turned to her then, his mouth curved in a smile, all the cynicism gone, and nothing left but a smooth and wonderful charm. "Would that be so terrible?"

"It could be . . . if you didn't fall in love with me."

"I see. We're back to that old stand again, eh? The glories of commitment."

Her anger rose, glorious, painkilling, a lump in her throat, a blindness in the eyes. Justin's charm had vanished. He sounded so cold-blooded, so cynical. She grasped the car handle . . . only to have Justin clamp his hand on her arm and hold her where she was. "Oh, no. You're not going to run away from me this time. Listen, Red. There's one thing you've said that's right about me. I do go after what I want. And I want you. I'll take you any way I can. But I won't lie to you. And I'll be damned if I can give you any bloody guarantees, not until we've been together for a while and we know whether this thing between us is a fluke or a miracle.

"Don't you see?" he asked in a voice husky with pain. "To go into this, telling ourselves it's a forever thing when neither of us knows for sure is just asking for heartache. I don't want that for either of us. I want you to be happy. I want me to be happy."

"What does it take to make you happy, Justin?"

"Being with you. Watching you undress, lying down beside you. Making love to you, burying myself in your body. Listening to you cry out with pleasure. Having you sleep beside me and wake up in my bed. That would make me happy."

She tried not to succumb to his seductive plea. Words were his tools and he used them well.

"You must know that ... I want that, too."

Justin moved toward her, but Shelly put her hands up to fend him off. "Unlike you, I'm not used to getting what I want."

He muttered a word, relaxed back against his seat and stared out the windshield into the darkness. There was an uneven layer of clouds in the night sky and slivers of silver where the moon shone through. He had the feeling that their conversation was like that, layers upon layers, hiding the truth.

His body quieted and his mind began to work again. "You don't make sense," he said. "You accuse me of being self-absorbed, yet you want me to make a commitment to you." Filled with a sudden, blinding insight, Justin turned to face her. "This commitment thing is just a smoke screen, isn't it? You're hiding behind a standard, safe, easy argument that you knew would rouse my ire."

She shook her head but she clasped her hands in her lap and looked down at them. Justin had interrogated enough witnesses to know she was afraid to let him see how close to the truth he was.

"Shelly." He reached for her chin and gently, as gently as if she were a child, he turned her head toward him. "It's time for the truth. I deserve that much from you, at least."

The dark form of his head, so dear, so familiar hovered close to hers. He did deserve the truth from her. But she wasn't sure she could articulate it. She didn't have his gift with words. She had a feeling, that was all, an overwhelming feeling that his life had taught him to cherish the illusion of perfection, while her life had taught her to deal with reality. Maybe that was what Justin needed, a touch of reality. She plucked his hand from her cheek and brought it down to the seat between them, spreading his palm flat on the expensive leather.

"How much did you pay for this car?"

"What?"

He was frowning, startled and puzzled.

"How much did you pay for this car? Twenty-five thousand? Thirty-five? Never mind, it doesn't matter. I'm sure it was the top of the line, with all the added extras. How about your shirt, Justin? That isn't just an ordinary checked shirt. It's a Clyde Clark shirt. The jeans I know were the best and most expensive in the store. I was with you when you bought them. Your boots are old, but they're the finest money can buy."

"I don't understand what the things I buy have to do with us—"

"They have to do with your expectations. You expect the best. Always. You expect to have the best, be the best, win the best. And," her voice dropped to a whisper, "you usually do. That's your reality. It's not mine."

"If this isn't the biggest load of unadulterated nonsense I've ever heard—"

"I'm not perfect, Justin. I drop things, break things, lose things, forget things. I get broken nails, cavities, and PMS. I don't believe in perfection. I believe in reality."

"You think I'm not realistic? If you could see what goes through our office every day of the week—"

"But how do you deal with what goes through your office? Don't you throw yourself at every case, an all-out effort, no holds barred?"

"I can't deny I'm good at my job, but I don't see what that has to do with us—"

"You will, if you think about it."

Justin frowned. "All I can see is you know me too damn well. It seems I didn't adequately assess the dangers of trying to take a woman to bed who's seen me flash Morley." He leaned over her suddenly and opened the door, his arm brushing her breasts. "But don't forget that's a two-way street. I know you just as well as you know me." He sat back, patiently waiting for her to get out of the car. "It isn't my supposed perfection that's putting you off. The reality," he accented the word heavily, "is that you're afraid. Afraid to put yourself on the line, afraid to take what you damn well want like hell."

Trembling, she swung her legs out and slid from the car.

He pulled the door shut behind her with a final little snap, his face visible in the open window. "I was wrong about your courage. You're only brave when you're sitting in the cockpit of a plane. In the arms of a man, you're a craven coward."

IT WASN'T THE PLACE to search for serenity, up there in
that secret sky that held sudden surprises, lifts and sinks
that even Shelly with all her experience couldn't antici-
pate, but she was filled with a reckless need to prove
something to herself. What, she didn't know.

*I need to soar. I need to cut loose the fetters of time
and space and just...be free. Free from my...thoughts.*

It wasn't a good day for a freedom search. One eye on
the altimeter, the other on the variometer, Shelly con-
cluded it was a day when the sink matched the dropping
of her heart.

She headed for a cloud street, a series of cumulus
clouds lined up in a row in which a sailplane can fly under and count on a steady lift, neither gaining nor losing
altitude. Of course, today the cloud street was wet and
worthless.

Along the valley ridge, she found a thermal with weak
lift. She worked it slowly, but the end result was that she
managed to maintain three thousand feet only by circling endlessly. She was in a thermal rut. There was no
way up... or out. Like her relationship with Justin.

She gave up working the thermal and pulled out to
drop down in a spiral toward the landing field. She told
herself the day wasn't right, but unbidden came the
thought that, for the first time in her life, soaring lacked
the excitement of flirting with danger that she loved.
She'd been exposed to a level of danger much greater
when she lay in Justin's arms, a danger that held all the
heart-stopping elation she'd only known before in the
sky, a danger that was...addictive.

She'd flown in another dimension, and now the old
one seemed too tame.

She touched down, coming to earth in more ways than
one. Unbuckling her safety harness, she lifted back the

canopy and climbed out, feeling disillusioned. She'd paid Pat to take her up and spent an hour of her own time, only to discover that Justin had destroyed her last refuge.

The unwelcome thought came that the last time she'd walked across the field, she'd looked up to see Justin wheeling his car into a parking place.

She felt a sudden, deep irreparable ache. Today the space was empty, the field barren. Derek was gone for the afternoon, but he'd promised to come back around three for his lesson. Pat had towed her up, returned to the field and gotten in her car to scoot home and prepare dinner. Mel was in the hangar, tinkering, the clang, clang of his wrench coming eerily to her ears from across the ridge top. Everyone had a busy, demanding life, uncomplicated by thoughts of what might have been.

Empty. She felt so empty. She pushed her red-gold hair back and struck off across the grass toward the shack. A cup of coffee. A sandwich. Maybe then the empty feeling would go away.

She was lying to herself and she knew it. For days she'd been telling herself that a cup of hot coffee, a warm bath, a good book, a good night's sleep, a great thermal would make her forget the sound of Justin's voice telling her good-bye. Nothing did.

She had to get hold of herself. Tomorrow was Saturday and Mel had, by dint of promising faithfully to take his medicine for a week, coerced her into saying she'd go with him to the airfield where Strom housed his B-17, and where the air show would be held. Mel had promised Strom he'd help him with some of the million chores that needed to be done before the show, fences along the flight line rigged out with string and sticks, plots laid out for food tents, inspection and painting of the FFA tower.

She was gambling on the hope that Justin wouldn't be there.

She lost. He was not the first person she saw, but he was the second. He was kneeling in front of a marble monument, dressed in an old pair of khaki pants, a gray sweatshirt and a pair of gloves. He had his head bent as he wielded a trowel in the earth, a breeze, the kind that always seemed to be blowing across the empty expanse of an air field, ruffling his golden hair. Scattered behind him were rocks randomly tossed on a pile. In front of him was a neatly laid half circle of rocks alternating with golden mums and ruby asters. He was making a rock garden in front of the monument dedicated to those airmen who'd lost their lives in World War II.

It was strange to watch him for those few precious moments before he saw her. Typically Justin, his whole attention was bent to the task of creating a spot of beauty in the middle of a pasture. But there were lines of fatigue on his face and a frown creasing his brow that had nothing to do with the job at hand. The week hadn't been easy for him, either. Lost in the need to somehow undo, retrieve, make amends, she walked to where he knelt.

When her shadow crossed his work area, he looked up. Something came and went in his green eyes. Stubborn male that he was, he didn't say a word, just bent his head and resumed tamping dirt down around the roots of a yellow mum. "You'll understand if I don't get up," he said in a tone that was softly even, cruelly precise. "I'm in the middle of creating a perfect rock garden."

Her own pride came to the fore, mixed with anger at his rudeness. "I wouldn't think of bothering you for a minute. I'll let you get on with it—"

She moved to walk past him. He reached out and grabbed her ankle, wrapping her jeans pant leg in his gloved grip. "Where are you going?"

He hadn't meant to look at her or talk to her. Most of all, he hadn't meant to touch her. She lowered her head, he raised his. The wind ruffled her red-gold hair, making him long to feel its silky slide against his fingers, while Shelly gazed at him and knew that even on his knees, he had an arrogant sureness that made her the supplicant.

"I came here to work."

He thought that over for a minute. "You can help me."

"Doing what?"

"Finishing this." His fingers relaxed their grip on her ankle, but his eyes were alive with a sardonic mockery as he continued to gaze into her face. "It will be a first for us—finishing what we started."

His bravado hid pain, a pain she shared. She dropped down on her knees and put her hand on his cheek. He recoiled from her touch instantly. Mortified, she snatched her hand away. "I'm sorry."

"You should be. Didn't any man ever warn you about the danger of setting off false alarms?"

She flushed, but held his gaze steadfastly. "The subject never came up."

He let that one go. He didn't want to think of her with other men. He wanted to think of her with him.

"Want me to hand you a rock?" she asked, her eyes watching him with their blue clarity like diamonds sparkling in the sun. He'd been missing a lot making love to her in the dark. He hadn't been able to see those sapphire eyes, that pale sheened skin that only a redhead could have, that fiery glorious hair. She was wearing denim pants that had seen better days and an old khaki flight jacket hanging loose in the first warmth of the morning, but under the khaki was a white T-shirt that hugged what he knew to be a slim, very feminine body.

"You'd better let me haul the rocks," he told her. "You can handle the flowers."

She might have protested such chauvinistic division of labor, but the rocks looked heavy. She decided to practice discretion. It would be easier on her spine.

Justin got to his feet, went to the pile and picked up a stone. He brought it back and placed it next to the flowers she'd started to plant.

"Wait a minute," she said, as he started to seat it in the loose earth. "That one's not quite the right shape." She jumped to her feet and scurried to the rock pile, indicating her choice with the toe of her shoe. "Maybe you should use this one."

He gave her the long-suffering look of an abused male, plucked the offending rock out of the earth and hauled it back to the pile. While she watched, he picked up the one she'd pointed out. When he'd placed her favorite to her satisfaction, she planted a mum next to it.

He went to fetch another rock. They were substantial rocks, about the size of a round loaf of bread and quite uniform. He was careful this time to pick one exactly the same shape as the others so her sensitive aesthetic sense would not be offended. But when he placed his choice next to the flower she planted, she shook her head. "You don't want that one. It has an ugly black streak down the middle."

Black streak. He'd been so busy getting the right size, he hadn't noticed the black streak. "It looks fine to me."

"It just won't do. Trust me. If you put that one in, you'll look at it when it's all done and wish you hadn't."

He stood staring at her.

"You did say you were making the *perfect* rock garden, didn't you?" she asked, her smile sweetly innocent.

Justin clamped his lips together, hoisted the rock out of the garden and tossed it to the back of the pile. Getting a little smarter now, he nudged a stone with his foot to bring it to her attention. "How about this one?"

She shook her head. "Maybe you should use this one."

He picked up the rock she chose and placed it next to her flower. She dug in the dirt, planting the next mum, thinking it was a beautiful day and they'd be lucky to have weather like this for the air show.

Justin looked down at her red-gold head and wondered where she'd ever gotten the asinine idea that she wasn't just as much of a demanding perfectionist as he was. "How about looking the stones over to see which one you want next?" Justin asked, his tone dry.

"It's okay," she said, enjoying the planting of the flower and the way the rock garden was taking shape too much to be dragged away to examine the rock pile. "Any one you choose will be fine."

Justin plucked up another rock and dropped it into the garden, making the leaves of the mum jiggle.

In the silence, Shelly surveyed it with dismay. "Oh, dear. That one's not right at all. Look at it, it's almost triangular when the other ones are nice and round." Her attention was all on the garden. "Maybe you should..."

Justin snatched up the offending rock and hurled it back onto the pile. It slammed against another pointed rock and cracked neatly in two.

"...take a break," Shelly murmured.

Justin turned to her. "Maybe you should take a hike."

With great dignity, she dusted off her hands. "My pleasure."

Justin watched her go, the short jacket swinging across her hips as she walked toward the hangar. Nice, neat hips, the nicest set of hips he'd ever seen packaged in denim. She was wearing a smudge of wet earth on her rear end. Well, he thought with an ironic twist on his mouth, his eyes dropping to the rock garden, that was one more thing they'd started and hadn't finished.

He thought about the things they'd started and hadn't finished and an explicit word resounded in his mind. Just thinking about touching her brought him to a fine-tuned peak of readiness. He wasn't accustomed to sexual frustration. He didn't like the feeling. And most of all he didn't like the niggling thought that if, the last time he held her in his arms, he'd been more lover and less prosecuting attorney, he wouldn't be watching her walk away from him, wishing he could wring her neck.

They ate lunch in the old hangar, gathered around a rickety iron table that was most often used to hold tools while they worked on an airplane. There were eight of them, Strom and Mel and four other men whom Shelly knew by name as well as Justin and herself. She had insisted on covering the table with old newspapers before they ate, which earned her an ironic glance from Justin. They'd spread their fast-food burgers, fries and salads out on top of the relatively clean papers and fallen into the food hungrily.

Justin sat at the opposite end of the table from Shelly. Without much effort or being too obvious, she avoided looking at him. He seemed determined to do the same.

Shelly kept a watchful eye on Mel, but as far as she could tell he seemed fine. He always seemed fine in the company of his World War II buddies. She didn't know whether it was because he was determined not to show any weakness, or whether he was genuinely so at ease that his symptoms subsided. Strom, too, appeared to be enjoying himself. The talk rolled around, as it always did, to the war.

Hal Henderson, who had the dignified air of a man who had been to hell and survived, told the story of the early days of Eaker's Eighth, when his staff arrived to settle in at the new headquarters, an imposing country home that had been an exclusive girls' school. The men had carried their bags upstairs, when suddenly there was a wild ringing of bells. Investigation revealed placards left over in each room of the old girl's dormitory that announced primly, Ring Twice for Mistress. Eager to take advantage of all the amenities, the men had complied vigorously.

Henderson talked of how green the Americans had been, how, in the first few battles, the German pilots had fooled them into grossly overestimating their kills by playing possum, flipping their planes over and plunging earthward, smoke pouring from the exhaust provided by smoke pots. At a lower altitude, the pilots righted their planes and flew home, laughing all the way.

They talked of the hours of boredom, alleviated by five minutes of excitement during a successful bomb run. They talked of trekking through the mud to the latrine in the morning to shave off their whiskers in order to ensure a good fit with their oxygen masks. And of course, Henderson reminded them all about the mission that had earned Strom his Congressional Medal of Honor.

"Our target was a munitions plant," Hal said, his face wearing an absorbed expression as if he were living it again. "Messerschmitts were chewing away at our fighter-pilot escorts, and we took a hit or two from ground flak. Still we went in and wheeled around the IP—" he paused and looked at Shelly "—that's the initial point in the bomb run."

She nodded her understanding.

"We opened our bay doors and dropped our load, but by the time we returned to the rally point, we had no power equipment, no landing gear, and the bomb bay doors were locked open. Strom nursed the Fortress along until we were over England, then he ordered everyone out of the plane. When the rest of the crew was safely away, including me, Mel and Strom prepared to parachute out. That was when they discovered the bombardier in the back of the plane. His chute was riddled with fragments, useless. Rather than abandon one of his crew to certain death, Strom made the decision to try for the airfield and make a 'pancake' landing."

Smiling, Hal glanced around at his captive audience. "As you can see, the attempt was successful. Strom brought the plane skittering down on its belly. When the emergency crew boarded, they found the bombardier unconscious from loss of blood. Strom and Mel were pretty shaken up, but all three men survived. That story was told and retold throughout the Air Corps." Hal looked across the table at Justin as if to drive the point home to the son what a brave man the father was. "What made the telling better was that the flight was Strom's twenty-fifth mission, the one that would give him his ticket to rotate out of active duty. The decision to stay with the plane wasn't an easy one for him to make."

"It was the only decision I could make," Strom said gruffly.

"Nice of you to go along for the ride," Henderson said to Mel.

"Yeah," Mel drawled, "wasn't it?" There was a strange note in her father's voice that made Shelly glance at him. He'd never been an easy man to read, but he seemed to turn even more impassive during the recital of Strom's derring-do. In contrast, Strom looked uncomfortable. This struck Shelly as odd. The congressman was a man of great self-possession. After years of life in the public eye, he shouldn't have been uncomfortable hearing the recounting of his heroic deed.

She tried to recall another time when the story of Strom's bravery had been told in his presence and found she couldn't. She'd known the essence of the story, but this was the first time she'd heard the event recounted in vivid detail.

Strom was the first to rise from the table, saying he wanted to get back to work on the B-17. Shelly cleared away the debris of the meal, thinking that some things never changed. The men ate and expected the female in their midst to clean up after them. She gathered up the newspapers she'd spread, aware that Justin was walking out of the hangar on those long legs, and that he probably wouldn't speak to her again that day. If he ever did.

CHAPTER SEVEN

ROBERT HANLEY, district attorney of Jefferson County, stood at the diner counter elbow to elbow with Justin, layering mustard, catsup, chili beans, onions and horseradish on his hotdog. With a smile on his face like Christmas, Hanley gathered up his drowned dog and headed for a back booth. Justin wondered how his wife stood the man's dragon breath. When he followed Hanley through the aisle of the ten-foot-wide room and squeezed into the seat opposite the man and his mountain of condiments, he wondered how *he* would stand it.

The diner was redolent with the smell of hamburgers, hotdogs, sauerkraut and coffee, but Justin found he wasn't very hungry. He ignored the burger and bun on the plate in front of him and cast his green eyes over his boss, wondering how a man who had half the city after his blood and the other half after his hide could sit there looking as if his worst worry was how to keep the horseradish from falling out of his bun.

Hanley's distraction was deceptive. Justin knew the real exercise of this lunch, besides providing Hanley with an opportunity to eat something other than the oat cakes and raw vegetables his wife thrived on. It was to convince Justin to keep his word and escort Miss Denise Beatty, the daughter of a county court judge, to a Friday-night fund-raising dinner for the Democratic candidate to the state senate. Hanley confirmed Justin's suspicions by saying, between munches and without meeting Justin's eyes, that he hoped Justin hadn't forgotten his arrangement with Ms Beatty.

"Maybe I wanted to forget."

That brought Hanley's attention away from his hot dog. He examined Justin with a quizzical look in his eyes. "What can I say, dude? That there's no justice in the world? You know that. You found that out when I handed you the Stewart case."

The strong odor of onions drifted to Justin's nose. "I knew it a little bit before that." Justin had control of himself but it wasn't as easy as it should have been. He didn't want to go to a fund-raising dinner and he especially didn't want to play the adoring ape for the beautiful Ms Beatty. Still, he had given his word to Hanley. The man was his boss. He liked Hanley, Hanley liked him. Hanley saw Justin as the A.D.A. most likely to be his successor. "You've got everything," he'd told Justin, "charisma, family connections, money, everything it takes to be successful in politics."

Bob had said those things, mercilessly dangling the carrot in front of Justin's nose at the same time he tossed Justin the Stewart case, the city's current hot potato. An off-duty sheriff's deputy, Teresa Stewart, had been shot to death by her former boyfriend.

Hanley knew better than to handle it himself. He was too politic for that. He was also too politic to let Justin slight Ms Beatty on a whim. Hanley and Clyde Beatty were already at daggers drawn over a case Hanley had handled while Beatty was on the bench. Hanley wanted no more trouble with the judge.

"You had no objection to the arrangement two months ago when we set this thing up. Why the sudden change of heart? Or need I ask? Has a new woman entered the picture?''

''No, there's no one new in the picture.'' *Someone old I rediscovered. Someone I know so well I can close my eyes and see her face in my dreams at night, hear her voice inside my head, feel her body under my hands.*

''You did say you wouldn't mind taking her.''

''I lied.''

Hanley paused in the act of lifting his hotdog to his mouth and shot Justin a shrewd look. ''Well, you've lived with the lie for two months, try to suffer with it for another thirty-six hours. Perhaps Denise will want an early night. Beauty sleep and all that.''

When Justin arrived at her door the next evening, Denise Beatty had had all her beauty sleep and then some. She was a gorgeous brunette with pale skin and coal-black hair, and she had brown eyes that danced with humor and intelligence. She was wearing a strapless, backless gown that looked as if it was held up by magic and made it impossible for him to provide a guiding hand without touching her bare flesh.

Mentally he cursed Hanley, cursed Beatty, cursed himself. If he hadn't been so distracted by a certain difficult redhead, he would have remembered his obligation soon enough to cancel out. ''You look lovely,'' he said dutifully, handing her the corsage box, his mocking eyes traveling over her bare shoulders. ''Although I'm not sure where you're going to pin this thing. I should have asked the florist to throw in a roll of Scotch tape.'' His dry tone made her laugh merrily as she took the box from him.

While he watched, Denise went to the mirror above the fireplace and pinned the roses at her waist. She lived in one of the old homes along East Avenue that reeked with money and antiques. The oval mirror had a Federal gold frame, the chairs were Chippendale, the carpet Aubusson, the glass Venetian. And Ms Beatty had the class to outdazzle it all.

He gazed at her long, sleek back and felt strangely unmoved. She came from a wealthy, privileged background similar to his own, and she was a personable, twenty-one-year-old woman. They'd met briefly at a party a few months ago, but tonight she was like an alien from another planet.

In the car she seemed not to mind his silence, but took over the responsibility of the conversation, chatting amiably about the weather, the dinner, her friends who would be there. She strongly supported the candidacy of the man whose coffers were fattened by the price of the dinner tickets, and strongly rejected his opponent.

But when they had gone inside the hotel dining room, were seated at the table and the main course had come and gone, Denise finished her conversation with the man on her right and turned her attention to Justin. "Mr. Assistant District Attorney, you're very quiet tonight. I seem to remember you being a little more...flamboyant."

He'd drunk the wine sparingly, eaten sparingly. Unlike him, she'd drained her glass once and then again. He wondered if she needed the wine for the courage to confront him. Guilt flickered through him briefly. "I'm sorry I disappointed you."

"You aren't sorry at all, but that's beside the point. Even if you sat in silence the whole evening, you couldn't disappoint a woman. She'd get pleasure out of just looking at you. Did I tell you how good you looked when you walked in the door tonight?"

"No," he said, in a tone that patently warned, *don't bother.*

"You have something on your mind. Is she blond, brunette, or red-headed?"

His eyes flickered over her. "Brunette," he said lightly.

"If you hadn't looked, you wouldn't have known which I was."

"You're wrong. Would you like some more wine?"

She arched one delicately shaped eyebrow. "Careful, Mr. Corbett. *In vino veritas.*"

"I have a hunch I'm going to get the truth, no matter how much wine you drink."

"Everyone says I'm very truthful. It's so much more convenient, being truthful, don't you think? It's too tiring to remember what lie you told to whom when."

He was beginning to feel uncomfortable but there wasn't a thing he could do about it. It disturbed him when women he barely knew turned chatty and confidential.

"Do you have a brother, Justin?"

"Yes. He was married not too long ago."

"Pity. I was hoping he'd be more amenable. And single, of course." She favored him with a sweeping examination that increased his discomfort. He wondered when this interminable evening would end.

"You're a different man than you were when last we met."

"I wasn't aware of any major change—"

"You may not be aware of it . . . but it's happened. I'd love to meet the woman who's made you so . . . cautious."

"So would I," he murmured.

"How gallant. But it's a lie, Mr. Counselor."

It was the only time in Justin's life he'd ever longed for a politician to begin his speech. The esteemed Democratic candidate did, at last, take the platform and Justin found himself applauding as heartily as Denise but for an entirely different reason.

The speech began, there were the usual warm-up jokes, the usual hearty laughs. Justin sat back in his chair, Denise's bare shoulder in his vision, and thought about how many similar functions he'd been to in the past three years and how he'd never noticed his own lack of interest in them. He had, of course, cut his eyeteeth on political meetings. But he remembered how he'd felt at the country hayride, alive and aware of Shelly at his side, and he knew that never again would he be able to sit through an evening with the bored tolerance he had practiced until it was a refined art.

Shelly had, with her gentle jostling of his perception of the dating game, shown him another world. Enjoyment didn't depend on expensive food, fine wine, the glitter of the city. Enjoyment depended on being with a woman whose heart beat in the same pattern as his own, a woman who thought and felt as he did. He was seated among the most influential people in the city, escorting one of the most beautiful women in the city, and all he could think of was that a part of him was missing. The best part.

He wished he was back in the dark car with Shelly, wished he could retract every word he'd said, wished he had done less talking and more kissing. He needed her. He needed her now. Not because he wanted to make love, but because he wanted to look at her, talk to her, be with her. He wanted her there beside him the way she'd been that night of the party.

He couldn't have what he wanted. She had gone out of his life, and he was left with empty evenings like this, doing things he didn't want to do with women he didn't want to be with.

The candidate's speech ended. When Denise murmured, with a flick of her gorgeous eyes, "It was a good speech, wasn't it?" he took the line of least resistance and nodded. She swallowed a word and said nothing as he helped her with her wrap and stood behind her while they waited for the people ahead of them to file out of the door. He was still grappling with his feeling of emptiness and his need for Shelly when the crowd flowed into the hotel lobby.

There were a couple of television cameras waiting there, with klieg lights. Instinctively Justin turned away from their glare. A camera bulb flashed in his face. He blinked and turned to protest, which was why he didn't see the man surge through the crowd until Denise screamed.

The next thing Justin knew a man had her by the throat. Justin chopped at his arms, but the big, bearded, six-foot-three giant held on grimly, and it was Denise who was bearing the brunt of his blows.

Fear gutted Justin's belly. Vulnerable. Hit a man where he's vulnerable.

He made a V of his fingers and jabbed them into the wild, dark eyes. The man howled and let go of Denise to fend off Justin's assault. Mad as a hornet, Denise grabbed his nearest hand and bit down hard. The man screamed in rage and came after her. Justin pushed her aside and gave the man a swift, hard kick in the groin. He cursed and staggered back, his hands going to his injured parts. By that time, the hotel security men had appeared and were subduing Denise's attacker. While camera flashes burst around them like popcorn, the team spirited him off to a room away from the crowd to await the arrival of the police.

Justin barely had time to ask Denise if she was all right and scoop up her shawl to wrap it around her shoulders when they were besieged by reporters. The television cameras were aimed at them and a microphone was poked under his mouth.

"Who was that man? Do you know who he was, Mr. Corbett?"

Justin looked into the camera, his eyes sardonic. "Call him a creep. He doesn't deserve a name."

"Was he attacking Ms Beatty seeking revenge on her father?"

"Your guess is as good as mine. Why don't you go ask him? I'm sure he'll be glad to get the free television coverage."

"While you're not, Mr. Corbett?" slyly asked a reporter. "You were a hero tonight and we've got it all on film. A little publicity like that can't hurt you. Especially when I hear you're thinking of running for district attorney. Now would be an excellent time for you to confirm that rumor."

Anger rose, heating him, mingling with the adrenaline already flowing in his veins. Justin was breathing hard after his exertion, but he was more than ready to battle it out. Before he could open his mouth, he felt a hand on his arm. Denise, cautioning him to be careful, acting as his protector now.

The world slowed, cooled. Stromberg Corbett's son came to his senses and realized he couldn't shoot off his mouth to the press any more than he already had. Grateful for Denise's intervention that gave him the second he needed to come to his senses, he shot the insistent reporter a look that would freeze water at fifty paces. "You will excuse us, won't you? Ms Beatty's had a shock."

Another man yelled, "Where'd you learn to fight dirty, Mr. Corbett?"

Justin's control cracked. "I've been watching the press."

"Is it true that you've replaced the artist Grant Wilding as Ms Beatty's lover?"

Justin felt a swift flare of irritation. Dandy. Wonderful. "No comment."

"Ms Beatty, will you be filing charges?"

"Ms Beatty can't discuss what's happened until she consults her attorney."

"But the police will want to question her—"

"Unlike her attacker, Ms Beatty is a responsible citizen. When the police need her, she'll be available for questioning. She has nothing further to tell you other than she thanks you for your concern," said Justin, shaking his head to indicate he would answer no more questions. Linking his arm through Denise's, he surged through the gaggle of reporters and stepped out into the autumn evening.

In his convertible, the top safely up, he turned to her and tried in the half light from a street lamp to examine the bare lovely neck that had nearly been broken. All he saw was reddened skin. "Are you all right?"

Her hand went to her throat. "Yes," she said huskily, "thanks to you. I may not feel like talking too much for a few days, but Dad will probably count that as a blessing. You were . . . pretty good out there."

"You're not so bad yourself. He'll probably have scars from those teeth of yours."

She gave him a weak smile. "In all the right places."

He had to give her full marks for courage. After what she'd been through, it was a miracle she could joke about it. She was a hell of a woman. She just wasn't his woman.

Justin started the car engine and pulled away from the curb. As if being transported from the scene made it easier for her to talk, Denise said, "I recognized him. He was the brother of a man my father sent to prison for killing his wife."

"Nice family," Justin murmured. "I remember that case. Are you sure you're okay?"

"I wouldn't have been if you hadn't been with me. I . . . thank you. I haven't said thank you."

He covered her hand with his. "You don't need to."

"You're very . . . competent."

"Don't you want to ask me where I learned to fight dirty?"

She laughed then, a nervous laugh, but a laugh nevertheless. The laugh ended in a shudder. "You think nothing can happen to you. When something does, it's like . . . a shock. It's like your world has been shattered."

"Is anybody going to be at home with you tonight? The police will probably keep the jerk in custody for a few hours, but just in case he has a brother—"

"Dad will be there." She turned to Justin, impulsively laying her hand on his arm. "But I don't want to go home. There's someone I have to see, now, tonight."

"All right," Justin said evenly. "Tell me where he lives."

Surprised, Denise subsided back into the seat and took her hand from Justin's arm. "How do you know it's a he?"

"I thought perhaps we might be going to see Mr. Grant Wilding."

She ducked her head, then turned to look at his profile. "You don't miss much, do you?"

"That's my job, listening to people, watching them, thinking about their motives. It seemed to me that if you were wild about me, you would have made some attempt to see me over the last two months."

"It's true. I was...trying you on for size. Da...someone told me you were exactly right for me...rich, well-connected, on your way up." She stared out through the windshield. "Grant lives on Maypole Street." She glanced back at Justin. "Does that tell you anything?"

"Only that he hasn't made his first million yet," said Justin lightly, swinging the car in the direction of a main street that would take him to the slightly seedy section of town where old houses perched on a hill across from the oldest cemetery in the city.

"You listen to...people...tell you what you're like and you think maybe they know better than you do. Somebody...tells you you can't exist without the nice clothes and the fancy home and the gourmet food that you're used to and you think maybe he's right." She gestured with her hand. "You don't know who you are until something like tonight happens to you. Then you find out that it's only the important things that matter." She gave a half laugh. "I'm not making much sense, am I?"

"You're making perfect sense," said Justin, and he meant it.

"Here, turn here."

The house was ramshackle, in need of paint. Justin pulled up next to the curb and shut off the motor. Denise stared at the house and didn't move.

"What is it?"

She lifted her chin and gave him a brave smile. "I'm afraid. Isn't that stupid? I've been here dozens of times, but this time, the time when I really need to know he'll be there for me, I'm afraid."

"I'll see you to the door."

She wrapped her fingers around the door handle but she didn't move. "We had a fight. He didn't want me to go with you tonight. But I was afraid that if I didn't, I'd regret it."

"Now you regret going."

"No, I don't," she said suddenly, fiercely. "It's made me see I can't live my life the way...other people want me to live." She looked directly at Justin. "The way my father wants me to live. I have to find my own way, make my own mistakes, learn to live without designer clothes."

Justin's mouth curved in a smile. "I've heard it said recently that all anybody needs is a pair of jeans."

She drew back from him in mock dismay. "Jeans cost a fortune."

"But I have it on excellent authority that a good pair lasts a long time."

"Well, then, there you see. Problem solved. I'll just make sure I buy a couple of pair while my father's still paying the bills and take them with me when I go." Impulsively, she leaned forward and brushed her mouth over Justin's. Then she sat back, trembling, smiling. "You stay here. I've got to do this alone."

He opened his mouth to protest, but she closed it with her fingers and gave him a fond smile.

"You're a bright, beautiful man and I like you very, very much, and I know you're just trying to protect me, but if Grant actually sees how good-looking you are, he'll start yelling at me all over again. Nothing's going to happen to me in the twelve feet between here and Grant's door. You can watch until I'm inside if it will make you feel better." She turned away to leave him.

"Denise."

"Yes?"

"After you go in, you'd better call your father first and tell him you're okay."

"First?" A black eyebrow climbed delicately.

"First," Justin repeated firmly. "And tell the judge that it was Wilding who insisted you call."

"I was right," Denise said. "You are a bright, beautiful man." She laughed then as he'd hoped she would and slipped out of the car. He moved to follow, but a small inner voice cautioned him to wait. She was on the porch already, ringing the bell.

The light over her head came on and a man appeared behind the screen door. His dark hair was tousled, his chest and feet bare. For a long, long instant of time, he stood in the doorway, staring at his beloved from behind the screen. Then he opened the door—and his arms. Denise moved into them and buried her head in his shoulder.

It should be that simple, Justin thought as he drove home through the dark streets. But it rarely is.

Inside his condo, he tossed his tie on the living room couch, and paced to the window to look down into the quiet garden behind his building. He wasn't tired. He was keyed up, restless.

He muttered a word. He'd never be able to sleep feeling like this. He—

The phone jarred him, nerves already on edge jumping with annoyance. Probably some damned reporter wanting to know whether he had Denise in his bed and the district attorney's job on his mind. To hell with them. He'd said enough for one night. He'd let the answering machine get it.

He threw himself down on the couch to listen. There was a silence then his father's voice filled the room. "Dammit, I hate talking to these machines. Where are you, boy? I swear every time I call you I get this damn thing—''

Justin reached for the phone. "I'm here, Dad."

Taken aback, Strom was silent for a moment, "Why didn't you answer?''

"I thought you were a reporter," Justin replied evenly.

"Humph. See why you might have thought that. Didn't it ever occur to you I'd be worried?''

Never one to show his cards before he had to, Justin asked casually, "Why should you be worried?''

"Why? Why? You were on the eleven o'clock news, son. That man could have made hash out of you.''

"Not hash," Justin drawled. "Hamburger, maybe, but not hash.''

"Hamburger then. You were crazy to take him on.''

"There wasn't anybody else there to do it. Is that why you called, to tell me I'm crazy? If so, you're wasting your time. I already know—''

"No. I called to tell you I'm proud.''

The wind properly knocked out of his sails, Justin laid his head back on the couch and threaded a hand through his hair. "Thanks." In earlier days, his father's praise would have meant everything to him. Now, other words echoed inside his head, Denise's words. *"The way... my father wants me to live..."*

Suddenly, he felt exhausted, washed out. The adrenaline had drained away and left him an empty shell. Maybe he would be able to sleep after all if it was past eleven o'clock... He bolted upright. "You saw everything on the eleven o'clock news?''

"Well, I don't know how much was everything, but I saw you defending your lady friend rather well and helping her with her wrap. I didn't know you were seeing a judge's daughter.''

"I'm not."

"Well, it sure looked like you were."

Justin muttered a curse and surged to his feet, nearly dropping the telephone. "Did I appear to be . . . fond of her?"

"I'd say more than fond. You looked like a enraged lion defending his mate."

"Great. Just great." At that moment, he realized that he hadn't accepted his estrangement from Shelly. He'd hoped, believed, known in some deep part of his brain that they'd get back together again. He was far less certain now, and far more disturbed.

"I'm all right, Dad. Don't worry about me." He remembered then what he had forgotten in the confusion and excitement, that his father was not a well man. "It didn't . . . make you ill, did it, seeing me on TV?"

"Hell, no. Best medicine I could have had, seeing my boy fight like a hero."

"I didn't exactly adhere to the Marquis of Queensbury rules, Dad," Justin said, his tone dry.

"You did what was necessary. You acted like a man. I've never been prouder."

"Thank you." Justin was uncomfortable and didn't know why. He felt like an imposter, undeserving of his father's praise. He'd done what had to be done because he was there. His father offered him more praise and Justin was equally adamant in rejecting it. Strom at last rang off.

Justin hung up the phone, his weariness gone, his mind working. If his father had seen everything on TV, the chances were good that Shelly had, too. He sliced his hand through his hair and paced to the window again. What would she think?

She would think he was seeing Denise, even while he targeted Shelly as fair game and laid out a line to get her in bed. Which, God help him, he had.

He had.

The enormity of what he'd done washed over him. Shelly had been right to shy away from him. From the first moment he'd tried to kiss her and she'd refused him, he'd considered her an exciting challenge in his life, a recalcitrant juror he had to persuade, a difficult aerobatic maneuver he had to master, a challenge he would, could, and must win no matter what the cost. Including his calling her a coward.

What a damned egocentric pigheaded fool he was.

Denise had made him see that women weren't a challenge to be won, a prize to be sought. They were people, real people, with blood and bone and nerves, who worried about their self-images and their life-styles and their honesty, who had the same hopes, dreams and fears that he did. All these years, he hadn't really seen that. He'd considered women a part of the game, the opposing participants in a love Olympics.

He felt a sudden, deep, complete and searing shame. He, who'd regarded himself as one of the few really tolerant and enlightened men in the world. Justin Corbett, who knew that women were bright and deserved as much money for their talents in the marketplace as men did, was, when it came to his love life, a male chauvinist of the first water.

Need burgeoned within him. He needed to see Shelly, talk to her, convince her that he wasn't the arrogant cretin she thought he was. A swift vision of the miles between them flashed through his brain, the moonlit miles of expressway, the mental miles of his stupidity. He ached to go to her.

If he did, he'd look like a fool.

After his performance tonight, played out for local, late-night TV news, beamed out over the land, she wouldn't believe him no matter what he said. He hardly believed the way he was feeling himself.

Worse, he had no right to go to Shelly and plead his case after the way he'd treated her. He had to stay where he was and take the punishment that fate had meted out to him. He cared for her too much to risk having her reject him again.

He cared for her—too much.

He felt gutted. He felt torn open, exposed, vulnerable. He'd never really cared for anyone in his life, not after his mother. He'd loved his mother. But she'd died and left him.

It wasn't safe to love people. It gave them the power to hurt you. That was the lesson his father had taught him and taught him well. Once he'd loved Strom desperately, wanted desperately to be loved in return. His father had treated him like a race horse judged solely on performance. His father liked people who won, so his son had learned to win.

A grim little smile played around Justin's mouth. He'd done what his father had taught him to do, turned his life into a game of winners and losers and made sure he was a winner.

Which was why he'd lost the biggest one of all. After years of empty sex, he'd learned to want one woman above all others. In the same instant he'd forfeited any chance to win her—

Dammit all! She wasn't a prize to be won. She was a woman to spend hours, days, weeks, years with. She was a woman who made a man want to step into the void of loving and not give a damn how far he fell.

He didn't have to worry about falling. Shelly knew him too well, knew him for what he was—and didn't want what he was.

Maybe if he could stop thinking about her, he could stop wanting her.

Maybe the moon could decide to stop orbiting the earth.

He had to get out of the condo. He had to go where he couldn't feel, couldn't want, couldn't think about what he'd lost through his own stupidity. He needed physical exercise. Swimming. He would go swimming. If he were very fortunate, he might drown.

SHELLY HADN'T RIDDEN a horse for years. But trapped in that silent house with Mel in bed and the blank television screen staring at her like a gray ghost, she wanted to get out and ride. Ride with the wind at her back and the stars in her eyes. Ride into a mindless state where neither time nor love existed.

After Mel had left her to climb the stairs and retire, she'd turned off the light and sat in the dark. The moon shone through the window, littering the room with moon glow. Thinking and feeling were two different processes and at the moment, she couldn't think, she could only feel.

How easy it had been to push Justin away. Easy. Because in pushing him away she had, in some foolish fashion, imagined she was bringing him closer. That was fantasy. The reality was that Justin was a human being with a life of his own. And life, as they said, went on.

In that room filled with moon-silvered shadows, the scenes she had witnessed on television danced through her mind. Justin, stepping out into the lobby looking very...Justin, irritated at the intrusion of the camera. The attacker appearing out of nowhere. Justin's face mirroring shock, rage, then deadly determination. Arms and legs flying. The camera tipping, as if there was so much going on the cameraman was confused about where to focus and in the panic, aimed at the floor. The scene righting with dizzying speed. The man, his face twisted with ugly emotion, going after the woman like an attack dog, then suddenly, doubling over in pain.

Only after it was over did Shelly's heart come up in her throat, thinking of the danger Justin had been in. She found herself trembling with a violent need to run her hands over his face and his body to assure herself that he was all right. Then she remembered how tenderly he placed the wrap around the woman's shoulders and how protective he was of her as he fended off the press, how his charm captivated the camera, even while his cynical words cut. As Shelly sat in the dark and thought of all those scenes, the deep wellspring of love that had been there for years, ages, eons spilled up out of her heart and overflowed into her consciousness.

Every tender emotion she was capable of feeling flowered inside her, love, pride, fear for his well-being, the need to be with him. She wanted desperately to be with him.

Justin's voice, inside her head. *You're afraid. Afraid to reach out and take what you want.*

Wildness of a kind she'd never known filled her. Wildness and recklessness and the need to claim what she knew instinctively should be hers. She was tired of being afraid, tired of being cautious. She who had never taken an emotional risk wanted to roll the dice and watch them fall. There was a chance that her instincts were entirely wrong, that Justin no longer wanted her, that he was spending the night with Ms Beatty. Still, there was something in his face, a detached way he had of looking at the lovely young woman that gave Shelly the courage to hope. Granted, if she was wrong and lost, she'd lose big. She'd lose her pride—and her love. But if she was right and she won...

She was crazy to contemplate going to him. Yet she couldn't stop thinking about what a coward she'd feel if she spent the rest of her life wondering what might have happened if she'd had the courage to reach for what she wanted now, tonight.

She lunged out of her chair and went to the phone in the kitchen.

Either Morley hadn't been sleeping, or he always sounded as if he were sitting around in the middle of the night waiting to answer a call. "Mr. Justin's address in the city? Who needs it?"

"I do, Morley," Shelly said as pleasantly as she knew how.

There was a silence, then he said, in that smooth, proprietary tone. "Yes, of course." He recited it, then added precise instructions about how to get there.

Shelly thanked him and hung up the phone.

On the other end of the line, Morley turned to Strom. "It's rather late at night. Do you think she's planning on driving into the city now, sir?"

Strom grinned. He looked in fine fettle, like a cat with a succulent canary under his paw. "I think she is, Morley. I think she is. In fact, I'm counting on it. Give me that phone. I'd better call that son of mine to warn him." But as the phone rang into empty silence in Justin's condo without even getting an answer from the answering machine, Strom's smile changed to a frown. Things were not going as he had planned after all. "Now where has that boy of mine got to?" he muttered.

CHAPTER EIGHT

JUSTIN RETURNED A LITTLE after two o'clock in the morning to find Shelly leaning against the wall next to his door. Her eyes were closed, her face pale under the scientifically softened light of the hallway, her hair a wild, tousled mass of red that made his gut twist with the need to bury his hands in it.

By what miracle was she standing there, propped against the wall like a tired traveler with no place to lay her head? He couldn't imagine. He only knew he was more than willing to accept Shelly in any form, hallucination, ghost or reality.

Her eyes opened, and something like pain flickered through their cool, blue depths.

"Have you been wondering where I was at this late hour?" he asked, struck immediately by the courage it must have taken for her not only to come, but to stand waiting for him until he returned.

In Shelly's eyes, he was the consummate Yuppie. He wore an expensive workout suit and carried a gym bag. His darkly gold wet hair was slicked back from his forehead, leaving his face naked and more vulnerable than Shelly had ever thought possible.

"Either you've been swimming...or Denise's water bed has a wicked leak."

His heart soared with laughter, relief and admiration for her quick wit. He smiled at her, thinking she was an endless treasure trove of surprises he'd never get tired of opening. "How did you come up with that so fast? You were asleep a second ago."

"I have fast recovery. What time is it?"

He gazed at her silently, and that quickly, the atmosphere turned heated, charged. "Time for us both to be in bed. That is why you came, isn't it?"

She shook her head, not in denial but in a refusal to answer. Without looking at her, he slipped his key in the lock, pushed open the door, and waited.

Without looking at him, she stepped over the threshold.

She tried not to catalog the luxury surrounding her, but it was too subtly perfect to ignore, the mauve-gray carpet underfoot, the huge picture window faintly lit with the glow of the city sky, the cushiony velvet furniture in a strange pumpkin color, the rank of books along the walls.

"Come in, sit down." Justin dropped his gym bag on the floor beside the couch and turned to her, wondering how long he could go on being civilly casual. He wanted to grab her and hug her breathless, but if he did, he'd scare her to death.

Shelly wondered why he didn't try to hold her. Chilled by his detachment, she wrapped her arms around her middle to keep from reaching for him.

"Would you like something to drink?" said the perfect host. "I'm having orange juice but I'd be glad to get you something stronger, if you like."

"No. Yes. Ginger ale."

His eyes flickered with a touch of amusement that he quickly stifled. "A stiff glass of ginger ale it is."

He brought Shelly's drink a few minutes later, handed it to her and stepped away to settle into the opposite

couch, with the oblong table between them. He drank
thirstily, as if his workout had drained the moisture from
his body, then set his glass on the table and leaned back
to look at her. Self-conscious under his shrewd and unrelenting examination, she took a sip of her ginger ale.
The ice cubes clinked in the glass, sounding like thunder
in the quiet room. He'd turned on only one small lamp,
the one that sat on a low table at the opposite end of the
couch. She felt caught in the pool of light and silence.
Nervously, she put her glass down on the table between
them. "Why don't you ask me why I'm here?"

"Strange as it may seem, I'm at a loss for words. Or
maybe I just want to cherish the fond hope that you've
come to say yes before you tell me otherwise."

Shelly lifted her head. "I know how to talk with you,
laugh with you, fly with you, but I don't know how
to...seduce you."

"That," he said softly, "is a matter of opinion. You
seduce me just by looking at me."

Her eyes caught, held his.

"Well, that seems clear enough," he murmured.
"Shall we start here on the couch, or proceed directly to
the bedroom?"

His words were a challenge, with a touch of cynicism
in them, but she understood why he was testing her. After the times she'd rejected him, she didn't blame him for
being a little rough with her. She'd have to show him that
he wasn't going to scare her off so easily. Bravely, she
held his considering gaze. "Whatever...suits you best."

He said a word, lunged up from the couch and went to
stand at the window with his back to her, his heart and
mind filled with the amazing knowledge that he didn't
know how to take a woman he cared for so desperately to
bed. The words, the gestures, the gallant, careless man-

ners didn't come so easily when his deepest feelings were involved. Deep inside him there was a need to strike out at her, to test her and see if she cared for the real him, the dark him that lurked below the charm, the wealth, the gift with words.

For the first time in his life, he wanted to be loved more than he wanted to make love. And it scared the hell out of him.

Shelly sat on the couch feeling stunned. Of all the reactions she'd expected from Justin she hadn't expected hesitation. Had she been wrong? Was he involved with another woman?

Before she could grapple with that disturbing thought, Justin turned around to her. "Why did you change your mind?" he asked.

She twisted around on the sofa, one graceful arm draped over the low back. *Because I love you. Because seeing you in danger made me realize how short life is, how much can happen and how every minute I spend away from you is a moment of time wasted.* "Why do you think?"

"I don't know. Did seeing me on television turn you on? Did you decide you'd like to go to bed with the local hero to see how it felt?"

She'd thought the test of her love for Justin would be finding him with another woman. She hadn't dreamed her real battle would be with Justin himself, that his bold audacity would fail him. Her damn-the-torpedos-full-speed-ahead man was afraid. Desperately, horribly afraid. Why? She didn't know. She did know he was protecting himself in the only way he knew, by striking out at her.

Understanding him didn't keep the feelings of hurt from welling up within her. Pride straightened her backbone. If he didn't want her, she would survive. She'd promised herself that on the long, dark, lonely road into the city. "If you think I'm that kind of woman you don't know me as well as I thought you did. I'll be going now. Thank you for the drink—"

"Shelly." Her name echoed in his quiet room, echoed in his ears. "Don't go."

She stood with her back to him, her breath held. "Why...not?"

"Because I...need you."

She turned around to study him. There was nothing of vulnerability in his face now. He looked coolly contained, detached, impassive. Those low, husky words might not have come from his lips at all. Yet they had. All she could do now was admit her own vulnerability and hope he wouldn't throw her need for him back into her face. "And I need you, Justin."

He stood waiting, his face changing imperceptibly, just enough to give her hope, asking her to make the first move. She wasn't too proud to comply. Carefully she skirted the couch and went to stand beside him. For a long endless moment, he studied her face. Then he simply opened his arms in the age-old gesture of vulnerability.

She went into them, her heart bursting with joyous relief when he enfolded her in his embrace. He was warm, damp around the edges, and smelled faintly of chlorine from the swimming pool, just as he always seemed to. Through the soft velour of his suit, his hard swimmer's body was both a challenge and a refuge.

She sighed softly, and to her amazement, he trembled.

"Shelly," he muttered in a heartfelt husky breath of relief and satisfaction, his mouth seeking hers, his hands burrowing into her hair.

She kissed him back hungrily, wanting to get closer, feel more of him, feel him deep inside her. The depth of her hunger shocked her. She wanted him now, burned to feel again the heat his touch created in her.

At the feel of her body pressed to his, Justin felt his stern resolve to take his time and not rush her explosion in a conflagration of need. His body demanded the satisfaction it had craved for weeks from this woman, even though his mind told him he would never again feel like this and he must savor every delicious second of anticipation. Still, he wasn't sure how much longer he could hold off. He'd never before believed he was capable of throwing a willing woman to the floor and burying his body in hers, but he knew now he was.

Deliberately he drew away from her, put his hands on her hips and turned her. "That way," he murmured, steering her toward the dim hallway.

She swallowed and began to walk. In the silence, the phone rang with ear-splitting intensity.

She stopped. He shook his head. "Let the answering machine get it."

But she didn't move. Sighing, he went to pick up the receiver.

"Well, you're home at last. Just wanted to let you know Shelly's on her way to see you."

"At this time of night?" he said blandly, reaching for her and pulling her against his hip so that she could hear what Strom was saying. "I hardly think so."

"Never kid a kidder, son. She's already there, isn't she? Mel called me a few minutes ago, worried as hell—"

Justin thought of Mel's condition and his father's heart and decided he'd better tell the truth. "Yes, Dad, she's here."

"Is she staying the night with you?"

His eyes knowing, amused, he covered the receiver. "Dad wants to know if you're staying the night with me."

Shelly returned his gaze steadfastly. "Tell him yes."

"She says yes," Justin repeated into the receiver.

"Well," said Strom in a satisfied tone.

"Well, indeed," drawled Justin.

"Call me tomorrow when you . . . wake up."

"Yes, Dad." Justin hung up the phone, his mouth quirking as he turned to Shelly. With his free hand he gestured toward the hallway. "Will you come into my fishbowl, said the spider to the fly?"

She laughed, her heart soaring. "If you think there's room for me," she turned to him and raised her hands to his cheeks, "I'd love to share your fishbowl with you."

His eyes roamed over her face. How good it felt to be with her, to know that she understood his father well enough to stay, despite Strom's interfering, heavy hand. He couldn't think of another woman who would have such forbearance. But no other woman knew his father—or him—as well as Shelly did. Underneath his desire for her burned an intense joy, as if he'd found gold. "Have I told you lately how much I . . . admire you?"

"Not . . . lately," she said carefully, her heart accelerating at the tone of his voice and how dangerously close he was to telling her that he cared for her.

He turned her, guiding her toward the bedroom. "Have I told you lately how much I like your red hair?"

"No," she murmured, thinking he'd cleverly defused the moment of revelation. They were inside his bedroom now, standing locked together in the middle of the room, the soft light shielding the expression in his eyes from her gaze. She just had time to notice clothes tossed on a chair, the first thing she'd seen out of place since she came into the apartment. He'd evidently been in a hurry to go for his swim. His bed was a huge round circle, a masculine puddle of brown velvet, big enough for a quartet to sleep in. Then she forgot to look around for clues of the man she loved, for he was getting down to business. His hands tugged her sweater off both her arms, while his mouth brushed her cheek. Carelessly, he tossed the garment in the general direction of the chair.

He kissed the roses in her cheeks, kissed her mouth, kissed her eyes, kissed her nose. "Relax," he murmured in the soft, throaty tone that had the power to unnerve her completely. "You're in good hands."

She was in expert hands. Shelly tilted her face up to his restless, hungry tasting and savored each brush of his warm mouth, the hunger building alarmingly inside her. She hadn't known it could be like this, this wild, hungry spiral carrying her aloft with a reckless need for total abandonment to a man's caresses.

His hands wandered up her back. When he found her bra and the clip opened, he muttered a groan of satisfaction and brought her freed breasts against his body. Her body stinging with pleasure, she slipped her hands under his velour top and slid her palms up his smooth, warm back, feeling the muscle and bone moving as he caressed her.

His hands cupped her buttocks, pressing her hips into his. She felt his heat, his hardness, his readiness. All his hesitancy, all his fear had vanished. He was a male in pursuit, his mouth claiming hers, his hands intimately possessive, his thighs encircling hers.

He made her feel totally wanton, totally beautiful, totally womanly in a way she had never felt before. He caressed and possessed, but he allowed her the same liberties. His body was hers, he told her in a language that had no words, hers to touch, to taste, to do with what she would.

He savored her mouth, tugging at her lower lip with a gentle lover's bite. He mapped her spine, his touch exquisitely gentle, bringing chills of pleasure to her flesh. He discovered her breasts, cradling one, rubbing the cotton fabric of her T-shirt against the already swollen nipple.

She clutched at his back, feeling the skin heat and slick from the intensity of his desire. Her knees weakened with a languorous need to lie down and open her body to him.

As if he sensed her surrender, he became impatient with her clothes. Her shirt came off with stomach-twisting ease and so did her bra. She stood before him, soft, smooth, pure feminine enticement. He leaned down to taste the roseate peak that was already tight and ready for him, but she pushed him back. He raised surprised eyes to her.

"My turn," she said softly and grasped the zipper at the top of his velour shirt to pull it down with a long, singing rasp. When she deliberately brushed it from his shoulders, watched it fall to the floor, and even more deliberately flattened her palms on the nipples buried in tufts of crisp, golden hair, his eyes darkened.

"Brazen woman," he murmured.

She slid her hands around to his back and pressed her soft breasts against his chest. "I've only just begun."

He gazed into her face, his eyes an emerald glitter at such close range. "If I'd known my appearance on TV would bring you into my bedroom tonight, I'd have been nicer to those reporters.''

She rubbed her mouth on his cheek, savoring the saltiness of his skin.

''You weren't very nice to them, were you?''

''I'm generally not nice to people who attack me.'' His hands cupped her hips, pulling her into him. ''Present company excepted, of course.''

She laughed and he raised a hand to her cheek. ''I like making you laugh. Especially when you're in my arms and so delightfully bare.''

''I like making you laugh, too. It gives me a sense of power over you.''

''Brazen, power hungry, what other faults are you hiding inside this delightful body, woman?''

A deep, abiding love for you. ''If you think I'm going to give all my secrets away, you're crazy.''

''Not all of them, perhaps. But you've already given me one or two,'' he said with deliberate sensuality, his gaze locked on her face, ''and you're about to give me more.''

''Justin—''

At the look on her face of soft feminine shock and arousal, he bent her over his arm and took her breast in his mouth, suckling her with the care of a man who holds a precious treasure. She gasped in surprise and then moaned as he took her deeper into his mouth and suckled her with more intensity, as if he meant to devour her.

He moved to her other breast and her body clenched with surprise, contracted with delight. She reached for his bare shoulder, felt the rock-hard bone and muscle and clasped him, needing something to hold on to for support. This was the Justin she knew too well, boldly tak-

ing what he wanted with a charm and expertise that had
the giver aching to give more.

He clasped her, lifted her. Velvet rubbed sensually
against her back, her legs dangled off the side of the bed.
Justin's mouth was still locked to her breast; he had followed her down with relentless precision. She plunged her
hands into his hair, asking for relief from the hot, aching longing.

As if he understood, he lifted his head, his face
wreathed in the dark, satisfied look of a male about to
mate with the female of his choice. He unzipped her jeans
and, pulling them expertly from under her hips, he
stripped them off and tossed them aside. Her panties
were thin strips of fabric that bared her buttocks and hips
G-string style. He muttered a sound of satisfaction, and
thrust his fingers under the thin strip of fabric. When he
stripped away that last, final tiny barrier that kept him
from seeing her, and his eyes roved hungrily over her
satiny slimness down to the auburn curls that strip of
fabric had covered, she found herself waiting tensely,
desperately needing him.

He returned his gaze to her face, read the apprehension he saw there, and leaned over her, his mouth touching hers as he said tenderly, as if he knew she needed to
hear the words, "I've never seen anything so beautiful.
You're awesome, love. Truly... awesome." His mouth
wandered lower, his tongue wetting the valley between her
breasts, the circle of her navel, the flat valley of her abdomen. Then he was home, tasting her.

She gasped at the feel of him probing her softness with
his tongue. As always, he was bold in his taking, leaving
her with no recourse but to lie and writhe with pleasure
under his ministrations. He was alternately bold and
tender, lifting her up on a wave of taut sexual ecstasy and

then letting her down gently to do nothing but wait for the shuddering lift of the next wave.

Over and over again, he took her to the brink. Over and over again, she urged him to come up and into her. Over and over again he refused to sacrifice her pleasure for his. His hands cupped her buttocks, holding her locked close to him, allowing only the lift of her hips in response to her pleasure-driven restlessness.

At last, when he had taken her expertly through crest after crest of erotic ecstasy that stopped just short of the final explosion, he lifted away from her to pull off his pants.

While she lay watching in a dazed, aching dual state of satiation and hunger, his strong swimmer's legs emerged from their covering. He was wearing a jock strap and that too, came off, releasing his body from the confinement of the white cotton. Before she had time to fully appreciate the body she'd admired on that hot summer night when he'd swum nude in his father's pool, he was beside her, lying on his back and lifting her over him.

Gently, watching her face with an intensity that monitored her every expression, he lowered her onto him.

The erotic relief was nearly unbearable. He filled her emptiness with a superb rightness that could not be denied. She swallowed and said his name in a soft sigh that made his eyes glow with an emerald brightness and his mouth curve into an evocative smile of supreme male satisfaction. He was beautiful: bronzed skin glowing under the soft light, broad shoulders blocked out below the strong column of his throat, the display of muscle and bone glazed with the flow and sculptural symmetry of a work of art.

"Are you all right?" he asked, looking as smug and as arrogant as only a self-assured male who knows he's pleasing his woman can.

"I'm fine." Deliberately, she rotated her hips. "How about you," she asked in a sultry tone.

At the first lift and rub of her belly, his eyes widened, darkened. Watching him react to her loving was almost as enjoyable as loving him. "Are you all right?" she asked him, anxious in spite of her show of assurance.

"Never—" He groaned softly and closed his eyes, missing the flash of concern in hers. Then he opened them and read her face correctly "—better." He smiled at her concern, teasing her. "Well worth the wait."

For reminding her of the nights she'd fled from his arms and left him unsatisfied, she punished him with a delicate circling of her hips. It was a punishment he was perfectly willing to endure for as long as she felt the need to chasten him. She was a formidable foe, and he might just die of pleasure before this battle was over. He smiled, wondering how soon he would be able to concentrate enough to capture one of those silky breasts swaying above him and get a little of his own back.

The balance of power was hers now. He'd given it to her deliberately, but he hadn't expected her to ply it so mercilessly, so ruthlessly. Throughout an endless, blinding span of time, there seemed to be no end to the pleasure her smooth feminine body could mete out. The brush of her breasts, the touch of her hands, the warmth of her mouth gliding over his jaw, the flick of her tongue against the pulse in his throat, his earlobe, his nipple, made his body tighten with intense pleasure. And there was ever and always the warm clenching of her body around his, sending the ebb and flow of a sensual delight washing through him in ever higher tides. She was woman supreme, as secure in her power over him as he had been in his over her.

"Brazen, power-hungry, awesome and wanton," he murmured, his hands finding her breasts, gently supporting them as they swayed above him. "You're sending me into the stratosphere, woman. Without a parachute."

"Good," she whispered. "We'll fall together." She undulated, pleasuring him.

Shelly..." He gripped her arms warningly, but she went on plying her erotic torture until he was driven half mad with the need for release. As much as he wanted to go on receiving her pleasure, he couldn't stop himself from retrieving the power he'd given her. He rolled her onto her back, going with her, driving deeply into her until her cries of shuddering satisfaction told him he could at last release his own tight control and let the exploding ecstasy flower within him.

He lay bound to her in the sweet aftermath of ultimate relaxation. Every nerve and muscle seemed branded with the imprint of her soft yielding body under his. He moved to release her, but she caught him. "No, don't leave me. Not yet."

Her words, the touch of her hand on his head seduced him. "I'm too heavy—"

"No." With a determined grip, she pulled him down on top of her. He collapsed into her softness, her sweetness, thinking he just might die if he didn't give her what she wanted, for he needed to stay caught in the echoing sweetness of her, snuggled into her body, the body that had the power to make him feel as if a thousand incandescent lamps burned inside him.

"Well...worth...waiting for," he murmured, pressing his mouth into her warm neck that was flushed with sexual arousal. He raised his head to look at her, his woman, his lover. Her hair flowed around her head, a red glow in the soft light, alive with golden highlights. Her blue eyes shone darkly, the pupils black with the aftermath of passion. He was filled with a tenderness that nearly consumed him. This self-contained, wonderful woman had made love to him with abandoned enjoyment that was unmarred by self-consciousness. Now she was his. Needing to reaffirm his ownership, he licked her lips in a playful gesture.

She wrinkled her nose. Delighted that he'd annoyed her, he tongued her cheek, her chin. She wriggled, making a small sensual tremor course through him.

"Interesting," he murmured and tried another experimental lick on her ear.

"Justin," she protested, but she was smiling. She wriggled again, bringing him more pleasure. He caught her face in his hands and forced her to look at him. He read the truth in her eyes—that she knew full well what she was doing.

"You need severe disciplining," he said with exaggerated severity, his hands holding her head imprisoned, his eyes gleaming with mock warning.

She reached up and enclosed his face between her palms, holding him just as he held her. "What will you do to me that you haven't already done?"

His eyes gleamed as if he were the devil's own. He cast an affected, lascivious glance over her bare shoulders, her vulnerable throat. "I might have another trick or two up my sleeve."

She slid her hands down his bare arms. "You haven't got a sleeve." With his hands occupied holding her face, she had free access to his torso. She let her fingertips glide teasingly along his ribs down to his rounded hip bones and over his buttocks.

"You haven't got a scruple."

"Nope," she said cheerfully. "Not a one. They're much too heavy to carry around."

She patted his taut cheeks playfully, then circled their roundness lazily, letting her hands drift. Her exploring fingers brought his body to life.

"Red, you're playing with fire." His thumbs circled her ears as lazily as her palms circled his buttocks.

Her eyes lifted to his, caught and held them. "Relax," she said with cool deliberateness, her eyes slanted and as mischievous as a cat's. "You're in good hands."

"Do you remember everything I say?"

That quickly, the teasing vanished from her eyes. "Yes."

The surrender in that steady gaze seduced him more powerfully than any playful seduction. She acknowledged his influence on her, both mentally and physically. He felt impelled to do the same but the words stuck in his throat. What could he tell her? That she was his mate, his match, his equal and that he never wanted to let her go? Surely she must know that. He'd made love to her with all the expertise and control at his command. After it was over, and he felt sated and satiated with her, one little movement of her body against his and he was ready to love her again.

She waited, breath held, hoping he would admit her power over him as easily as she had his over her. His green eyes never wavered, but he said nothing. She smiled, more with bravado than amusement. "But then you were my teacher. It was my job to remember what you said."

Relief surged through him, along with admiration and affection. She wasn't going to put him to the test. She accepted him as he was. He was overwhelmed by his love for her. His body responded, burgeoning to life.

Justin's evident pleasure at being rescued gave her a twinge of pain. Yet even while she struggled to hide her disappointment, she felt her desire rising to meet his. If he wasn't ready yet to admit that their intimacy was more than physical, she would wait. A deeply primitive feminine wisdom told her that Justin cared for her more than he was willing to say.

With a groan he lowered his head and kissed her, claiming her mouth, claiming her body, enjoying the pleasure of taking his time, knowing that he no longer needed to fight the resurgence of desire. She had issued the invitation and he was more than happy to oblige her.

His mouth locked on hers and playfulness gave way to a newer, more intense passion. She claimed him again, taking him in, inciting him to new heights of hunger before she gave him succor.

JUSTIN CAME AWAKE to daylight and the sight of a bare, lovely back turned to him. He gazed at the long, slim loveliness unmarred by a blemish. Unlike many redheads, Shelly wasn't freckled. Her skin had the pure creamy look of satin.

He wanted to let her sleep, he intended to let her sleep. But he found himself wanting to touch her more. He reached out and traced a Cuban eight on her bare flesh.

Shelly murmured a protest and rolled over, bringing the sheet with her. He realized too late that he'd outsmarted himself. Asleep, she'd presented him the view of her lovely back. Half-awake, she'd covered herself. He tried tracing a hammerhead dive on her abdomen heading straight down . . .

She came awake with a soft cry and propped herself up on one elbow, all tousled, indignant woman. "What do you think you're doing?"

"Practicing maneuvers. That was a hammerhead dive headed for—"

"I know where it was headed for."

"—ground zero." His smile was nearly irresistible, but she made a Herculean attempt to resist. She sank back down on the bed, partially annoyed, partially aroused. "You're taking unfair advantage, Justin."

Instantly contrite, he tugged at the sheet and kissed the top of her breast. "I'm sorry." It was done with such reverence that she couldn't tell whether the apology was sincere or not. She raised her hand to touch his golden head, not quite sure she wasn't dreaming. "What are you sorry for?"

"Taking unfair advantage. Waking you up when I should have let you sleep and generally acting like the spoiled brat you said I was."

Her eyes darkened. "Do you remember everything I say?" She echoed his words, wondering if he would acknowledge her effect on him.

"Yes," he said simply and she knew it was the partial admission of love she wanted.

"You . . . wouldn't happen to have a spare toothbrush, would you?"

He leaned over her, his hands flat on each side of her, pinning her under the sheet, his grin wolfish. "You planned to stay the night, didn't you bring yours?"

"I planned to stay the night, but I didn't know what you planned. For all I knew, Denise was here. Do you have a spare toothbrush?" she repeated more insistently.

"Yes," he said, watching her.

Her eyes flickered away from his. "Kept on hand for occasions like these."

"Kept on hand for occasions when I travel." Coolly, he leaned over and kissed her, an unromantic smack on the cheek.

"You're certainly in a good mood this morning. I can't ruffle your feathers no matter what I do."

"I can't remember you trying to ruffle my feathers. But if you're so inclined, feel free—"

She hit him and none too gently. "Do you have a robe I can wear?"

"If I did, do you think I'd admit it after that crack about the toothbrush?"

"I meant a robe of yours I could wear."

"Oh, a robe of mine." The devilish look came back full-blown. "What do you need a robe for?"

At her chastising look, he crawled out of the other side of the bed and stood up. "All right, all right." Gloriously naked and unself-conscious, he strolled to the closet and came back with a striped terry robe that would go around her three times.

"Will this do?"

"I certainly hope so."

One eyebrow slightly raised, he held it open in front of him . . . and waited.

She lay where she was, not moving.

"I have seen everything there is to see," he drawled.

"Not upright and drooping, you haven't."

He laughed, his shoulders twitching. "You don't 'droop,' love."

"I might be this morning, just when I don't want to."

He dropped down on the bed, his eyes dancing with laughter, his hands draping the robe over her sheeted body and pinning her to the bed. "You've already told me you aren't perfect. Broken nails, cavities—which I presume is why you're so concerned about a toothbrush—and PMS, if I remember correctly."

"You remember too darn correctly, Counselor."

He sobered and his eyes darkened. "I remember what it was like to make love to you." He lowered his head to kiss her.

She twisted her head away. "Don't."

He pulled back, frowning. "Is this the morning-after syndrome?"

He was genuinely annoyed. She sighed, thinking she owed him the truth. "I still haven't brushed my teeth."

He stared at her for a moment as if she were a puzzle he didn't understand. Then the annoyance fled, the devilish light came back in his eyes and he smiled. She stared at him, fascinated, thinking temptation had never been packaged so . . . temptingly.

Slowly he lowered his head. She wriggled, a halfhearted effort, but he tautened the robe across her breasts, pinning her more tightly in place. With deliberate intent, he fit his mouth over hers, nudging her lips open with his tongue, taking her.

She didn't want him to know her this well, be this close. She wanted space. He gave her none. He took what he wanted to take, exploring, teasing. She writhed under him, trying to loosen his hold on her. She didn't want to feel the rise of passion again, not like this, not before she was ready. He came too close, took too much.

He raised his head, his eyes dark with the beginnings of arousal, his mouth sensual. But one sweep of those green eyes over her face and his expression changed.

"You're angry with me."

"I made a simple request. I expected you to honor it."

He wasn't angry. He looked more astounded than angry. He withdrew his hands, his expression sober. "I'm beginning to see which one of us is really hung up on perfection." He stood up, his eyes on her face. "You use this bathroom," he gestured toward a door, "I'll take the one down the hall." Tall, magnificent, proud as sin and naked as a baby, he turned his back to her and walked out of the bedroom.

CHAPTER NINE

THE MICROWAVE WAS BEEPING when Shelly walked into Justin's kitchen. "I'm not a cook," he said. Yet the coffee was burbling in the automatic drip machine, and he was adroitly shifting the bacon onto a paper towel-draped plate and then returning to the stove to stir a panful of eggs that were turning golden.

"This is pure luxury," she said lightly. The atmosphere in the kitchen was cool and Justin didn't respond. He was dressed in a pullover shirt and the jeans she'd helped him buy. She'd gotten her clothes on, but it seemed as if she could have worn a harem dress with seven veils and he wouldn't have noticed. He was watching the eggs as if his life depended on it, keeping his total attention on his work as he dished them up, sliced the toast diagonally with a neat, deft hand and poured the coffee into two cups.

When everything was on the table, he said, "Sit," with his old arrogance, indicating the chair behind the round table, while he turned a chair and threw a leg over it, still not looking at her. "Do you want catsup with your eggs?"

"No, thank you."

"Well, go ahead, sully your clean teeth with some breakfast." He raised his head and met her eyes finally, his tone half-teasing, half-defensive.

The look on his face made her lose her appetite. "Justin, listen—"

"No, you listen." He put his fork down on the plate with a decisive little click. "I thought we settled something last night. I thought it was going to be you and me, babe, just like the song. But I can see I was mistaken."

She gazed at him, feeling as if her world were crumbling. "You're different than I thought you'd be."

Now she had his attention. "How did you think I'd be?"

"I thought you'd be more casual, not so...all-consuming."

"All-consuming?" He raised a golden eyebrow. "What do you mean by that?"

"I didn't know you'd want to get so...close."

"Close?" His mouth twisted. "We've been to bed together, but we aren't close. And that's exactly the way you want it, isn't it?"

She stiffened, her fork pausing on the way to her mouth. Slowly she lowered the uneaten food to her plate. "Is this a cross-examination?"

"No. It's an attempt to get at the truth. I was wrong about your reason for pushing me away. You're not hung up on perfection. You're hung up on privacy. Come close, but not too close."

She felt cornered, ground down by his persistent logic. He'd had far too much practice at playing the hostile question-and-answer game and she'd had none. "Has it ever occurred to you that you spend too much time analyzing your witnesses' motives?"

"Well, I'll tell you one thing, lady, with your hidden motivations you'd keep me busy for a long time."

Shelly dropped her fork on her plate and jumped to her feet. He was quicker than she and caught her before she'd gone two steps.

He muttered an oath and dragged her to him, relaxing fractionally when he felt her instant acceptance of his warmth and strength. "Dammit, Shelly, I don't like feeling like this. Feeling as if I need you, to breathe. It makes me . . . resent you. I want to know how you feel. I want to know I'm not in this alone."

"I don't like feeling the way I do, either," she said. "Right now, I don't like you much."

"Don't hate me, please." He stared down at her, his eyes all green fire and dark intensity, the bones of his face standing out against his skin. Almost to himself, he murmured, "I've never cared a damn what anybody thought of me . . . until now."

The soft sweet scent of her hair filled his nose. He relaxed his hold on her, leaning away from her to look into her face. "It's a sobering thing for a man who's supposed to be good at everything to find out he's damn poor at falling in love."

She was still for a long moment. It was a risk, he knew that, but he had to take it. She leaned into him, but her body was tense and he found himself tensing, too, waiting.

"Is that . . . true?" she said, her glistening eyes roving over his face. Shelly couldn't believe she'd heard the words. They were words she'd wanted to hear for a long time. Perhaps forever.

He stroked her hair. "Would I lie to you about how I feel? You must see what you do to me. I've been out of control since the first moment I separated your hair from Kim's veil at the wedding." He plucked at a curl, lifting it, then letting it fall from his fingers and watching the red-gold fan it made as it settled back into place. "You care for me, I know you do. You wouldn't have come to me last night if you didn't."

"I guess...I'm not any better at falling in love than you are. I haven't had much practice at it."

It was an admission made in a soft hesitant voice and it wasn't nearly as much as he wanted, but it would have to suffice.

"I'm more than willing to help you make up for lost time." His hands roved, coming up under her T-shirt in a way that was now achingly familiar to her. His palms were warm on her cool skin, his fingers gliding neatly under her bra strap so that he was nearly spanning her back with his long fingers.

"That wasn't what I meant...Justin. You're taking unfair advantage—"

"And will go on doing so, every chance I get. Especially when you melt in my arms the way you are now."

He brought her closer, fitting her into his body. "This isn't close enough. You're so beautiful and...elusive. I want all of you. Now."

It was an arrogant statement rather than a question, and she had every right to say no. She could and must say no. But his hands were plying their magic on her back, and the sweet ache was rising in her and her will to resist was gone. "Our breakfast will get cold."

His smile was pure fallen angel. He'd won, and he knew it. "Why do you think they invented microwave ovens?"

In the bedroom, as he began to help her undress, he watched her carefully for any sign of hesitancy. The shades were up, it was close to noon, and the light was unrelenting. It was another challenge to be met, and she answered it the way she did most of the challenges Justin handed her, with her chin up and her spine straight.

But when their clothes were scattered around them and he carried her down on the bed, Shelly learned that Justin brought a new dimension of intimacy to daylight loving. He carried out a sweet exploration of her face, throat, breasts, hips, and thighs, each lift and dip of satin skin exclaimed over and admired. It was almost as if he were deliberately taking the deep intimacy she had tried to deny him.

She retaliated in kind, running her hands over the curls of crisp antique gold hair coiled over the bronzed skin of his chest and thighs, exploring the paler girdle at his hips where the sun hadn't reached. And when his eyes locked with hers and he brought their bodies together in the final joining, the daylight enabled her to see the way his pupils darkened and expanded when he entered her and the way, when they lay locked fully together, his mouth relaxed into a sensuous smile that promised—and delivered—ecstasy.

JUSTIN REWARMED THE EGGS in the microwave and this time when they sat down to eat, they talked of inconsequential things, but the warmth and heat of their loving was still there, lingering between them.

It was long past time for Shelly to return home. Sunday was a working day on Eagle Hill and if she didn't get there soon, there would be no revenue from tourists who wanted to take a quick glide ride.

"I have to go. Dad can't take the tourists up."

Justin's eyes flashed at her in that way she was beginning to recognize, a combination of the memory of loving that had been, and anticipation of loving that was to come. Then the look disappeared. With a stoic and impassive face, Justin strolled around the table to pull out her chair for her. But when she stood and pivoted to walk away from him, he caught her and turned her into his arms, his impassivity falling away like a cloak. "Don't you ever take a day off?" A smile played over his lips, as if he'd already decided she was going to stay.

"I have to take two days off the weekend of the air show."

He held her by the arms, his smile changing subtly into irritation. "I almost forgot about it." Then, as if the thought just struck him, "Are we still flying together?"

"If that's what your father wants."

He grinned. "Oh, it's what he wants, all right, you and me flying together."

She shook her head, her mouth lifting in a helpless smile. "He's as bad as you are."

"We come by it naturally. It's in our genes—"

"Never mind." She raised her face to him. "I'm glad your father is so...broad-minded. But when we're out at the air field in front of my father, I'd appreciate it if you'd be a little more...discreet."

"You mean I shouldn't grab you and kiss you like this?" His mouth came down, not hard, but insistently. His tongue pried apart her lips, equally determined. She tried to resist him, but the residual heat smoldering in her from his long and languorous loving rose in full measure, and when the kiss ended, it was because he lifted his head, not because she wanted him to stop.

"That might do for starters," she said breathlessly.

"What else shouldn't I do?"

"You shouldn't look at me as if we've been to bed together."

"So sorry." Getting into the spirit of the thing, he stepped back and clicked his heels together, which didn't come off too well since he wasn't wearing shoes. "Your wish is my command, my lady."

SHELLY STOOD IN THE pilots' dining tent at the air show around noon the next Saturday and wished Justin wasn't granting her wish quite so zealously. She'd wanted him to be discreet not because she cared what people thought, but because, in some obscure way, if she stood alone at the air show, it helped her to preserve the illusion of her individuality. She still had the dread of being absorbed by Justin, of losing herself in him, for he, like no other man she'd ever met, had the power to take over her thoughts and feelings until there was nothing left of her own will. She wouldn't—couldn't—let a man become so important to her that she would be destroyed by losing him.

Shelly had to give him credit. Justin had given her nothing more than a brief nod when he strolled into the tent. Now he stood two tables away from her, one foot propped up on the bench, his attention on the World War II pilot recounting a story, his mouth lifted in a smile, his golden hair tousled.

Quite irrationally she wanted him to come over and put his arm around her, wanted him to acknowledge the closeness they'd shared. He was destroying her peace of mind, and she couldn't tell from his face or his stance if he was doing it deliberately, or if he was genuinely trying to comply with her instructions. While he had admitted he was teetering on the brink of caring for her, he didn't seem to be falling very far very fast, if the way he looked at her a moment ago was any indication.

She was a mass of contradictions. She wanted him close, she didn't want him close. She wanted him . . . She wanted him. It always came back to that.

Shelly had made the rules and Justin was playing by them, but he didn't like it much. She wasn't a fragile woman, but she looked fragile with her pale skin and her mane of red hair, and he wanted to gather her up and take her out of the heat and the dust, wanted to smooth her hair down with his hand, wanted to love her.

He'd come into the tent a moment ago to stand next to Strom, his eyes on Mel's face. He hadn't been sure what Mel's reaction to him would be. Mel knew his daughter had gone to Justin; Shelly'd left a note telling him that. And Mel was man enough to know they hadn't spent the night playing tiddledywinks.

Mel had said hello and nothing more. He was his usual contained, quiet self, as cordial and friendly as ever. Things appeared to be normal. Justin breathed a sigh of relief. Mel had always seemed fond of him, first as a boy, then as a man. If it were not for a genuine wish to keep the status quo, he would have tossed Shelly's request to the four winds, gone to her, and put his arm possessively over her shoulder.

Touching her. He wanted to touch her, was having the devil's own time not to go to where she was standing and just...touch her. Needing to feel her under his hands had gotten to be a habit with him. A habit he thoroughly enjoyed.

How long could he stand here pretending he was listening to Kleindist refight the war? His patience was stretched thin, his peace of mind gone.

Air shows were not conducive to maintaining peace of mind. There was chaos everywhere he looked. A gaggle of Piper Cubs bristled to the east of the flight line—the personal planes of the pilots who'd flown in for the show. Cars streamed down the one narrow road that led to the air field. The people in the money tents were yelling. The announcer was pleading with people not to ask that husbands and wives be paged over the public loudspeaker.

Two tables away Shelly, too, was taking in the sights and sounds of the air show. The smell of frying hamburger and onions, the smell she always associated with air shows, wafted to her nose. Her stomach clenched, but not from the smell of food. In another hour, she'd be taking off from that grassy runway and flying aerobatic patterns with the man she loved.

She'd come here for refuge and a chance to catch her breath before her part in the program. The pilots' dining tent was the place where, ostensibly, those who were flying in the show could rest and relax. The privacy was a mirage; the crowd surged around the outside of the tent on the other side of the snow fence. She was surrounded by twenty thousand people, but she felt very alone.

A woman and a man wearing jeans and matching peach-colored sweatshirts passed through security and came into the tent. In a swirl of long dark hair, like a pint-sized ship in the wind, the woman headed for Justin, dragging the man along by the hand she had locked to his.

"Hi," Denise said, and smiled.

It took Justin a minute to recognize her. The last time he'd seen Ms Beatty, she had been showing more of her luscious body and less of her teeth.

"Hi, yourself," Justin said, smiling back.

"We saw your name on the program and I threw my weight around to get in here. I wanted to introduce you to Grant."

Justin stuck out his hand. "Wilding. Pleased to meet you." He was used to measuring up men quickly, and he liked the clear-eyed straightforward look he got from the younger man.

"I owe you a debt of thanks."

"No problem."

Denise ignored the men and twisted her head, craning around Justin to scan the crowd.

"You've only been here five seconds and already my charm has worn off," Justin drawled.

"Short attention span," Wilding said, his eyes indulgent as they roved over Denise's indignant face.

"Obviously." Justin was in the mood to tease her. She'd gone to great pains to arrange the meeting she'd wanted to avoid a week ago. And Justin had a hunch he knew why. Denise, curious and enthusiastic creature that she was, wanted to meet Shelly.

Denise popped two knuckles lightly against his sleeve. "Don't be difficult. I was looking for your lady."

He raised an eyebrow in feigned surprise. "I never would have guessed. What makes you think she's here?"

"Well, I saw on the program that you were doing stunts with a woman flyer and I figured if she had enough nerve to take you on in the air, she might have enough nerve to take you on in b—" Denise stopped speaking and her cheeks colored "—a relationship."

"She's the one you really came to see."

Denise looked as guileless as a child and totally undisturbed at being caught out. "All right, so I was curious. Isn't she here?"

"She's right over there."

Denise craned her neck past Justin's shoulder. "The one with red hair?" Denise asked. Justin nodded. A moment later, Denise turned eyes large with surprise up to Justin. "I might have known. She's gorgeous. But why is she standing over there by herself?"

"It's a little game we're playing. She's pretending not to notice me and I'm pretending not to notice her."

"Well, you're both playing it badly. I think I'll get her over here for you."

"How are you going to do that?"

Denise raised her hand. "I can do it—without so much as lifting my little finger. All I have to do is smile at you." And she did.

"She won't fall for that old trick," Justin said dryly.

"Wait and see," Denise countered, her smile brightening, focusing on him.

Individuality was a fine thing to maintain, and Shelly meant to maintain it. She wasn't going to go rushing over to Justin just because the woman whose life he'd saved was standing next to him, laughing up into his face. After all, there was another man with her.

Who was probably her brother. Or a bodyguard.

Shelly gritted her teeth. Any woman with brains and principles wouldn't worry about another woman talking to her man. Shelly was a woman with brains and principles. She also had a body that moved without being told to do so. Her feet were moving, taking her to Justin's side. Her hand was moving, gliding possessively into the circle of Justin's arm as he stood with his hand stuck in his pocket.

She felt him tense in surprise, but when he turned to her, his eyes danced with laughter. What had she done that was so funny? Just because she hadn't followed her own instructions he didn't need to stand there looking so happy.

"Ah, there you are," he said lightly. He introduced her to Denise, whose eyes were as amused as Justin's. Evidently they'd just been sharing a joke. The man behind Denise was smiling faintly. It must have been a good joke.

Shelly found she rather liked Denise. The young woman was friendly, outgoing, unperturbed by her experience of the other evening. Actually she was glowing. Shelly didn't have to watch her very long before she understood that the man standing quietly beside her, listening to Denise bubble with enthusiasm was the source of her secure happiness.

Justin had, somewhere in the course of the conversation moved his hand and hers so that they were entwined together in the pocket of his flight jacket. She felt warmed by his touch, as secure as Denise.

Instantly, and as unobtrusively as she could, she retrieved her hand from Justin's. His frown told her he didn't like it. She felt a pang of guilt, but told herself she had nothing to feel guilty about. She'd warned him about her need for space.

"Excuse me. I have to go make a last-minute check on the plane."

Denise smiled, her face bland, her eyes full of mischief. "I look forward to seeing you and Justin...perform."

MEL AND STROM stood with their heads tipped, watching as their offspring created a ballet of graceful loops and circles in the sky. The sun glinting off the blue wings of the two planes invoked a silence that was universal and ageless. Aerobatics was an old sport begun in World War I by ace pilots as the best way of staying alive, but even after years of aerobatic demonstrations, two planes doing loops side by side in the sky still imbued people with silent, awestruck wonder.

Mel felt a little awestruck himself. It was a source of pride to him that Shelly could hold her own with a man of Justin's ability and experience. Perhaps it was a foolish pride, but there was an element of fantasy in it for him, too. Shelly was doing what he, Mel, hadn't been able to do. Strom had always had the edge on him. Corbett was the better pilot, with a quicker response and a keener eye. Most of all, he had the gift, that ability to combine the right-brain intuitive intelligence with left-side logic. A good pilot is an artist, processing information either intellectually or intuitively, whichever the occasion demands. That ability to pilot with both the "flying by the seat of your pants" intelligence and the thinking side of your brain was something a man either had or he didn't. Strom had it. He could assess a situation and make a lightning decision about it, a quick, correct decision. That ability made him an excellent pilot and an even better politician. Corbett didn't make mistakes. Except that once...

Strom was entitled to one mistake in a lifetime. Mel had made two.

"She's good, Mel. You must be very proud of her."

"I am."

Strom grimaced. "The years do funny things. I never thought the day would come when I'd be standing on the ground watching my son fly." Strom stared up at the planes. "They say they're working on engines that will respond to voice commands and instruments that can be activated by the glance of an eye. Did it ever occur to you that a man doesn't get old, he gets obsolete?"

"It's occurred to me," Mel answered, his tone dry. "I guess I'm not quite ready to get tossed up on the heap just yet. I hope to be back in the saddle soon."

"Feeling better, are you?"

"Feeling fine. Have to feel fine. Shelly needs me."

"Well, it makes me feel fine to see our two kids up there together again." Strom squinted into the sun, then shaded his eyes and looked at the man beside him. "Ever worry about her up there?"

"She's safer with Justin chasing her up there than she is on the ground." He spoke slowly, deliberately.

Strom scowled and looked unhappy, defensive. "About your daughter and my son—I know I said a lot of things, but I didn't have a thing to do with their getting together, I swear I didn't."

Mel stared up into the sky. "I reckon that's something they arranged all by themselves."

"I've warned my son not to hurt your girl." Strom dipped his head then tilted it to watch the darting, humming planes. "I'd be obliged if you'd do the same."

That brought Mel's attention to Strom. "What are you talking about?"

Strom shook his head. "In all the years I've known you, I've never heard you tell that girl no. You've encouraged her to think the world was her oyster."

"It is," Mel said in a low tone, his eyes going back to the sky.

"And you tried to give it to her piece by piece to make up for her mother's death. Mel, it was a fluke that your first wife died in childbirth and your second wife of an aneurysm three months after Shelly was born, just a crazy fluke. It had nothing to do with you. You don't have anything to make up to Shelly, not after what you've done for her..."

"Thanks to you."

"All right, so I loaned you a little money and you were able to buy the school and settle down. But believe me, right now I feel as if I've been paid back a hundredfold. It's thanks to your Shelly that my boy is finally interested enough in a woman to have her stay the night in his own home. That means a lot to me. Promise me you won't do anything to discourage them."

Mel's mouth quirked. "I doubt very much if anything I say or do will change their minds one way or another."

"Shelly cares about your opinion . . . and so do I."

"I like Justin. He has all your good qualities—"

"And none of the bad? He is a fine young man. He's all I had hoped he could be. Except that he's past thirty and still single."

"I think you'd better let him decide when and how to change that."

"But with just a little encouragement—"

"No." Mel frowned, adamant. "They have to work this out for themselves."

THERE WERE NO SURPRISES in the routine for Justin now. He knew where Shelly was going, and in some odd way, the knowing elated him. It was as if they were making love up there in the sky, in a way that was supremely unselfish. She seemed intent on making him look good and keeping him safe, while he watched her like a hawk.

Suddenly, when he hovered at the top of the turnover for the hammerhead dive, he knew the taste of fear. If she made one little misstep, applied her left rudder too soon . . . Then there was no time for him to worry about Shelly for his own machine was plunging toward earth. He pulled up at the fifteen hundred limit and did an eye check for Shelly. His heart plunked back into its proper place when he saw her flying beside him.

He was never going to fly with her again like this. Just now, he'd endangered his own life and possibly hers, worrying about her in that split second of time when he needed all his concentration on his own flying.

The simulated battle and chase was not as much fun as it had been the day they'd practiced. He felt an edginess in his nerves that he didn't want to feel. It was as if he wanted to control the other plane, wanted to *make sure* she was safe. There was no way he could do that. He had to fly his part of the routine, and let her fly hers.

As always she did it extremely well, eluding him just as she had before. But when at last the routine was over and they had landed, Justin sat in the cockpit and knew a strong, unremitting sense of relief. This was another side of his love for Shelly, a side he hadn't counted on. He didn't want to feel this way, torn apart by the need to protect her, to make sure there was no chance of harm coming to her.

He was no longer able to fly as an individual. He had been split in two—and the best part of him was in that other plane.

Justin said a succinct word, shed his parachute and his flight suit and tossed them carelessly back into the plane. He'd have a talk with that woman and he'd have it now, while he was still possessed of a few shreds of reasonable thought. He'd tell her...

Like him, she'd shed her chute and suit and was walking across the grass toward him in her light jacket and her jeans. Her smile would have provided the kilowatt power for Chicago. Exuberant, she launched herself at him and threw her arms around his neck. He stood stunned by the sudden onslaught of slim woman filling his arms so unexpectedly.

"Strom should be getting this hug instead of you, but I just had to give it to somebody. Thank you for letting me fly that beautiful plane."

All his good intentions drifted away. He'd worry until doomsday if that was what it took to recreate the Shelly he'd once known, the enthusiastic Shelly who loved flying so much that she forgot her need for space and independence and threw her arms around him while the whole world watched. And she did have her arms around him.

Justin was not a man to pass up a God-given opportunity. He grasped her around the hips, lifted her off the ground and twirled her around like a gyrating star.

She was breathless when he set her down. "What was that for?" she asked, her eyes sparkling with blue diamond lights.

"That was 'You're welcome.'"

Shelly's euphoria vanished. As she stood there in his arms, she felt the pressure of his hard body, saw the gleam of the sun in his green eyes, the golden cast of his skin in the hollow of his throat. Her man. Ready, Willing. Wanting.

Suddenly she too was ready, willing, wanting. "Please...let go of me," she murmured. He did, but the nerve in the side of his cheek pulsed from the effort it took to comply with her request.

There was an after-flight supper, and Shelly stayed for it as she and Mel had planned to do, but the talk drifted around her like a lazy summer breeze, touching her but not disturbing her. Her thoughts, her eyes, her nerves seemed attuned to one man, the man who sat three places and the other side of the table away from her. Suppose he walked away from her because that's what he thought she wanted? She didn't want him to walk away. She wanted to ride home with him in the soft darkness of his car, walk with him into the clean scented darkness of his house, sink with him into the soft, pillowed darkness of his bed.

Justin wouldn't push her, she knew that. It would be up to her to tell him what she wanted.

CHAPTER TEN

WHY DID GOING to Justin seem so hard? Why, when the meal ended, did it seem so impossibly difficult for Shelly to slip her arm through his and murmur the right words? She'd gone to him before. But it had been in the dark of the night, a private journey into her own heart. This time they were in the company of their fathers' old cronies, the men and women who'd known each other for forty years.

Not that anyone was paying attention to her. There was afterglow in the tent, a nostalgic euphoria of living again those days when common men had been heros, when the roar of bombers returning had made them rush out to scan the skies and count, praying that their comrades had returned safely.

Old stories abounded. The wives, scattered among their men, looked patient and proud. Many of them had taken up flying and were now excellent pilots themselves.

In the end it was one of the wives who provided both the entertainment and the excuse to end the evening.

"I'm getting cold," she told her husband, Luke Clark, a gray-haired man who'd been a bombardier. The woman, Betty, linked her arm through his. "I'd like to go home."

"All right, babe, if you want to go, let's go. I've got the perfect cure for your ills," Luke told her, his leer mockingly playful.

"That's your cure for everything." Betty was playing to the crowd now. "No matter what I have, a backache, headache, sore muscles, he has the answer."

One of the other wives, a woman named Alice, chimed in. "Betty, you know women are romantics, and men are just sex fiends."

There was a roar of laughter at this. Betty turned to look at Alice's husband. "Ed, I thought you were such a nice, quiet mannerly guy, an officer and a gentleman. There must be depths to you we haven't seen."

Ed colored all the way down to the V of his shirt but he made a brave attempt at rebuttal. "I don't know what she's talking about. I've never seen this woman before in my life."

"I'm the mother of your children, that's who I am," said his wife tartly.

Bravely Ed studied her. "I   thought   you looked . . . vaguely familiar."

Another roar of laughter went up.

"You bombardiers are all alike," said Luke Clark. "Silent . . . but deep. Very deep."

There was more laughter, then people began to climb out from the bench seats and put their coats on in preparation for leaving. Under the cover of the general confusion, Shelly strolled over to Justin. He was standing next to his father, his head bent, listening to whatever Strom was saying into his ear.

Strom's eyes fell on Shelly. He stopped speaking. "I didn't mean to interrupt," she said.

"You aren't interrupting. Did you have something to say to my son?" Strom was effusive. He was also watching her closely. So was Mel. If her courage failed her, it would be now.

Justin watched her through lazy, half-closed eyes. With both their fathers watching, his lady was definitely under the gun. Everyone knew what was on everyone else's mind, but no one said a word. Did she want him enough to run the gamut? He hoped to hell she did.

If he was a gentleman, he'd think of a way to come to her rescue. But if he did, he'd never know for sure how deep her commitment to him was. It was a test, just like the one they'd taken in the sky today. Shelly had passed that one alone. With a twist of nerves, Justin knew he had to let her fly solo once again.

Shelly tilted her head up and straightened her spine. The look on Justin's face wasn't encouraging at all. He was expressionless. A month ago, a week ago, she might have been fooled. But the intimacies she'd shared with Justin had taught her much. The blander he looked, the more vulnerable he was. He was on edge, needing her. Her heart filling with gratitude, she slid her arm through Justin's, her hand sliding down his wrist to touch his hand. Instantly he clasped her fingers in acceptance.

She'd passed her test with flying colors, Justin thought, her courage providing the thermal lift that sent his spirits soaring. He was glad that the long evening was almost over. He'd sat and wondered what she would do, if she would coolly tell him good-bye and walk away or if she would let him know that she wanted to spend the night with him. Now that he realized she was as anxious as he for the amenities to end so they could escape the crowd and drive to his condo together, his blood quickened in his veins. It would be a long drive. He ached to have her to himself, warm and naked in his bed. First he'd tease her about coming to claim him while Denise stood beside him. Then he'd tell her what a wonderful lover she was and he'd enumerate all the things he meant to do to her—and all the things he meant her to do to him.

Shelly felt warmed by his spontaneous reassurance, warmed still more by the flash of heat in his eyes as they moved over her face. It was all there for her to see, the dark need, the tenderness, the caring. And the promise. He promised her things with his eyes no man would—or should—say to a woman in public. She stood receiving those promises, her pulse racing, knowing that even though she had reclaimed her independence for a little while in the secret sky, she stood beside him desperately wanting every dark promise in his eyes to come true, not caring that she was in danger of losing her independence forever.

The tent flap lifted and a man and woman entered. "Hey, did I hear something about bombardiers? Was our glorious name being taken in vain?"

"Johnson, you old son of a gun," said Clark. "You haven't been here in years. When did you get here? Why didn't you fly in sooner?"

"Couldn't. Had a company bash at which my presence was requested. Hey, where's my lifesaver? I came especially to see that character."

In the lamplight, it seemed to Shelly that Strom had paled. Mel, too, shifted on his feet, as if disconcerted.

Justin studied his father, feeling the flick of fear. Strom looked ... besieged. Was his father ill? He wasn't reaching for medication. It was something different, something emotional rather than physical. Only a bad shock could make the congressman forget himself enough to let his emotions show on his face. But what was it that had upset his father?

Justin considered the possibilities. Strom had been calm enough when Shelly approached them. The change had come after Johnson's entrance into the tent. Jim Johnson, One-Way J.J. as the men called him, was the bombardier whose life Strom had saved with his courageous flight back to home base in a riddled B-17. J.J. had the youthful look of a man who'd kept himself in shape through the years. He was lean and wiry, but as he made his way through the crowd to Strom, he walked with a slight limp, a wound he'd sustained from the stray shrapnel that had chewed up his parachute. Strom waited for him, his face pale and strained.

Mel stepped aside, and Johnson clapped Strom on the back. "Hey, congressman. Save my life again. Reduce my taxes." He laughed at his own joke. To Justin, his father's answering smile looked strained rather than welcoming.

"Seriously, I need you to save my life and offer me shelter. Susanne and I didn't know for sure if we'd make it and didn't reserve a motel room. Now they're all full," Johnson told Strom. "These fat-cat fly birds have taken every one. Any chance you could put my wife and me up for the night? I hate to impose, but one of the guys at the gate said he thought you might have the extra room. Said one of your boys had just gotten married and flown the coop."

"Yes, I have room," Strom said a shade too heartily. "We'd be glad to have you stay with us, wouldn't we, Mel?"

"Of course," Mel murmured.

Strom turned to Justin, his eyes strangely remote. "No need for you kids to drive back into town. You can stay out on the farm, too. We'll make it a party."

Justin squeezed Shelly's hand, a silent signal of disappointment. Yet there was something in his father's face that made it impossible for him to refuse. His eyes scanned Shelly's face, wordlessly asking the question. What shall I do?

She smiled slightly and nodded, giving him his answer.

Justin turned back to Strom, knowing it was a measure of his father's disconcertedness that he hadn't seen the little byplay between his son and Shelly. "Sounds good, Dad," Justin murmured in a tone as smooth as silk.

AT CORBETT HILL Justin showed Shelly into his mother's old room, and handed her the shirt she'd worn the first night she'd stayed there. "This isn't the way I wanted to spend the evening."

Despite her own acute disappointment, Shelly had sensed Strom's uneasiness and his son's response to it. It warmed her to see Justin caring for his father so easily and so unobtrusively. She'd wronged him in so many ways. He wasn't selfish or uncaring. He simply didn't want anyone to see the depth of his feelings, perhaps because his feelings were too deep, too painfully acute to be acknowledged. Like her, he'd been brought up by his father. Unlike her, he'd never really been cuddled or loved by the man who sired him. Justin had been tossed out into the winds of life at the age of ten and coached to win, win, win. Little wonder he had barriers like concrete walls around his heart.

With his finely tuned instincts honed in courtroom battles, he sensed her empathy for him. He caught her hand, his eyes alive with a new intent.

"How tired are you?"

"Not very," she admitted, her heart racing.

"How about coming out to the patio? We could talk...or swim."

"I don't have a suit."

"You won't need one. Put my shirt on over your underwear." She shook her head, but he grinned at her. "Who's going to see you? Morley's in bed, and so is J.J.'s wife. The fly boys are battened down for the evening in the den."

"It's not the people in bed I'm worried about."

His grin was slow and full of sin. "I'm absolutely trustworthy."

"And pigs fly."

His grin brightened to a dazzling perfection. "Don't trust me?"

"As far as I can throw you."

"Scared to come out and play, Red?"

"That will be the day, when I'm scared of you."

Lazily, he leaned back against the doorjamb, considering her, his eyes dancing with a secret joke. "Last one in the pool is a sex fiend." She was still smiling when he pushed away from the door and walked down to the hall whistling tunelessly in a fashion she was beginning to know well.

JUSTIN WAS THERE in the pool ahead of her, as she'd known he would be, slicing through the water in a silent, distance-eating crawl that barely rippled the surface. The man wasn't human, he was part fish. He moved with a natural ease and precision, breathing on every fifth stroke, which meant he was halfway down the pool before he lifted his head to check for her presence. Shelly perched on the edge of a chaise longue and watched, mesmerized.

Just when she'd decided he was going for a marathon swim of thirty laps, he surfaced, swirled the water and hair out of his eyes and headed for the side of the pool.

Nerves tightened along Shelly's spine and under her navel.

Water streamed from his shoulders and arms as he hoisted himself to the patio. He sat dripping, his eyes fastened on her. "Take off that shirt, woman, unless you want to sleep wet."

He expected her to protest. Amusement and mockery lurked in his green eyes. That mocking mirth drove Shelly to stand up and slide the shirt from her arms. Her bra covered her like a swim top, but her bottom was scantily clad in the briefest of bikini underpants. Justin breathed in sharply, and in one lithe motion, got to his feet. He was nude and as unself-conscious about it as Adam.

In that instant before he reached for her, she had the feminine satisfaction of seeing the darkness of his eyes, the altered state of his body. Then he pulled her to him as easily as he'd cut through the water. She came into his arms with the same fluidity that the water glided around him.

"You were the last one here. That makes you the sex fiend," said her accuser, his hand traveling lazily down her spine with an avidity that made him guilty of his own indictment.

"You weren't listening. I'm the romantic, you're the sex fiend. By definition."

"Well, now that I know who I am..." Justin growled in a deep mock-ferocious voice and made a playful swipe at her neck with his teeth that left her pale skin untouched.

She flinched, but not from fear. A sweet explosion blossomed in her. Playing with Justin was as dangerous as being held in his arms against his cool, bare skin, making her want sweeter, more intimate games. "You're wet and cold," she told him.

"You're dry and warm. But we can fix that—"

He moved like lightning, clasping her tighter and dropping like a stone with her into the pool just as he had the day of Paul's wedding. She went under the silken water with a giant splash, her arms and legs tangling with Justin's.

Warm. The water was warmer than the air, a smooth enveloping cocoon of warmth. She came up sputtering, her hair wet and clinging, stretched out a hand and clutched the side of the pool. "Would you consider learning a new diving technique?"

"You don't like my technique?"

"I was talking about diving."

"Ah, yes, diving." He came up beside her and encircled her in his arms, tugging her away from her secure hold.

She'd never trusted anyone to keep her from drowning, but now she had the impish urge to lie back in Justin's arms and let him do all the work.

His protest was immediate. "Hey. Cut that out. You're not exactly a lightweight."

"One hundred and twenty-five pounds of blue-twisted steel."

"More like two-ton lead."

"You dragged me in here, I'm your responsibility."

He splashed his responsibility in the face. She retaliated in kind. It was a free-for-all battle, childish and playful, one faceful of water after another coming Shelly's way until at last she put up her hands and surrendered, declaring him the winner.

Clinging to the side of the pool, she pushed her hair back out of her eyes. Manlike, he stayed in the middle, showing off, hardly having to work at bobbing upright in the water. Hair slicked back, facial bones sheened with water, all the good grooming and expensive clothes pared away, he was nothing but primitive male. She could feel him reaching out to her, with his eyes, with his mind. He looked . . . vulnerable. That was why water was sexy. It made a man look both strong and vulnerable. Which was not to mention the appeal of bronze skin sheened with a wet gleam.

Justin absorbed Shelly's lovely face, beaded with moisture, alive with elation, and knew he'd never felt this way before in his life. Desire coiled inside him, knotting, making him ache. Not with wanting. With the pain of knowing that he would never be able to put his life together unless she was a part of it.

His body throbbed, urging him to reach out and take her. He wanted to strip off those two pieces of cloth and claim her in the most primitive way a man can claim a woman. It frightened him, this urge he had to possess. He was a civilized man, taught to adhere to the rules of society. Yet his father had schooled him to reach out and take what he wanted. A Corbett man had an inalienable right to grab for the prize. His hands curled at his sides. A deep instinct told him that, trust aside, Shelly would resent this male compulsion.

He had never learned how to woo. Good grades, athletic ability, women had all been his for the taking. For the first time he needed to practice subtlety. He had taken her to bed but she wasn't his. Not yet. He had to reach for control. He had to woo her. He was used to manipulating witnesses. He didn't want to manipulate Shelly. He wanted to give her choices. It was up to her to make the right ones.

"Are you cold?"

Shelly shook her head. "The water is warm. Heated, I suppose."

"Dad doesn't drain the pool until the really cold weather comes after Christmas. If we get any sun, the thermal heat helps."

She should have been grateful for his sudden switch into the prosaic. Instead, she found it confusing. She'd expected to be stripped of her token garments and made love to. Instead she was being given a weather report. That the explosion inside her hadn't died away but had merely grown more persistent wasn't helping. She ached. In her confusion, she turned to the ladder, found the bottom rung with her feet and climbed out of the water, uncaring that she was giving him a good view of her backside. Obviously it wouldn't bother him.

She sought refuge in the towel, wrapping it around her and burying her face in its cool, scented cleanness.

Justin kicked his legs and ducked his head, aiming at the side of the pool. He came up, water sluicing from his loins. All fluid muscle and easy grace, he walked to the patio table where the other towel lay, and, after thoroughly drying his head, swathed the white terry around his hips.

"Had enough?" His green eyes were hidden from her by the reflection of the pool that nearly matched.

Was there a hidden mine field in the question? Shelly didn't know. She didn't know what to think about this newly restrained Justin. "Yes," she said lightly.

"Relaxed enough so you'll sleep well?"

"Oh, absolutely," she lied.

In her room, sprawled in bed, she explored the height and depth of that lie. Her body was cooled and slightly exhausted, Justin's shirt loose and comfortable. She should have been able to fall asleep instantly. Instead she lay awake listening. And hearing nothing.

She went back over the events of the day, looking for some incident that might have angered Justin. Yet he'd seemed friendly enough at the pool. Friendly, natural, normal. Was he just letting her down easily?

No. The undercurrents had been there, she knew they had. They were just . . . deflected.

Shelly had never lied to herself and she didn't intend to start now. She wanted Justin. She'd seen physical evidence that he wanted her. Yet he hadn't made a move toward her. Why?

In a flash of insight, she had the answer. He was giving her the control. He was handing her the decision.

She didn't like having to make the decision. She'd taken the initiative once, so why was he making her take it again?

Her mouth quirked. Whatever his reason, it seemed she'd already made up her mind. But when she got inside Mr. Corbett's room, she was going to have a talk with him. If he didn't toss her out on her ear.

The hall was moonlit, the wood floor clean and cool under her bare feet. Justin's door was ajar, but the light was off. She felt her breath catch in her throat, knew the urge to turn and flee.

He was in bed, lying on his side, a sheet pulled up under his arm, his body still. He was asleep. Swallowing her disappointment, she twisted around to retreat. The bedcovers rustled. When she turned back to look, he had rolled over.

"Now that you're here, you might as well stay."

She faced him and pressed her spine against the door. She had never been in his room before and the darkness seemed intimate with its faint smell of leather and man, the scent of Justin all round her. "I couldn't sleep. Did I wake you?"

"From a sound sleep," he drawled, taunting her with the obvious lie. He lifted up slightly, and bare shoulders shone in the moonlight.

"I wanted to talk to you."

"Couldn't it wait until daylight?"

She took a step into the room, her annoyance overcoming her shyness. "You do believe in having your pound of flesh, don't you?"

"Right at the moment, one hundred and twenty-five pounds is more to my taste."

She thrust away the thought of being more to Justin's taste and took a step closer. Against the white pillow, his tousled hair, the planes of his face stood out in bold relief. His eyes were shadowy mysteries, uncharted waters.

"You don't have to treat me like spun glass. In the beginning, you didn't. I thought...that is, it would be better if you'd...make your wishes known."

"I wish you'd stop talking and come to bed."

The huskiness in his voice made it easier for her to strip off his shirt and take those last few steps. When she slid in beside him, he was waiting to receive her. The full body hug told her he was as needy and as wanting as she. Kissing followed, a gentle tasting of lips and tongues that already knew how, when and where to savor. Hands touched, hands with an ancient knowledge and a newly acquired one. Cool skin turned warm, then heated and moist. Lips that were languid and lazily exploring became intent and hungry. And when at last on a long, gasping sigh, she took him into her, the moon had risen beyond their window, leaving them in a darkness that no longer mattered.

SHELLY MOVED to leave, but Justin restrained her. "Stay."

"I shouldn't."

"Yes," he said, "you should," and kissed her until she no longer thought of leaving—or anything else.

THE SUN FILTERED in the window where the moon had shone the night before. Shelly lay awake, watching Justin prop himself up on his elbow and look down into her sleepy eyes.

"How long are you going to lie there, lazybones?"

"As long as I can get by with it." She snuggled into his shoulder. He lifted barely interested fingers to trace the hollow of her throat. "We have another show to do today, Red."

"Ummm." The subject didn't interest her. Nothing interested her except the way Justin's hair curled in front of his ear and how there were light-gold strands and dark-gold strands and a few shades in between.

"What are your plans for next weekend?"

"I'm participating in a four-day soaring competition at Harris Hill." She touched his mouth, the mouth that could look both sensuous and daunting at once. She'd hate to face him across the witness stand. "Will you come with me?"

He was pleased to be asked, she could see that. "Can't, love. I'll be up to my rear end in work. I go into court the next Monday."

She didn't like thinking about his having to return to the real world, the world where he'd been given a case so difficult someone would hate him no matter what he did. "The Stewart case."

His lazy fingers drifted lower and found more interesting terrain to explore. She felt her pulse quicken, her breathing hesitate.

"Who told you that?" he asked, as if he didn't care about her answer. He was more interested in seeing how lightly he could touch her and raise chill bumps on her flesh.

"The hurricane with the thirty-pound lump on her hip."

"Barbara?" He didn't want to think about Barbara, about his work, about the world outside. He wanted to think only of the silken flesh under his hand and how her nipple was tightening, lifting even after an exhausting night of lovemaking.

"Barbara. Does that mean we won't be able to be together next weekend?"

He liked that faint note of regret in her voice. "'Fraid so, love." He leaned over and tasted her mouth. "Unless you drop out of the contest and come stay with me, instead."

She went very still beneath him. Regret filled him instantly. He'd hit a nerve. And he'd destroyed the lovely, languid fall into more lovemaking.

"Justin, I can't. I've been planning on entering this competition for nearly a year. I'm hoping to win my first diamond."

The darkness cooled, his ardor cooled. "There will be other competitions—"

"Not this close, not for another year." She could feel his withdrawal. She didn't want him to withdraw. She wanted him to pursue the lazy path he'd started down her body.

Suddenly his hand was back, cupping her breast with such gentle possession that her breath stopped in her throat. "It means a lot to you, doesn't it? Competing. Winning."

There was a strange note in his voice she didn't understand. It was impossible to think clearly with his fingers plying those gentle caresses that roused her flesh and stole her sanity. "I enjoy competitions, yes."

"And you like to win."

"No one likes to lose—" Shelly brushed his hand away. "Counselor, you're doing it again. You're examining the witness under false pretenses."

"Close. The legal syntax is a little confused, but you've captured the essence." His smile was triumphant and possessive. "You're right, I am trying to make a point. I'm saying that you, my lovely pot, have been airily telling me, the kettle, about how single-minded I am and how much I like to win, when you are just as bad. Further, you say my father instilled in me this unholy competitive streak. It's my contention that you, love, have been endowed by your father with the same lust for victory, but like him you hide it, thinking it's not so virulent if it isn't obvious."

She started to protest but the words died on her lips. The clench of nerves in her stomach told her there was more than a little truth to his words.

"Should I apologize?"

He leaned over her, all male satisfaction. "Not for me, love. I like having you fit me . . . in every way."

He looked too smug, too self-satisfied. She shouldn't let him make love to her after he'd just sliced her psyche open and looked inside. He knew her too well. He could see inside her soul.

He could see inside her soul . . . and he still loved her. The thousand lonely days and nights, the endless pain of being the new kid on the block, blew away from her like leaves banished by the wind. A feeling, strong, hard, hot, welled up within her. She, who'd never had a long-lasting friendship or been dependent on anyone else for her happiness, had allowed another human being to become the center of her universe.

Accumulated fears, old and new, bubbled to the surface. Only one fear made sense. She'd been so careful never to let anybody penetrate the core of her heart. But Justin, as she'd known he would, blasted through her last fragile barrier. He was the man she loved with a depth that would last for an eternity.

"I've been so alone..."

The smugness vanished. In his deep, dark, intent eyes lay the knowledge of every one of her vagabond days, her lonely years. "I know, love, I know."

His hand covered her breast as his mouth covered her lips, telling her in that ancient way of a man with a woman that she was no longer alone. She was flooded with an overwhelming love for him. *He knows. He understands.*

Caught in the throes of her newfound feeling for him, Shelly shuddered with the old, simmering pleasure he'd given her moments ago and the new pleasure welling up from her discovery of the depth of her feeling. She was in the arms of the man she'd been born to love.

The exquisite rise of anticipation and the glimpse of ecstasy shattered her fears, scattered her thoughts. "You're taking unfair advantage again, Counselor," she told him softly when he lifted his mouth from hers, but she raised her hand to cup his head and bring his mouth down for another kiss.

"Objection noted and overruled. You're a special case that calls for special...handling. Besides," his mouth was a feast of sensuous delight, too provocative to look at, too enticing to refuse, "I have every right to take unfair advantage. If you won't give up your weekend for me, I have to make the most of the time we have left."

There was a new and enchanting darkness in Shelly's eyes and a beauty in her face that aroused Justin to a primitive possessiveness he hadn't known he could feel. Soft, melting arms that belonged to his woman were his for the taking. And he took them, exploring their finely downed backs, their finely boned wrists. Her soft melting mouth was his to explore, dark, salty, disturbing, full of secret, velvety caverns. Her feminine, yielding body was his to pleasure, smooth and supple, strong enough to bear his weight. And take the pleasure he gave. And sought. His woman. His.

THAT DAY, JUSTIN and Shelly flew their routine like two perfectly tuned parts of the same machine. Their lovemaking, and the understanding that followed, had enhanced that invisible tie between them. Within the disciplined confines of their carefully worked out aerobatic patterns, they anticipated each other even more acutely. The crowd, knowing they were seeing something unique, applauded the two aerobatic pilots enthusiastically when they landed and taxied along the flight line.

Late that afternoon, adhering to tradition, the yellow-tailed B-17 made a pass over the air field, opened its bomb bay doors and released its load of pumpkins. The Great Pumpkin Drop, it was called. While the orange globes plummeted to earth on the other side of the flight line well away from the crowd, Shelly and Justin, standing wedged in between the neck-craning adults and children, clasped hands and smiled.

That night, they lay in bed together wrapped in each other's arms for a quiet moment after making love. In the darkness, Shelly said nothing but Justin could feel her relax against him. It was a new world to him, but a world that was becoming wonderfully familiar, a world made up of the supple bareness of his lover and the murmur of voices drifting up the stairwell. Mel and Strom were in the den as usual, talking.

"What part of World War II do you suppose they're refighting now?" Justin asked, tracing a finger down his beautiful red-haired woman's throat.

"The missions over Germany," Shelly said promptly, her eyelids drifting shut, her head finding a comfortable place in Justin's shoulder. She thought how right it was to lie with him in the dark, cool quiet, and how much she wished they could drop out of the real world with its choices and problems and stay locked in each other's arms forever.

Shelly awoke with an odd, prickling fear. She was too old to be frightened of things that went bump in the night, but nerves were tingling in the back of her neck. A light breeze moved the sheer curtain but everything else was quiet in the Corbett house. She hadn't been dreaming, she'd heard something. What?

Carefully she slipped out of Justin's arms and went to stand at the window and look out over the moonlit countryside. She hadn't awakened in the middle of the night since she was a child. She caught a faint whiff of barn smell, a potpourri of dried leaves and horse dung wafting in on the night air. Yet her straining ears heard only the usual night sounds on a country farm: the nicker of a horse, a car zipping by on the road.

She sighed and turned around, feeling chilled in the cool night air. Justin lay in bed, his arms open in the space where she'd slipped away from him, his golden head half turned toward her pillow. That was where she belonged, locked next to his strength and warmth. She circled around to her side of the bed, hoping she could slip into his arms again without waking him.

She was leaning over the bed, one knee raised, when she heard the thump again. *Strom*. If he were having a heart attack and in severe pain, he might have fallen out of bed, knocked something over. Her stomach clenched in fear. Not stopping to think, she ran out of the door and down the hall.

Outside Strom's door, she halted. Suppose she was wrong? Suppose she went bursting into Strom's room and woke him from a sound sleep? She'd acted like a fool, running out of Justin's room without waking him. But he'd been sleeping so peacefully and this whole thing could be her imagination. Cautious now, and having a dozen second thoughts, she turned the knob carefully.

Illuminated in the moonlight that flooded the room, Strom lay on his side, snoring peacefully, a solid, endearing lump in the bed. Shelly released a sigh of relief. Quiet as a shadow, she backed out and closed the door. What a silly worrywart she was. She hadn't known loving Justin to distraction would turn her into an idiot. Yet here she was, prowling through the hall in an attempt to shield him from the pain of discovering his father was ill.

Calm and reason returned. Strom wasn't ill. Everything was fine. The stimulation from her own adrenaline faded, and she was left cold and chilled. She needed Justin's arms around her to bring her back to warmth and sanity. She turned back, the moonlit threshold of his room like a beacon in the darkness.

This time, the nearness and clarity of the thump made the hair come up on her nape. Worse, it seemed to come from her father's room.

She'd been mistaken about Strom, so Mel was probably sleeping just as peacefully. But she wouldn't be able to relax until she saw for herself that her father was all right.

Mel wouldn't like it. He'd chafed under her watchful eye the day before, telling her she worried too much, that his blood pressure was fine and he was all right and she was not to worry. Knowing how sensitive he was about having to take medicine in front of his cronies, she hadn't checked with him after dinner about his medication. Her eyes and heart had been full of Justin. Carefully she twisted the knob on her father's door.

Shelly stepped into sheer, solid dark. She edged forward cautiously, praying she wouldn't stumble over a chair, wake up the whole household and put that long-suffering look of disgust in Mel's eyes.

She tripped on something odd-shaped and soft. She groped out wildly and caught herself on the edge of the bed.

She'd stumbled over her father. Mel lay sprawled on the floor on his stomach, as if he had gotten out of bed and tumbled headfirst onto the floor.

A cold chill of fear clenched every nerve in her body. "Dad. Dad!" She stooped down to lift him into a more comfortable position. He was warm and alive and breathing, but the sound that came from his throat was inhuman.

She got him over on his back, and ran her hands over him, not sure how she could tell if something was broken. He moaned a growling sound of disgust and distress. He was telling her in his own way that he had no broken bones and wanted to get into bed.

He'd had a stroke. He could move one side of his body, but the other side was paralyzed. "Dad. Let me call an ambulance—"

A hand gripped her fiercely. He didn't want that. He raised his head, showing he wanted to get back into bed. Frantic, terrified, Shelly squatted beside him, torn between what she knew she should do and what Mel obviously wanted her to do. While she hung there hesitating, he gripped her hand harder and growled. Shaking, fighting back tears, she tried to prop him up. But thin as he was, his muscled shoulders and upper torso were too heavy for her to lift him onto the bed. Justin. She needed Justin.

Her throat bursting, her eyes filling with tears, she laid him back carefully. "I can't do this alone, Dad. I have to get help."

He banged his foot on the floor in agreement. That was the sound she'd heard, her father's inarticulate, primitive plea for help. She shot to her feet and raced out of the room and down the hall.

The moonlit room and the sleeping man in whose arms she'd lain only moments ago seemed like a dream. She grasped his shoulder, relieved to discover that he was warm, alive, healthy. She'd never needed his strength and courage more.

"Justin. Justin!"

Panic. Panic was wrong. She was a pilot, she'd learned not to panic. Then why was she shaking so? Why couldn't she think or breathe? Why couldn't Justin wake up? The world had gone into slow motion and nothing moved fast enough. Oh, dear heaven, let him wake up. He was asleep and her father was dying . . .

Justin dreamed he was in the courtroom. The jury was solidly against him. He was losing the case. He was hurting someone. A woman. A woman said his name with such hurt and desperation that he wondered what he had done to cause her such pain. Shelly's voice. He didn't want to hurt Shelly. He wanted to see her smile, listen to her laugh. But she was crying. Crying and calling his name as if she were dying and he was the only one who could save her...

His dreamworld dissolved into reality. Her fingers on his arm were warm and hard and transmitted the message of panic and fear with perfect clarity. He sat up. "What is it?"

"Dad. He—"

Justin sprang out of bed, reached for his pants and was on his feet and pushing her toward the door with a speed that gave her back part of her heart. In the dark hallway, Justin asked questions.

"What's wrong?"

"I think he's had a stroke. He's lying on the floor, and he can't move one side of his body, and I can't move him..."

Inside Mel's room Justin knelt and ran a quick hand over him, then grasped his wrist, searching for a pulse. "It's strong but fast. Nothing broken. Let's see if we can get him up on the bed."

Mel mumbled and tossed his head in an attempt to assist Justin and Shelly. Grasping him on each side, they managed to lift him onto the bed. When they had straightened his legs and made him comfortable, Justin sat down beside Mel and switched on the light. At the look of Mel's face, he reached for the bedside phone and dialed. Numb, Shelly sank to the other side of the bed.

"This is 2354 Langston Road, Corbett residence. We need an ambulance right away. One of our guests has had a stroke."

He went on giving other information while Shelly, no

longer able to listen, grasped her father's hand. She felt
the pressure of his fingers, the amazingly hard grasp of
his hand on hers. His eyes were glazed, his face oddly
distorted, one side normal, the other side slack, his eye-
lid, cheek and mouth drooping. A thin film of perspira-
tion lay on his brow. His mouth moved soundlessly and
his eyes clung to her as if she were his only reality.

Justin hung up the phone. "They said to make sure
he's kept warm and comfortable and they're on their
way." Justin picked up Mel's other hand and felt his skin
crawl at the lifelessness in Mel's fingers. "We're getting
help for you, ace. Just hang on a little longer, okay? Let's
get you under the covers." As easily as if he had been
doing it all his life, Justin pulled the quilt down from
under the dead weight of Mel's body and back over him.
"I'll get an extra blanket for his feet."

He went to the chest on the opposite side of the room,
his back bare and tanned as he bent to the bottom drawer.

Shelly watched, drawing sustenance and calm from the
sight of him, solid muscle and bone sheathed by tanned
skin in a room where her father's fragility made her shake
with nerves.

Justin flipped out the blanket over Mel and tucked the
end under his feet. His eyes flickering to Shelly's for a
brief second, he sat down beside Mel and took his hand
again. "So, ace. Help is on the way. Can you shake your
head?"

He did, but it was an awkward movement of his head
on the pillow.

"Try blinking your eyes. Once for yes, twice for no.
Are you hurting anywhere?"

Mel's eyelids came down slowly once, then again.

"Are you warm enough?"

Mel blinked once.

In the distance, the sound of a siren wailed through the night. Justin's eyes met Shelly's. "They're almost here."

The relief in her face was beautiful to see. She clasped Mel's hand tighter and said to him, "Help's coming, Dad. Hang on."

Mel stared at her and then blinked once deliberately. She swallowed, fighting tears.

"Shelly." Justin's tone was gentle. "You'd better go put something on before the guys get here." He nodded at the long length of bare thigh visible in the spill of the lamplight over the bed.

Mel blinked once in quick, furious agreement.

Caught on the edge of laughter and tears, Shelly stared at her father. Justin, watching, thought he had never seen any woman look so beautiful. "Go on, love," he said in that same, soft tone. "I won't let anything happen to your dad while you're gone."

Shelly looked into those calm, controlled, caring green eyes—and believed him.

CHAPTER ELEVEN

HE LOOKED SHRUNKEN, diminished, both arms connected to tubes, one to an IV, the other to the machine that showed his heart rate in a stabbing, peaked line. His right cheek hung slackly, the right eye barely open, the right side of his mouth drooping. His left eye tracked her path into the room, asking her silent, anxious questions.

Controlling her face as well as she could, Shelly moved toward her father and brushed her lips over his forehead. "Dad." Hospital smells rushed up to her, the scent of antiseptic, soap and helplessness freezing her tongue. Bright words, funny words, glossy, meaningless, comforting words deserted her, leaving her with nothing but the searing knowledge of her father's mortality.

She covered his left hand with hers. Instantly he grabbed her fingers in a grip that made her want to cry out with pain. It was as if all the strength he'd lost had returned to focus in that one bone-crushing grasp.

"Not . . . here."

Not understanding, she shook her head, emotion welling up from within, bringing the unwanted tears to her eyes. She who had always known what her father was thinking didn't know what he meant, whether he didn't want her there, or didn't want her crying all over him in public. Valiantly she strove for control.

He grimaced, looking grotesque with only half of his face responding to his bodily command. "Not . . ." he struggled, his eyes a little wild, and at last brought out the word he wanted "be . . . here."

She clasped his hand tighter, understanding at last. Mel did not like lying in bed, felled, impotent. She wrapped both her hands around his and brought their joined hands up to his cheek. She wanted to tell him how sorry she was, but she denied herself the luxury. He would like her pity even less than he liked being confined in the hospital. "I'll get you out of here as soon as I can. But for right now, you've got to concentrate on getting well." She infused the words with a passionate intensity, the doctor's words ringing in her ears.

"It's possible your father will recover some movement on his right side but he is sixty-five. His age is a factor against him . . ."

A nurse touched her shoulder to tell her the time was up. Mel clung to her, his eyes anguished. She smiled at him. "I have to go so you can rest. I'll be back, don't worry. Nobody's going to keep me away from you."

Panic flared in his gray eyes, and she looked down at him and saw the misery, the wretched aloneness of lying ill on a hospital bed, not being able to talk or control what went on around him. Mel was—had been—easy-going and good-natured, but he liked control. It was that restless need for autonomy that had sent him from place to place when Shelly was a child. She gripped his hand again, trying to give him the reassurance he needed so desperately. With a flickering of the old pride, he attempted a head shake and made a gruff, dismissing sound, a dark resignation coming into his eyes.

A scene flashed into her mind—Mel, smiling up at her as she climbed into the pilot's seat for her first solo flight. His smile had been carefully impersonal, his manner casual. He'd refused to acknowledge that she might be afraid. If he didn't see her fear, it didn't exist. "You'll do fine. You're my daughter."

Now Mel had his own trial by fire to face alone, the first long, dark night of many to come. As if he read her thoughts, he loosened his hand and closed his eyes, dismissing her. She turned, unable to forget that one dark look of despair she'd seen before he'd shuttered his thoughts from her. He was in pain, he was frightened, he was lonely, but he wouldn't turn to her for support. He fought his fears the way he lived his life. Alone. But his determination to face adversity with solitary courage left her feeling more desolate than ever. Why couldn't he, just once, need her? Then perhaps he could forgive her for needing him....

After the quiet of her father's room the waiting room was too brightly lit, too full of sound and life. Somewhere out in the hall, someone laughed, a raucous sound of an emotion she'd forgotten existed.

The two Corbett men stood waiting for her, one tall, slim, indolently leaning against the wall, the other shorter, rotund, anxious.

Shelly willed herself not to give in to the bitter regret, the wild need to dissolve into tears. She had to stay calm and in control, be worthy of the man who lay with such quiet courage in the room she'd just left. Chin up, back straight, she walked toward Justin and his father.

The pain, vulnerability and fragility in Strom's face hit her a second blow. *Not Strom, too.* The need to put on a good face intensified. If she wasn't strong, Strom might end up lying beside her father.

Justin's eyes met hers, a wealth of understanding in them. "How is he?" His voice was warm, subtly comforting.

"He's doing well. He has a little speech," her mouth lifted in a rueful smile, "enough to make himself understood. The doctor thinks he's out of danger, but they are going to continue to monitor him for twenty-four hours." She felt cold and chilled and had the irrational need to seek the warmth of Justin's arms.

That sharp green gaze of his wandered over her face, stripping away the facade of cool, calm control that she had constructed so carefully. Softly, so that his father couldn't hear, he said, "How are you doing?"

She shook her head and said, "Fine," but his eyes mocked her gently as his arm slipped around her waist. Instinctively she tensed. She'd spent a lifetime meeting trouble alone. Surely she could go on doing so. But his hand on her hip was insistent, forcing her to lean into him.

"The hardest part is reaching out for help when you need it."

Reaching out for help. Her father had never been able to reach out for help. And he'd taught her the lesson well. But he hadn't taught her how to shunt aside generous caring like Justin's.

She didn't remember moving. One second she was alone and bereft and the next she was in Justin's arms. She gripped the lapels of his blue jacket and buried her face in his throat, strangling the sound of pain and outrage she could no longer contain.

His arms, strong, comforting, life-giving arms, held her steadily against the warmth of his body. He said nothing, offering her silence and physical comfort instead of meaningless words. He gave her what she needed most, a place to hide, a place to rage and grieve.

"Put her down on the couch, son. Then you can sit next to her."

Strom's voice. She lifted her head and saw him, flush-faced, breathing a little too fast. So much for her fine control and her concern for Strom. She gripped Justin's shirt tighter in a spasmodic response to the pain and muttered in Justin's ear as they sank down together, "He shouldn't be here."

"He's better here than at home, not knowing what's going on and pacing the floor worrying," he murmured back. From comforter to comforted, they became loving fellow conspirators against Strom. "It won't kill him to see a little honest emotion between us."

"I couldn't bear it if anything happened to him, too—"

"I know. I know." Justin's soft-voiced agreement was as calming as a summer breeze on her heated cheek. He eased her back against the sofa, still holding her in his arms. His jeaned thigh brushed hers while her head nestled in his shoulder.

She lay in his arms feeling guilt-stricken. She should have insisted her father take his medicine. She would have if she hadn't been so wrapped up in Justin.

Guilt engulfed her, filled her throat with unshed tears. She pushed away from him and straightened. Justin's face smoothed into a mask that concealed his emotion—or lack of it—from her. She said, "I appreciate your being here, but there's nothing you can do now. You'd better take your father home."

"Not till I've seen to you." In that instant when she'd come apart in his arms, all the barriers between them had collapsed. A wild and reckless hope had surged through him that things were resolved. Premature, that hope. Shelly had replaced her defences with a vengeance, and all he could do was smile and pretend he hadn't noticed.

To Shelly, Justin's smile was easy, familiar, beguiling even while it concealed. "Morley's here. He'll drive Dad home. You'll need a place to stay in the city while Mel is in the hospital. My condo is close. I'll go with you and help you settle in." At her look of protest, he added smoothly, "Dad and I will feel much better knowing you're settled and comfortable, right Dad?"

Blatant blackmail, that's what it was, and the gleam in his green eyes said Justin knew exactly what he was doing. There was no way she would take the slightest chance of causing damage to Strom's emotional stability and health on top of her father's. And she needed to be close to Mel.

"All right."

They walked out of the hospital together, Strom following Justin. He said good-bye to his dad, then bent his head to say something to Morley, who sat behind the wheel of the silver Cadillac. Straightening, apparently satisfied, Justin strode back across the lot toward his own car where Shelly waited.

She was feeling calmer when they reached the condo. Or perhaps it was numbness setting in. With a sense of inevitability, she followed Justin through the cream-soft living room and up the stairs.

She stood waiting while he went around turning on lights. The shadows fell away, leaving the brown velvet bed enormous in the light; darkly sensuous, inviting. His gaze followed the path of hers and he smiled an oddly self-deprecating smile. "You'd better take a hot bath to relax before you go to sleep. I'll bunk down on the couch."

At her look of surprise, Justin said a word. "What kind of an insensitive fool do you think I am? I know what you need, and it isn't sex."

His blunt declaration shattered her last defense. She'd expected him to take her down on the bed and make love to her without a second thought. She hadn't expected him to be self-sacrificing for her sake.

Her eyes darkened with pain. He thought he knew what she needed. Dark. Sleep. Solitude. Forgetfulness. He was wrong. She wanted life, in its rawest, most vibrant form. "Don't . . . go."

The look in his eyes would have stopped a regiment. "Are you saying you want to go to bed with me?" He came closer, hunter stalking prey.

"I need . . . to touch you."

He stopped coming toward her. He didn't want to be a damn security blanket. He wanted to be the man she ached to have in her body, her heart, her life. "Why? As an antidote to ward off fear?"

The tone of his voice chilled her. This was her worst nightmare, needing him desperately, being denied. She wrapped her arms around her middle. Before she thought, she said the words screaming in her mind. "I need . . . to be with you."

He'd never wanted a victory more—or been more ashamed of his triumph. He swooped and enfolded her in his arms. "Ah, love. I'm sorry. It's just my old instinctive need to win."

"One of these days you might discover," she found his mouth with hers, "that losing has its advantages."

JUSTIN LAY BESIDE HER in bed, his face illumined in the small night-light, his mind on Shelly. There were only two hours left until dawn and Shelly looked as if she would sleep through both of them.

He folded his arms and clasped his palms under his head, his brow furrowed in thought. For one small moment of time earlier in the evening, in that waiting room, she'd accepted him. She'd come into his arms willingly, and it had felt good. Later, as he'd stood looking at her in the intimacy of the bedroom, he'd known he couldn't take advantage of her when she looked as she had then, battered by life, needy.

She hadn't been needy when she stepped into his arms. She'd been fierce as a tigress, taking his mouth avidly, running her hands possessively over his body, making love to him like a desperate woman. When they sank down on the bed together, she'd driven him wild with her hands, her lips, her tongue. After their first frenzied coming together, as they lay in the sultry aftermath that followed, Shelly turned to Justin and began touching him all over again, sending him into a prolonged, intense heightening of senses that nearly drove him out of his mind. He hadn't known a woman could take him to the brink again and again until, in that final blessed moment of completion, he felt as if he were dying.

She was complicated, his woman. Complicated, sexy and beautiful. Whether she recognized it or not, she needed him. And he needed her. Too much. Far too much. He, the expert swimmer, was in over his head. Justin tried to still the small voice that asked how he'd let that happen . . . or what he was going to do about it now that it had.

JUSTIN DROVE SHELLY back to Captain's Corners Monday evening to pack an overnight bag and pick up her toiletries. The house seemed desolate, silent and dusty. She spent an hour on the phone, canceling her lessons at the soaring school. When she went to see Pat to tell her what had happened, tears shone in the older woman's eyes. Pat liked Mel. Everyone liked Mel.

During the next few days, Justin inserted himself into Shelly's life effortlessly, smoothing out the bumps in her suddenly turned-upside-down days. He helped her establish a routine, seeing to it that she ate breakfast each morning, driving her to the hospital before he went to work. Her hours there were interspersed with visiting Mel and waiting outside in the atrium where a split-leaf philodendron grew toward the sky. She sat contemplating the plant with Jack and the Beanstalk aspirations while the nurse changed her father's bed. At six o'clock, when Justin pulled up outside the hospital entrance, Shelly climbed into the car beside him, thinking there must be no more exhausting way to spend a day.

The next few days passed in fragmented hours of despair and boredom, splintered minutes of hope, nights filled with worry and Justin. If it hadn't been for him, she'd have been totally alone, isolated from the rest of the world. She knew the medical staff and greeted them by name, but it was Justin's visits to Mel and his morning and night appearances that were the flashes of gold in her life, infinitely rare, infinitely precious.

At night when they lay together in the big bed, he made no sexual demands on her. He simply held her, offering the warmth of his body and the strength of his arms to drive away the nightmare about Mel.

Seeing her father each day, watching with desperate hope for some sign of improvement took its toll. She began to feel like a juggler doing a balancing act. In Mel's room, she was the picture of cheerful optimism. Away from him, her spirits plummeted to the depths.

One evening toward the end of the week, Justin insisted that Shelly let Strom sit with Mel while they went out to dinner. Shelly complied, only because it was easier than arguing. After they had eaten a delicious meal in a small intimate dining room done in pink and maroon, Justin covered her hand with his. "Has Mel's speech made any improvement since he started to work with the therapist?" ·

She looked down at their intertwined hands. Against the pale pink tablecloth, Justin's fingers were bronzed, tiny golden hairs sparkling on their lean length. "He can swear." She looked up, her eyes seeking Justin's for understanding, a smile curving her lips. "Dad's from the old school, never swear in the presence of a female. I didn't know he knew half those words. The doctor says it's quite common. But it's hard to hear him say those things. I know he's angry and he's hurting, but I just wish he would...let me inside. It's almost as if he hates me because I can walk out of there and he can't."

"Maybe he does hate you a little. That's a common reaction, too. He's like a lion in a trap, angry and roaring, flailing out at anybody who happens to be in range."

"I know that. I just can't...accept it."

The green in Justin's eyes darkened. "It doesn't fit your image of your perfect dad, does it?"

Justin had caught her on the raw, he could see that. Her eyes were brilliant blue sapphires in her pale face and her fingers tensed in his. "I don't know what you're talking about."

"Yes, you do. You put your dad on a high pedestal when you were a little kid, the same way I did mine." He stroked her hand gently. "You have to let him come down now, Red. Let him be human."

She thought of Mel turning away from her in the hospital room and pulled her hand away from Justin's. "I'm more than willing to let him be human. He's the one who thinks he's impervious to wind and weather and all the other human failings the rest of us mortals have. He—"

"Excuse me, Mr. Corbett?" The waiter was polite, but determined. "There's a telephone call for you. If you'd care to take it at our hostess station?"

Justin frowned in irritation at being interrupted. But when he looked at Shelly, his irritation died. Irrationally she'd thought the message was about her father.

Justin rose with a lithe grace, his smile easy. "Probably just Hanley with a brainstorm about the Stewart case he wants to share. Have some wine," he said to Shelly. Her face relaxed slightly. Justin trailed his hand caressively over her shoulder. "I'll be back before you know I'm gone."

Shelly watched him stride away, her heart clenched in foreboding. Surely he was right. If it had been about Mel, they would have called her, not Justin. She lifted her wineglass and tried to obey Justin's order to relax, but even the wine she'd sipped didn't help when he came striding back and she looked up to see his bronzed face had gone a shade paler. "It was the hospital. They say there's been no change in Mel's condition, but he's been asking for me."

She shot up out of her chair, fumbling for her coat. She'd known. "Where's Strom?"

"Still there. According to the nurse who spoke to me, something my father said seems to have upset Mel."

The world tilted on its axis. The little oasis of relaxation was torn from her as if it had never been. She fell back into an icy pool of anxiety and dread, feeling as if she had never left it as she followed Justin out into the cool air.

Inside the convertible he pulled her close to him and turned on the heater, but nothing helped. Her teeth wanted to chatter.

At the hospital the nurse calmly pointed toward Mel's door and told them to go in. Strom was still there, but he looked years older, shrunken, as he leaned against the foot of the bed.

"What's going on with you two?" said Justin, his voice edged with irritation.

Mel looked wild-eyed, distraught. "Tell...him...no," he ground out in a hollow, guttural voice. "Tell him...crazy. Make him see...hurt you." A string of obscenities followed, bringing a flush to Strom's cheeks.

Justin turned to Strom. "What did you say to him?"

"Nothing." Strom's eyes darted around the room as if he longed to escape. The smooth politician had disappeared. He had the look of a hunted animal.

"You must have said something—"

Shelly laid her hand on Justin's arm. "Please don't upset your father."

"He sure as hell seems to have upset yours." Justin thrust his hand through his hair and said a companion word to Mel's. He felt buffeted on every side. What the devil was going on here? The hospital room was brightly lit, pristine and neat. Each face was illuminated well: Strom's tortured one, his hands clutching the bottom of Mel's bed; Shelly's tense and lovely countenance, her attention focused on her father; and Mel's distorted profile, one eye full of Mel's intelligence and spirit, the other nearly covered by the drooping lid.

Justin tried to view them with the cool logic he used in the courtroom, but he couldn't. All the people he loved were in this room. They'd known each other for years. They should be able to understand each other. But there was something going on between the two men that defied logic.

Strom shook his head as if coming out of a dream. "All right, Mel, all right," he said. "You win. I won't say anything."

The sick man's eyes closed in relief. When he opened them again, his gaze shifted to Shelly. "Want... you...to...go."

While Justin watched, Shelly absorbed the blow, the color rushing up into her cheeks. Justin's hands curled into his palms. Mel couldn't be so cruel.

"You want me to go?" Shelly asked in a cool tone that held a wealth of pride, strength and hurt.

A terrible grimace brought one side of Mel's face up in disgust. "Not go...good-bye. Go...com—"

Shelly shook her head. She seemed to relax a little, but she was still fighting to comprehend Mel's meaning. "I don't understand what you mean."

Mel swore. Suddenly understanding, Justin laid his hand on her arm. "I think he wants you to go to the soaring competition tomorrow."

Furious eye blinks expressed Mel's agreement, his expression a bizarre parody of hope.

"I can't leave you, Dad."

Mel grunted, said a word, pointed at Strom. "He...stay. You...go. No good...hanging around... here." He fixed Shelly with another hot, oddly half-intense, half-indifferent gaze. "You...go."

"I think you'd better do as he asks," Justin murmured softly.

Shelly shook her head and opened her mouth as if to protest. A cool, clear gaze from Justin's green eyes made her change her mind. "All right, Dad. If that's what you want, I'll go."

They filed out of the hospital room a few minutes later, a chastened and confused group. Strom climbed into the Cadillac and Justin put Shelly into his car.

Riding beside him through the city streets, Shelly pushed a hand back through her red mane of hair and gazed into the darkness, seeing nothing. To her amazement, Justin seemed to be smiling.

"What's so funny?"

"I was thinking about Mel. He's flat on his back, but he has the three of us dancing to his tune. He brought me running to see what he wanted, got you to say you'd go to the competition and won some kind of crazy standing argument he has with my father. That's quite a feat for a guy who can hardly talk."

"He's ill," said Shelly, "and illness gives a person power."

"Mel's always had strength. He's stronger than my father."

Shelly twisted her head to stare at Justin. "How can you say that? Your father is a congressman. He meets with dozens of people, gives speeches, talks with presidents—"

"But he relies on Mel for strength. Haven't you noticed that before?"

"No. No, I hadn't. I just assumed that my father enjoyed being with Strom because of the prestige..."

Justin made a sound in his throat. "You know your father better than that."

"I'm not sure I do," she answered softly. "I've never known my father very well. He doesn't...reveal much of himself to anyone. That's why it's so hard to go in and see him lying there caught in all that...raw emotion."

"Maybe that's why he wants you to go to the competition so badly. He wants to feel alive and successful again—through you."

"I hadn't . . . thought of that."

Justin let her sit in silence the rest of the way home. But when they reached the condo, he followed her into the bedroom. "Want me to help you pack your bag?"

She turned to him, her face a lovely combination of desire and tense expectancy. "That's not what I want you to do."

At the look of her, something old and hard seemed to crack and shatter inside him. Standing very still, he said in a mock-serious tone, "I wonder what it is I could possibly do for you."

She walked toward him slowly. "Make me feel alive again."

"That's a tall order. What makes you think I'm the right man for the job?" His tone was serious, yet teasing. He stood waiting. She stepped into his arms and offered him her mouth, kissing him in a way that erased any lingering doubts he had about being the right man for the job.

SHELLY EASED A HAND out from under the sheet and laid it lightly on Justin's chest. He didn't wake. His breathing continued deep and rhythmic. He was exhausted. Besides ferrying her to and from the hospital, he'd been working hard, bringing work home from the office, reading depositions, calculating strategy. She'd been so caught up in her worry about Mel she hadn't asked him how his preparation was going for the case that was to go into court next week.

The room was dark. The bed was warm, scented with Justin's body and hers. The shadow against the wall was the tall chest of drawers where Justin's brush and comb lay. Across from the bed was the dresser they shared. The contents of his pockets, billfold, coins, scraps of paper that seemed to multiply around Justin like subdividing amoeba lay on one corner, on the other sat the tapestry bag she used for her makeup and her comb and brush.

They were living together, sharing their lives the way a husband and wife did. Under the stress of worrying about her father, she'd done what she'd vowed she would never do. She'd entered a man's life and let him enter hers. She'd accepted everything Justin had to give: shelter, support, comfort.

For one terrible, delicious moment she let herself dream about what it would be like to continue on this way for a month. Or a year. Or the rest of her life. To marry, raise children and grow old with Justin.

Her stomach clenched with nervous fear. It was a dream, an impossible dream and it would never come true. Life didn't serve up fairytale endings. Life served up cruel twists, surprise denouements, betrayals to the heart. Life dealt cruelly with those who loved and tried to hang on to their love.

What if, because of this interlude they'd spent together, Justin felt he was obligated in some way to her? Suppose he asked her to stay with him out of a sense of responsibility? It would be difficult for him to break things off because of their familial ties.

She couldn't bear to think she'd trapped him into a relationship. She would have to be the one to break it off. She could do it as naturally as it had begun. Tomorrow she would return to Eagle Hill, gather up her crew, rig the sailplane for travel and head for the southern tier. When she came back to the city after the competition, she would take a motel room. Possibly Mel would be ready to leave the hospital shortly after that. There would be no need for Justin to feel obligated or trapped into a relationship he hadn't initiated.

"Is THERE A NUMBER where I can call you?" Justin asked the next morning over the breakfast table.

"I'm not sure. I'll find a phone when I get there and call the hospital to let them know where I can be reached."

He stilled suddenly, like a wild deer sensing danger. "What about me? What about letting me know where you can be reached?"

She was silent, toying with her toast. In the deathly quiet that fell in the bright kitchen, Shelly felt Justin's gaze roving over her face. "Justin, I really appreciate what you've done for me, please believe that. But I can't go on . . . living off you—"

"Isn't living with me the correct term?"

"We haven't been precisely living together—"

"We were precise enough about it last night."

He saw her absorb the blow and told himself he didn't care. He did. He felt as if he were flailing himself. He could stand—just barely—letting her go for four days. He couldn't stand letting her go for good. And that was what his red-haired, sexy little double-crosser had in mind. He rose from the table and went to the sink to empty the contents of his coffee cup. His special coffee, *crème de noisette*, made from imported beans and ground in his own grinder, tasted bitter this morning. He put the cup down and braced himself on the sink, his back to her. He thought of her life, of the isolation she'd lived in. He thought of Mel, of the two women he'd lost and the pain he must have suffered. For years, Mel had taught Shelly to shun love and commitment and depend only on herself. But last night, and on several other nights, Shelly had opened her arms and invited him in. She'd come to him in his father's house and she'd talked of her loneliness and isolation. He'd believed they'd achieved an understanding. Now they stood in the kitchen together, but they might as well have been on separate poles of the earth.

He felt betrayed. He thought she was learning to trust him. For that was what this was all about. It wasn't about loving or not loving. It was about trusting. She had to trust him to be there for her all the days of her life—and trust herself to want him that long. "We'll talk about this when you return."

"As you like," she said quietly.

Justin knew damn well he'd lost, that she was moving out and wouldn't come back. She was going to play it safe. She was willing to soar for diamonds, but she couldn't risk going for the gold hidden in her heart.

His eyes traveled over the fringed edges of the raffia place mats that she'd dug out of his linen closet, the rose she'd insisted they buy one night in the supermarket because it looked lonely, the black-rimmed dishes she'd told him were sinfully opulent. Everywhere he looked there were things to remind him that she'd shared his life with him.

"If it bothers you that we're living together, we could . . . get married," he said in a diffident tone.

His eyes, green shards of glass, flew down to hers. She flinched as if he'd hit her.

He hunched his shoulders. "Well, I can see that idea really appeals to you."

"Don't."

He lifted his head and addressed the ceiling. "'Don't,' she says. Don't embarrass her by asking for her hand in marriage." His eyes flashed to her face and there was hurt and vulnerability in them. "What is it about me you can't stand? Is it the wet towels on the bathroom floor? Do I hog the bed, snore, eat like a pig?"

She met his eyes. Justin had recovered with a vengeance. The arrogant lawyer was back, playing to the jury box. She said, "I've already told you. There's nothing wrong with you. That's what's wrong with you."

"Let's not talk about what's wrong with me. Let's talk about what's wrong with you. Let's talk about how you run at the first sign that I'm getting close to you. Let's talk about how afraid you are to let me into your life. Let's talk about how badly your father has infected you with his stay-strong, stay-independent, never-love-too-much garbage."

She'd planned to explain about how she didn't want to obligate him. She'd planned to tell him how much she hated the thought he might feel obligated to propose marriage whether he wanted it or not. He had proposed. And he couldn't have made it more obvious that he was doing it out of a sense of responsibility. There he stood, feeling obligated just as she knew he would—and blaming her for refusing to play along with his game. "I have to go." She reached down for her bag.

For a moment she thought the depth of pain and longing in his eyes would make her falter, turn back, and say...yes. Then he said in a soft, lethal tone, "We all gotta do what we gotta do."

THE WEATHER. Sailplane pilots were at the mercy of the weather. Particularly in autumn, when, like a teenager, the climate vacillated between the maturity of summer and the raw newness of winter.

Shelly felt the tug of two opposing forces herself. Part of her concentrated on the weather briefings and the contest requirements. Part of her remained in Justin's plush condo.

She couldn't think of him. She had to concentrate on the contest, on flying, on the skill of her competitors. There were pilots from all over the country holed up in every available motel room within driving distance of Harris Hill, the soaring capital of New York State. The favored Bill Brown from Texas sported a brown leather cap, barnstormer style. Zach Kingston from Indiana, who'd been labeled the Dark Horse Hoosier, had a shy smile and a tendency to duck his head when anybody addressed a question to him. There was no chance she would win against these men. Still, the sky held its own secrets—and surprises.

By seven o'clock the next morning, Shelly's sailplane was rigged to fly. She'd done the usual checks. Her ground crew, Pat and Derek, were ready. When her turn came, she took the tow and went up, knowing that in the sky her mind would have to be on flying and nothing else.

There were excellent cumulus clouds. Conditions were as good as they looked. Fantastic. Wonderful. She would be in the running.

In her euphoria she got careless. She went too high and was accidentally pulled into cloud. Disaster. Her speed picked up, in what she knew was a spiral dive earthward. She was plummeting blindly to earth unable to see sky or ground.

Panic gripped her, followed by its companion nausea. She tried to spin out. Mistake. Try something else. Keep the needle centered. If the needle is centered, flight is in a straight line. Keep the ball in the ball bank centered.

Ball centered shows the plane is approximately level. Check air speed: ten miles over stall.

As if she was being thrown out of a whirlpool, Shelly came out of cloud at 400 meters. There was no lift any-where and she circled back to the airfield shaking, dis-heartened that she'd made such a disastrous mistake. The Hoosier had made sixty miles, she found out that night in the little motel dining room, where the pilots who'd landed close enough all congregated to bemoan their might-have-beens and celebrate their victories. She'd gotten nothing but a lesson in humility.

The second day wasn't much better. As if Shelly needed to be reminded of the changeable nature of soar-ing, the third day was one for the textbooks. Thermals everywhere. She could do no wrong. She flew three hundred and twenty nine miles that day and earned her first diamond for her Golden C pin. She also beat the Hoosier who'd made two hundred and eighty two miles.

She celebrated that night and bought Pat her favorite, a bottle of imported Canadian beer. Derek toasted Shelly with his Coke. She was a hundred miles east of the city where Justin was, and as she sat in the country restau-rant with a beaming Pat and a grinning Derek, the ela-tion she expected to feel—should have felt—was missing. Justin should have been sitting beside her, lounging back in his chair, his long legs crossed at the knee, his eyes raking her with that aren't-you-the-foxy-lady and wait-till-I-get-you-alone look.

"Hey," said Pat suddenly pointing to the TV set that hung over their heads, silently flashing scenes of the news. "Isn't that your man?"

Shelly hadn't been watching, her chair was too much at an angle. She turned her head. Justin's face filled the screen. He was coming out of the courthouse and he was angry. Reporters were poking microphones at his mouth, he was shunting them away. Another man, older, his face darkly flushed, walked beside Justin, his arm linked in Justin's.

"What do you think it is?" Pat stared upward in fascinated awe, as if she couldn't believe she was seeing someone she knew on television.

"It must be something about the case he's working on."

What had Barbara told her? *He's been handed a firecracker of a case, his turn, I guess.*

Shelly ached to hear what was being said, but as quickly as Justin's image had flashed on the screen, it was gone. The two newspeople, one female, one male, both deadly attractive and serious, were saying something with great earnestness. Was it about Justin?

Back in the motel, she settled down with Pat on her bed to watch the eleven o'clock news. No mention was made of a court case or an assistant district attorney named Justin Corbett.

Pat glanced at Shelly. "You could call him. You do have his number, don't you?"

"Yes, of course."

"You had trouble, he helped you. Seems like you might do the same."

"Seems like," said Shelly, picking up the phone.

CHAPTER TWELVE

"HELLO?" In that one syllable, Justin conveyed a wealth of annoyance. If he was in as bad a mood as he sounded, she was lucky he had even answered.

"How are you, Justin?"

When he recognized her voice, the silence rang in her ears. "Passable." He wasn't going to give away a thing. "How are things going for you down there?"

"Actually, I'm not 'down there.' I had a great day yesterday. Earned my first diamond and ended up west of Syracuse." She felt guilty telling him about her good fortune, but it seemed best to speak naturally.

"Congratulations." He spoke coolly, but without rancor.

She waited for him to confide in her, but Justin was shutting her out. Nerves tightened, sending out signals of pain. She would have to probe, and she wasn't nearly as adept at that as he. "I saw you on television this evening."

"The wonders of electronics."

"I couldn't hear what was being said," she rushed on, feeling as if she were heading pell-mell into disaster, "I was in a restaurant and they had the sound turned down."

"So you had to call to satisfy your curiosity?"

"That's below the belt, Counselor." She was losing her willingness to be reasonable. She wanted him to acknowledge the intimacy between them, and her special right to share his troubles. She gripped the phone, wishing she could see his face. It was dreadful, trying to cut through his pride long distance. "Justin, I need to know what's happened. I just caught the end of it as you were coming out of the courthouse—"

"Ho, ho. Then you missed the real show. The charming Mrs. Stewart tried to scratch my eyes out."

Shocked, she struggled to absorb his words. They didn't make any sense. "Why would she want to do that when you're the one who's prosecuting her daughter's killer?"

"The defendant decided to plea bargain. We agreed. Of course that means a reduced sentence. The woman's family want their full pound of flesh, not a lighter sentence for Teresa's killer. I want a sure conviction. The judge wants the case off the court docket. Everybody's got their special interest." He paused and then said in a softer, more lethal tone, "Just like you and me."

"That's another low blow, fellow. Knock it off."

Sprawled on his couch, his shoes kicked off, Justin laid his head back and let the pain wash over him. Shelly was the only woman in the world he'd let talk to him like that. He even liked hearing her no-nonsense tone. He liked everything about her. An aching loneliness for her swept through him like a wind through an empty canyon. He needed her. More than ever, now that he'd heard her voice. It had been a hell of a day and now here she was, offering him nothing but the tantalizing illusion of her that the telephone provided.

"Is anybody with you?" she asked.

"Oh, yeah. Mata Hari dropped in earlier but she had to leave. She had a big spy deal pending—"

"I meant your father or Morley."

"You do wish cheery company on me, don't you?" There was another long pause. "There's only one person I need to be with right now. A lady named Shelly Armstrong. Ever hear of her? Some people dig for gold, she soars for diamonds." A pause, a gathering for the attack. "When she's in my bed, I soar."

"Justin, I wish I could be with you, truly I do—"

"'If wishes were horses, beggars would ride...'"

"Are you drinking?"

"No, but it's a damn good idea. Don't know why I didn't think of it. Always did say you had a good head on your shoulders, woman. The rest of you isn't so bad, either."

"Now you listen to me, Justin Delaine Corbett. You take a hot shower and go to bed."

"What fun is that without you?"

"It won't be fun at all. It will be good for you. It will be what you need—"

"You're what I need."

He'd said it in a dozen ways while they were together, but she'd never been struck with the stark truth of it the way she was when the dry, unadorned words came to her ear through a telephone receiver.

"I'll come to you as soon as I can."

"Yeah," he drawled.

"Please, do as I say. Shower and bed."

"I'll see how I feel about it after I've had that drink. I...thank you for calling, Shelly." The teasing man was gone. In the blink of an eye, he'd reverted to cool, polite, military-school correctness.

"I...no problem. Good night, Justin."

"Good night, Shelly," he said distantly.

She hung up the phone thinking she'd lied. She did have a problem. The problem was six feet, two inches tall.

and weighed a hundred and ninety pounds soaking wet. Soaking wet. Naked, wet, wonderful man, emerging from the pool and scrubbing himself with a towel. She should have known the first night she saw him like that that she was lost.

Her handsome devil was a clever one, too. During those first few weeks, he'd wanted to take her to bed and he'd done everything in his power to get her there. But somewhere along the way, his feelings had changed. He liked taking her to bed, he made no secret of that. But there was more than his desire for her. He liked her as a friend. And loved her as a woman. Those were two powerful weapons in his arsenal of arrows aimed straight at her heart.

Pat had gone into the bathroom to allow her to talk to Justin in private. Shelly supposed she should tell her friend it was safe to come out now. Instead, she lay back on the bed and stared up at the ceiling.

Something strange was happening inside her. A barrier was crumbling and it didn't feel good. It felt painful. It felt risky. Its collapse left her vulnerable, exposed.

Justin was right about her. She wasn't afraid of his being perfect or growing tired of her. She was afraid of wanting to spend the rest of her life with him.

She didn't know how to love, not really. She'd told herself she loved Justin but she hadn't been willing to take that final step that would make him a part of her life. She didn't want to love someone that much, risk that much. She'd learned the lesson of independence early in her youth when her father had ferried her around the country with him, and she'd adhered to the principle of self-sufficiency ever since. She'd been careful never to get too involved with a man she couldn't pull away from. That was why she'd been wary of Justin from the beginning. In the deepest part of her heart she'd known Justin was the one man who could vault over the barrier and plumb the depths until she let him in.

She didn't know when it had happened. Maybe when she was sixteen, maybe on the day of the wedding when he'd wrapped his arms around her and taken her into the pool. When didn't matter. Why didn't matter. The only thing that mattered was telling him so. Now, when he needed to hear it most. She must go to him.

She lay frozen on the bed, unable to move. It wasn't giving up the contest that bothered her. She'd won her first diamond and Mel would be pleased. There would be other contests. What bothered her was making the final, fatal declaration to Justin.

She was brave in the air but she was a coward on the ground. A spineless, mindless coward, caught in the trap of a thousand yesterdays. Maybe tomorrow would be soon enough to be brave....

A small voice told her that if she didn't go to Justin tonight, she'd lose the infinitely precious gift he'd given her. Trust.

She lunged off the bed. "Pat. I'm leaving."

Pat appeared from around the bathroom door, her face flushed from her shower. "Leaving? Tonight? Now?"

"I have to see Justin. He...needs me." She spoke firmly, but her hands were shaking. She knew if she waited one more minute she'd lose her nerve. Already a lifetime habit of self-preservation had conjured up little voices to whisper in her ear, voices that warned her she was taking a big fall off a precipice with no guarantee of a safe landing. Her stomach was tighter with nerves than when she'd fallen out of that cloud yesterday. That was what she was doing, falling out of a cloud, plunging straight into the gray fog of taking a chance on another human being.

"You and Derek can trailer the plane back to the hill tomorrow morning. I'll take my car into the city."

"What will we do until you get back?"

"I've already canceled the lessons for the rest of the week. Take some days off. I'll call you when I want you to come back to work." Shelly threw her makeup into the suitcase, muttering a word when a tube of lipstick rolled away from her onto the bed. She snatched it up and tossed it on top of her clothes.

"Hey," Pat said, catching her arm. "I'm glad you're going. Good luck."

For a poignant moment Shelly studied the face of the only woman she'd ever really called friend. There was concern for her there, along with admiration. "Thanks. I'll need it." She shut her suitcase and grabbed up her coat, knowing she was burning her bridges behind her in a way she'd never done before.

THE PHONE WAS AN instrument of the devil, Justin knew. All it ever brought was trouble. But when it rang again, he couldn't ignore it. Shelly might be calling back to say something he wanted to hear.

"Are you all right?"

He relaxed against the couch, his head on the low back, his eyes closed against the pain.

"Yes, Dad, I'm fine." *A patent lie, but never mind, Dad. You only want to hear the good news.*

"Is that true what I heard on TV that that woman wanted to scratch your eyes out because you agreed to plea bargain?"

"Yeah, it's true."

"You're sure you're doing what's best for your career?"

Justin's mouth twisted in ironic mockery. A young woman had lost her life, but he was supposed to worry about his career. "Probably not."

"Dammit, boy, if there's one thing I thought I taught you it's to watch out for your hind side."

"I'm a slow learner." He looked up at the ceiling, his eyes tracing the starburst pattern imbedded in the plaster. He felt like a starburst, shattering from the inside out.

"Have you heard from Shelly yet?"

"Yes."

"Things any better between you?"

Irritated, Justin closed his eyes and tried to think. His brain felt numb. He'd been battered too many times today. "We're still talking to each other if that's what you mean."

"Are you going to mess up there, too, and let her get away from you?"

Justin gritted his teeth and fought to control his temper. "I'm doing my best not to 'mess up.'"

"Have you told her how you feel about her?"

"More or less."

"Humph. My guess is it's mostly less and not much more."

"A lesson well learned from you."

In the silence that followed, Justin castigated himself heartily. It was hard to remember he couldn't spar with his father as he once did. Yet he was tired of lying, tired of putting up a facade. Shelly's call had left him aching. There was so little truth left in the world. He wanted a piece of it for himself and his father.

"You always knew how I felt," Strom said at last.

"I never knew how you felt—except that you wanted me to win."

"I wanted the best for you—"

"And I wanted the best *of* you. I never got that. You saved that for your constituents."

Strom inhaled sharply. "You make me sound like an utter failure as a father."

"I didn't mean that, Dad. I just meant you've never been able to tell me how you felt about me, good or bad. It's not surprising I'm afflicted with the same disease."

There was an endless, bottomless silence. "I've always thought you were the best son a man could have."

Justin gripped the phone. "Yeah, Dad. I always had to be the best for you, the best athlete, the best son. You didn't tell me you wanted me to be the best lover of women, but the implication is there. Well, let me tell you something funny. I didn't just learn the lessons you wanted me to learn, I absorbed all you had to teach. I'm a good lover, but I'm damn poor at loving."

"You . . . can't mean that."

"I'm afraid I do, Dad." He shook his head in frustrated pain. "I don't want to hurt you, or imply that you've been a failure. I just want you to admit to the simple truth that we haven't been . . . all we could be to each other."

"The . . . truth is important to you."

His father sounded as if Justin had reached through the phone and hit him. Justin tried to ease the force of his blow. "Tonight it seems like the most important thing in the world. I can't go on mouthing polite lies. I can't pretend to you that I'm worried about my career when a mother is grieving over her dead daughter. She's lost her daughter, Dad. Maybe she's entitled to scratch my eyes out because I'm going for the conviction that's sure and easy, instead of taking a chance on the one that's uncertain and hard. And I can't pretend that things are wonderful between Shelly and me because they aren't. I need...to be able to tell the truth to somebody. I'd like to know that just once in your life you were there for me, that I don't have to create a facade of perfection for you. I'd like you to let me have problems, let me be less than perfect and tell me you understand and you still love me. Maybe if you could, just once, let me be a little less than perfect, I could come a lot closer to it."

"I've always tried to be a good father to you. I've given you every opportunity..."

Justin had asked for too much. He'd asked for something Strom couldn't give, had never been able to give—the admission that his son had problems just like everyone else. For if Strom admitted that his son was human and made mistakes, that must mean that he, too, was human and made mistakes. Strom didn't believe that could never believe it.

"Oh, hell, Dad, I know you did the best you could. In the end, that's what we all do. Look, forget what I said. I appreciate everything you've done for me. And don' worry about my career. I'll survive. I always do. That' what life's all about, isn't it?"

Strom tried again to justify his position while Justi listened. Justin answered in the soothing, placating wa his father was accustomed to. In the end Justin agreed t have dinner with his father in a few days, but when h hung up the phone, it was with a sense of relief.

He'd walk across hot coals before he'd intentionall hurt Strom. It was only since the advent of Shelly tha he'd felt the old, intolerable need for closeness to ar other human being he hadn't felt since the death of h mother. Funny. Since he'd learned to want emotional ir timacy with Shelly, he wanted it with his father, too. For that one moment it had seemed terribly important to have Strom acknowledge the truth: that though the Corbett men had all the visible riches, they lacked the one thing that counted most in the world, the need to give and receive unconditional love. Without that, nothing else was worth a damn.

His father couldn't admit to a weakness like needing love. Like a fly in amber, Strom was trapped in his own vision of perfection. Was it too late for him to break out? Maybe it was. Too late for the father—and too late for the son he'd molded in his image.

OUTSIDE JUSTIN'S CONDO, her nerves singing, Shelly raised her hand to ring the doorbell. It was two o'clock in the morning, and if he'd taken her advice, he'd be in bed. Her finger poised over the button, she hesitated. If...

If. When. Maybe. It was too late for doubts. She was here, she had to go through with seeing him or lose respect for herself.

She rang the doorbell three times and was almost ready to give up when the door opened. His gold hair ruffled, his eyes empty, Justin stood looking at her as if he'd never seen her before in his life.

"I'm sorry. Were you asleep?"

"No." He stood blocking the doorway. She slipped around him, stepped onto the beige carpeting, gently eased the door out from under his hand and pushed it closed.

"Would you like to come in?" His voice was dry, an ironic steel tone he'd never used with her before.

"If it's not too much trouble." She turned away from him to look around the room as if she didn't know what it looked like, trying to hang onto her poise. He wasn't going to make anything easy for her. She hadn't really expected him to.

"I see you did have that drink."

"Actually, I've had two. Would you care to join me in a third? No, your first, my third."

"Keeping the record straight, Counselor?" she said lightly.

"I try, I try."

Justin's voice made her knees feel wobbly. She'd had a long day and it was hard to hang on to her optimism when he looked at her with detached indifference. She walked to the couch and settled into a corner of it.

"Make yourself at home."

She didn't flinch at his cutting comment but she could feel her cheeks warm. He came closer, walked around the low table on the other side and poured the drinks with great concentration. His eyes darkly mocking, he handed her the glass.

"About keeping the record straight." He settled into the chair across from her and stretched his legs out. He was wearing the suit pants he must have worn to work that day but his feet were bare. So was his chest. His unbuttoned pale blue shirt fell aside, the two dangling ends of his untied tie framing his flat stomach.

She'd explored his navel with her tongue, felt his hard abdomen ride on hers. The first tightening of desire tingled through her, driven by memory and anticipation. He, obviously, didn't feel a thing.

"Yes?"

He hadn't lifted the glass to his mouth. Now that she was there in person to bedevil, he no longer seemed to need the alcohol to dull his senses.

He sat back, studying her with those shard-glass eyes. "Let's straighten the record by asking the question, why are you here? What is it you want? The last I knew, you called, made the perfunctory inquiry after my well-being, told me you were staying to finish the competition and hung up without telling me where you were or how you could be reached. Status quo. The relationship back on the same footing it was when you left. I was yours to take and enjoy when you wanted, put back on the shelf when you didn't want."

He continued casually, as if he didn't know he was destroying her. "Two hours later you show up on my doorstep, a suitably tolerant look on your face for the man who failed to take your excellent advice to shower and go to bed. You come into my home uninvited and you sit down on my couch uninvited. I can only conclude, Ms Armstrong, that you are endowed with a great deal of nerve."

"It would seem so, Mr. Corbett."

"Now you sit there with that look on your face that makes me feel as if I'm hurting you. But I'm not sure it's possible to hurt you, Ms Armstrong. You're the strong, silent type, impervious to injury."

"You're being ridiculous—"

"I know but I'm rather enjoying it. So the impervious Ms Armstrong has come to call. Which brings us back to the original question: Why? Driving all night is hardly likely to improve her concentration in the clouds tomorrow. Therefore, in asking the question 'Why is she here,' we have to first assume that she has dropped out of the competition, is that correct, Ms Armstrong?"

She nodded, knowing he wasn't quite sober and knowing this verbal examination was a catharsis he needed.

"So we have it verified that Ms Armstrong has made the decision to drop out of the race and come to her lover. But when she arrives on her lover's doorstep, she finds him unwilling to open his arms and receive her. Now what is she going to do? And more important, how long is she going to stay?"

She wanted to say "As long as you want me," but the look on his face didn't invite that kind of vulnerability. If she handed him a weapon like that, he might decide to use it. The words stuck in her throat. She swallowed. "How long do you want me to stay?"

"You're the one who came knocking on my door in the middle of the night. You tell me."

"I'm here . . . for as long as you need me."

He looked at her and his eyes were black with anger. "I need you all the bloody damn time. Either get all the way into my life or get the hell out."

Her back stiffened. "In other words, the relationship has to run on your terms or not at all."

"Not on my 'terms,'" he said. "If I wanted to dictate to you, I would have told you I didn't want you to go to the competition. I didn't ask you to stay home. I asked you to let me know where you were. I think that's a reasonable request between two people who love each other."

"It is." Her eyes met his, her pupils huge and dark with shock. He'd said he loved her, as if there was no question about his feelings.

"I don't want you to give up the competition. You can stay the night here and go back tomorrow—"

"No," she said.

Anger, exasperation and frustration shone from his face. "You are one hell of a stubborn woman, lady."

"Yes," she said, waiting.

"I've had hostile witnesses who were more forthcoming than you."

"I suppose that's possible."

"Why did you come?"

"I came because you needed me," she said simply, sitting very still, facing him. "At least that's what you said a couple of hours ago."

"A couple of hours ago, a couple of years ago, a couple of lifetimes ago." He considered her, his green eyes moving unforgivingly over her face. "I should do you one big favor and tell you to get the hell out. You deserve better than me."

Despite his words, the look in Justin's eyes told her he wasn't going to throw her out. He had something entirely different on his mind.

"I'm sure I do."

"But you don't have sense enough to walk out of here and go looking for that something better, do you?"

She smiled in the age-old way of a secure woman. "Do I look like I'm going anywhere?"

"You keep smiling like that, and the only place you're going is into my bed."

"Talk, Counselor, nothing but talk. Is that all you can do? I feel like Eliza Dolittle. Words, words, words. All talk and no action."

His eyes gleamed. "Are you going to come here, or shall I come and get you?"

"I'll meet you halfway." Deliberately she stood up and walked around the low table to stand at its exact midpoint. Just as deliberately he straightened his long, lean frame and came to where she stood. He reached for her— and she caught her hand in his.

As soon as he touched her, her courage failed her. "Justin, I'm . . . frightened. I want to ask you a million things . . . but I'm afraid of what you'll say."

He remembered his own plea to his father. *Just listen and share my pain with me.* "Try me."

"I know there aren't any guarantees, but I feel as if I'm stepping off a high building without a net."

"I know, love." He waited, his eyes watching her steadily.

"Just because I love you and you love me doesn't mean that we own each other or that we're going to spend our days living in each other's back pockets. You have your work and I have mine—"

"I know, love." Justin moved slightly, his eyes flickering over the soft skin at the base of her throat. "I'll give you as much distance as you want." He slid an arm round her waist to pull her into his arms, contradicting his soothing words. At the feel of her warm, slender weight against his chest and hips, his patience faltered. He bent, slid a hand under her knees and lifted her into his arms. "If we're going to talk the night away, I suggest we do it where it's warm and comfortable."

She closed her eyes to shut out the sight of his beautiful, intent face and said, "If that's what you want."

"Docile at last. And suddenly satisfied with words and no action. Will wonders never cease?"

The velvet of his bedspread felt softly provocative when Justin placed her gently on the bed. He began to undress. "You're taking off your clothes to talk?" she asked.

"I hear better without my tie."

Shelly had seen him undress many times before, but this time was special. He was hers, his unself-conscious, single-minded pursuit of her a part of his charm. Just as it always had been.

Had she accused him of being all talk and no action? He had her out of her clothes as fast as he'd shed his own.

"Justin—"

"Shhh. Time to get under the covers."

He adjusted the sheet and blanket over her, snuggled next to her and began to stroke her hair away from her face in a way that both soothed and excited her. "Now what was it you wanted to say?"

Justin leaned over her throat and kissed that soft hollow that had been enticing him.

"How can I think when you're doing that?"

With an instant meekness that aroused all her suspicions, he lay back down on the pillow beside her.

"Now what are you doing?" she asked.

"Letting you think."

"Who said I wanted to think?"

He raised up over her, his eyes catching hers and holding them, the teasing mockery banished by the dark seriousness. "I'll do my damnedest to be there whenever you need me for the rest of our lives. And I'll do my damnedest to disappear when you want me out of your hair. I can't promise any more than that."

"I can't ask for any more than that," she said, raising her arms to slide them around his neck.

Shelly pressed against him, surrendering more than her body to him. She surrendered everything she was, all the hopes, dreams and fears of the skinny little kid who'd never had any friends. She'd learned, at last, that there was no way to keep a little part of herself detached and safe. She had to risk all, or risk losing it all.

He took her to him, exploring her with his hands and mouth, all the while wondering if he was worthy of the gift she gave.

Shelly. Everything came down to her, her smooth, satin skin, the way she wrapped her legs around his, the scent of her glorious red hair. With her he could find the truth.

Truth. Shelly accepted the truth from Justin in the brush of his hands over her breasts, in the caress of his mouth on their aching crests. When he suckled her, she accepted his possession, let it reverberate inside her, quivering like a whispery voice in a dark tunnel.

Again and again he came to drink at the well of her generosity, and again and again, she offered him what he needed most. The well was nearly inexhaustible. She couldn't get enough of him, nor could he get enough of her. His fingers molded her flesh, discovering soft slope of breast, rounded curve of navel. His mouth descended lower to the nest of red-gold curls, finding her, taking her apart and putting her together in a new way that made her more hungry for him than before. When she could bear no more, she turned to him to reciprocate, retaliate, regenerate him with her mouth. Her hunger heightened his, led him to seek her. Their seeking led to new hunger and to ecstasy.

WHILE JUSTIN LAY beside Shelly in the still darkness, tracing a lazy finger over her ribs, around her belly and up to her breast bone, she said, "What are you thinking?"

"I'm thinking I'm not going to like going to work tomorrow when I know what I could be doing if I were at home," he drawled.

She smiled up at him. "We couldn't just lie around making love all day."

"Why not?" It was a mistake, giving him encouragement. That marauding finger meandered, bringing chills to her bare flesh.

"I can be here when you come home...if you'd like," she said.

"I'd like. Are you going to eat breakfast with me in the morning the way we did before?"

"Of course. You don't think I'm crazy enough to turn down a free breakfast, do you?"

"I hoped you weren't. It would bode ill for our children."

"Are we...having children?"

"I assume so. That's what most people do after they get married, isn't it?"

"I don't...know. Never having been married—"

"We can remedy that. Are you going to want one of those big, fancy affairs in a church?"

"No," she said instantly, before she realized she knew the answer. "I want to get married at Corbett Hill." In that instant, she knew all the old resentments had vanished. Corbett Hill was hers—in a way she'd never dreamed it would be. But the house, the grounds, the wealth no longer mattered. What mattered was that all those things were a part of Justin. Maybe that was the secret reason she'd always wanted to belong at Corbett Hill.

Her blunt request to be married in his home earned her a kiss. "Sensible woman. I knew there was a reason I liked you."

"That's the only reason you like me, because I'm sensible?"

"No, there are many reasons why I like you. One is here," he kissed her mouth, "and here," her earlobe, "and here," the tip of her breast, "and here," he moved to lean further over her abdomen. She pulled him back beside her, loving the look of self-satisfaction on his face. He was a menace in bed, this man with no scruples when it came to sexual provocation, and he knew it, but she wouldn't change him if she could. He was as self-assured as ever, but there was a new vulnerability about him that she found infinitely endearing.

"Justin, you should . . . rest."

He took his hand away from her breast and lay there, silent and unmoving beside her.

"What are you doing now?"

"Resting, just as you ordered."

She glared at him in mock exasperation. "Must you always do everything I tell you to do? Don't you have a mind of your own?"

He proceeded to show her that he did indeed have his own mind, and he meant to use every clever cell in it to bring her to sighing devastation.

THE NEXT MORNING, there were kisses outside the bathroom, kisses inside the bathroom, and much struggling and mock protesting about better ways to spend the day and snatching away of underwear before Justin finally let Shelly get dressed. Fully clothed, she left the bedroom battle zone and retreated to the living room to wait for him to finish getting ready. When he appeared in the doorway, clean-shaven and dressed in a gray three-piece suit, her heart came up into her throat with love.

"You look wonderful," she said, knowing she sounded besotted and not caring.

"It's all that debauchery that does it. Better tonic than vitamins."

"Alice was right. Men are sex fiends."

"Naw. I just need another little shot of tonic." Grinning at her, he strode across the room and was reaching for her over her unconvincing protests when she stopped suddenly and shook her head.

"No more...tonic. You have to go to work and I have to go see my dad."

Justin looked at the ceiling and appealed to some nameless deity, "Why did I have the bad luck to fall for such a hard-hearted woman?"

CHAPTER THIRTEEN

THE GLOW OF SHELLY'S loving still clung to Justin when he walked out of the courtroom a few hours later, steeling himself to head over to the diner and slather relish on an overdone hamburger. The plea bargaining had gone as he'd expected. They were nearly at an agreement, only a few details left to be ironed out. It wasn't perfect, but it was going to be a good compromise. The world seemed a better place.

A man stepped away from the pillar where he'd been leaning and Justin's euphoria vanished. "Dad? What are you doing here?"

His father looked as if he hadn't slept a wink. Fatigue didn't sit as well on him as it did on his son. "I came to see you. Lunch? If you're not busy, that is. If you are, we'll make it another day."

Justin felt decidedly odd. His father had never, in living memory, adjusted his schedule in order to seek out his son at Justin's convenience. "My pleasure. Is Morley here?"

"No. I drove myself. I...wanted to talk to you alone."

Justin immediately changed the location of his planned lunch. The congressman had gone to great pains to get into the city to see him, and the diner was no place to have a discussion that was obviously very important.

Justin led his father on foot over the Skyway, a span of enclosed hallways, tunnels and escalators that created an internal path through the city's three major downtown buildings. His father's breath quickened as he walked through the tunnel.

"Maybe I should have picked some place closer—" Justin began.

"Nonsense," his father sputtered.

"Are you having pain?"

"No."

Justin didn't think Strom was lying. He didn't seem to be suffering, he was just short of breath. At last, blessedly, they were seated in the old, elegant top-floor tea room that had been the center of the city until a decade ago, when elegance became old-fashioned. Tall pillars of marble rose to ceilings thirty feet high. The tables were spread with rose tablecloths and set with fresh flowers, there was soft classical music coming over the loudspeaker.

Strom was recognized and seated with effusive attention. "Nice to go out with a celebrity," Justin murmured.

"You'll be one yourself one of these days."

Justin's mouth quirked. "Let's hope not."

Strom sat back in the chair and studied Justin. Justin was used to those examining looks, but there was something different about Strom's demeanor today that made Justin uneasy. He seemed almost desperate to see what he looked for.

"You never did like it much, did you? All the hullabaloo, the commotion, the reelection strategies, the campaigning. You never loved it like I did."

"No, Dad, I never did."

"That's why you're dragging your feet on this district attorney thing."

"You've got it."

"From what you said last night, I gather you might even have been a little jealous."

"It's entirely possible I was when I was a kid. I'd lost one parent at an early age. I suppose I wondered why I couldn't have the other one around when I wanted him."

"I guess you might have." Strom sounded as if the thought had never occurred to him.

"You soon set me straight. I remember grabbing you around the waist and hanging on after we came out of the church from Mother's funeral because I had the crazy idea I was going to lose you, too. You pushed me away and told me to straighten up and act like a man."

Strom stared at his son, his eyes bleak. "I don't remember doing that at all. You must have thought I was an unfeeling bastard of a father."

"I just thought you didn't want me touching you."

"Maybe I didn't. Maybe it . . . hurt too much."

Justin sat back, apprehension filling him. His father was in a strange mood, one he had only seen once before, the night he'd found him drinking alone in the library before Paul's wedding.

The waiter came. Strom ordered white wine and looked at Justin, who shook his head. "No way, Dad. Not if you're driving." Strom sighed and changed his order to coffee. Justin held up two fingers. The waiter nodded and left.

"That's one reason I don't like to drive to hell and gone to eat lunch."

Justin forced himself to relax. "Why are you here in 'hell and gone'?"

Strom scowled at him, his eyebrows drawn together. "I came to talk to you. I've been thinking about what you said last night and I—"

The waiter returned, carefully setting the coffee in front of the two men. Strom clamped his lips together, waiting.

The waiter asked if they were ready to order, Strom told him yes, and said he'd like a steak sandwich. Justin gave his father another meaningful glance, but Strom stood firm. His mouth quirking, Justin ordered broiled fish and a salad.

The waiter went away, but Strom remained silent. "You were saying," Justin prodded lightly.

"Should have known better than to try to tell you the secret in a public place."

"Secret? What are you talking about?"

Strom stared at Justin. "You look like her, you know. Have her eyes, her hair, her smile. Maybe that's why I never tried—why I couldn't see—hell! I can't do this."

Justin sat very still, feeling his blood go cold. "Are you trying to tell me something about my mother?"

"No. This doesn't have anything to do with your mother. This has to do with me." His eyes flickered to Justin's and there was desperation in them. "And it has to do with us. I realized after last night that I've spent most of my life hounding you to be perfect because I wasn't. A long time ago...before you were born...I...made a mistake. I see now that it's standing like a barrier between us. It's always been there. I just didn't see it until last night."

Justin was often thrown wild curve balls by defense lawyers, but trying to follow his father through the logic of that speech defied his skill at concentration.

The waiter came with the food. Strom gave it a quick, disinterested glance. When the waiter left, he took a deep breath. "I'm not...I've never been...what you think I am." At the question in his eyes, Strom said in a choked voice, "Perfect. A hero."

Justin smiled. "I did suspect you weren't perfect."

Strom scowled. "No, I mean I didn't . . . that is, I—" He cursed. "This is harder than I thought it would be."

Puzzled, curious, Justin gazed at his father. What had the master politician groping for words?

The steak sandwich that Strom ordered sat untouched. He raised hazel eyes to Justin, eyes that were tortured, eyes that stirred compassion and apprehension in Justin. Strom straightened his shoulders and looked for all the world like the soldier he had been, preparing himself to face a firing squad. In the soft lighting, his face was pale. "I'm drafting a letter to the president of the United States to tell him that I have no right to the Medal of Honor that was awarded me, that the medal belongs to Mel. When I told Morley what I was going to do, he pointed out that I should tell you first. When the contents of the letter become known, the backlash will affect you, too. You'd have to forget about running for district attorney. Your name will be anathema to the public. As mine will be."

He looked down at his plate, leaving Justin to struggle with a surge of emotions, the uppermost, disbelief. He didn't give a damn about running for district attorney, that was Strom's dream, not his. "What do you mean, the medal belongs to Mel?"

"Just what I said, dammit."

This was the Strom Justin knew, the Strom he'd learned to deal with. "Tell me how it happened."

Strom slumped back against his chair. "You've heard the story enough times to know it was my last mission before being rotated home. We were coming back from bombing a munitions dump in Munich. We'd taken flack. We were in bad shape, limping home. We had no altimeter, no power equipment, no landing gear and the bomb bay doors were stuck open. We made it back to England and then the crew began to bail out. Mel and I were ready to go when Mel insisted we make one last sweep through the plane. That was when we found the bombardier. He was shot in the thigh and unconscious. Still we could have jumped with him...if his chute hadn't been riddled with fragments.

"We stood looking at each other, Mel and I. Then Mel said in that quiet way of his, 'We'd better try to fly her in.'"

Strom shook his head. "All I could think of was that missing landing gear, and those bomb bay doors stuck open. In my mind, we didn't have a hope in hell of surviving a pancake landing. But I didn't want to show Mel how scared I was. We went back into the cockpit...and that's when I panicked. I was tired, dead tired, and strung out on nerves. There I was, so close to being shipped out I could taste it, and Mel was telling me I had to die. I knew I was going to die. I could see the plane exploding and me trapped inside that little tin can of a nose, my flesh burning. I could feel it right through to my bones, that horrible trapped feeling, knowing I was going to die, knowing there was no way out. I grabbed up my chute and was halfway out of my seat when Mel turned and landed a haymaker on my jaw that put me right back in it. While I sat there trembling with fear, Mel brought the plane down on the air field in the best damn pancake landing you'd ever hope to see."

Through the maze of shock and disbelief, Justin heard the pride in Strom's voice for his friend and marveled at it.

Strom shook his head. "What happened after that was crazy. While we both sat there, shaking and scared in the aftermath, the medics came racing out on the field, and everybody behind them. One eager beaver hoisted himself into the plane to see what was going on and why we weren't coming out." Strom's eyes caught Justin's. "I was the pilot, I was in the pilot's seat, they assumed that I'd made the landing—"

"And you said nothing to contradict them."

Strom's eyes turned dark and fiery. "Dammit, no. What would I have said? That when the test came, I proved beyond a shadow of a doubt that I was a coward? You know what an old war horse your grandfather was. He would have died of shame."

"Why didn't Mel say anything? Why didn't he knock your block off?"

"Before we went on that mission, he'd just received the news that his first wife had died in childbirth. When he climbed into that plane to take off, he didn't care whether he lived or died. He may have felt guilty for making the decision that endangered my life and decided I deserved the credit, I don't know. I could have taken my chute and bailed out, leaving him alone at the controls. I didn't. That's the only thought that helps me stay sane. Anyway, after we were debriefed, we agreed to let the story stand the way everybody else had written it. We also agreed never to divulge the secret unless we both decided it was time to tell the truth. But if anything happens to me, no one would ever know the whole story. Mel will never break his vow of silence. But . . . in the past few years, I discovered I don't want to go to my grave carrying this burden."

"That's what you said that upset him in the hospital room."

"Yes." Strom made a gesture with his hand. "We'd talked about it before he got sick, and his position was always the same. He didn't want anyone else to know. He's . . . a good man."

"A hero," Justin murmured. The elegance of the room was a mockery. Sham, all of it. Marble pillars, rose tablecloths, painted daisies, nothing but a facade. His life was a facade, built on a lie. "All these years you've held a lie up to me and asked me to live up to it."

"Don't . . . look at me like that."

"You did everything in your power to make sure I had the courage you lacked."

Strom paled as if his son had hit him. Justin shook his head and turned his eyes away from his father. It all seemed a terrible waste. His whole life built on a sham. How could he face—

Shelly. She would be thrust in the limelight along with her father if the truth came out, limelight she didn't like, wouldn't want. "You can't send that letter, Dad. Not until Mel's well enough for you to discuss it with him."

Strom's eyes narrowed. "Thinking of your own hide now, are you?"

He was furious, coldly, deadly furious. "Dammit, it's not my hide that matters. It's Shelly's, and Mel's and Paul's. Somehow in your self-sacrificing little urge you seem to forget how many other people's lives this—thing—touches. But that shouldn't surprise me, should it, that you haven't stopped to consider anybody else but yourself, that you didn't once think about the reporters who will swarm into Mel's hospital room and ask that ill man a thousand questions he can't answer. And as for what they'll do to me—Morley had to remind you of that." Justin's eyes blazed with years of hurt, anger and pain.

"You despise me because I'm a coward," Strom said.

"I don't despise you because you had a moment of fear. That makes you human. I despise what you did afterward. You selfishly took a medal that belonged to somebody else because you needed that bit of metal and ribbon to save face. You weren't a coward, Dad. You were selfish. And you still are. At this very moment, you're acting like a little tin god who walks around aloof and alone and doesn't need another damned person in the universe. You didn't come here to ask me what to do. You came here to tell me what you were going to do. Well, I say go ahead and do it. Destroy Mel, Shelly, Paul, all of us. If it makes you feel better, that's what counts.

His father looked stunned.

Muttering in disgust, Justin stood and tossed his napkin on the table. "If you'll excuse me?"

Strom reached out and caught Justin's wrist, his face anguished. "Wait, son. I . . . want you to stay with me. Just now, I . . . need somebody to be with me."

Justin looked down at his father's hand on his arm. "Then find somebody. I'm unlucky enough to be your son." Justin tugged his sleeve loose from Strom's grasp, turned his back on his father and walked out of the dining room.

WHISTLING, SHELLY UNLOCKED the door of Justin's condo with the key he'd given her. Clutching her bag of groceries, she waltzed inside and pushed the door closed with her hip. At the kitchen door, she reversed her course and let it waggle shut behind her. She swayed her backside in a rhumba to match the metronome swing of the door, her whistle shrill and a little off tune.

She felt so good. Mel was so much better. He'd improved greatly over the last few days. He'd smiled at her and clutched her hand when she told him about winning her first diamond, and he hadn't even seemed to care that she'd dropped out of the competition and returned a day early.

There was one small fly in her ointment of happiness. When she'd told Mel about her engagement to Justin, he'd gotten the oddest look on his face.

Maybe he was just tired. Maybe it was difficult to look happy for your engaged daughter when you were lying on a hospital bed wondering when you were going to get out of there. Mel was already nagging her about leaving. To her surprise the doctor had said he could leave at the end of the week.

She hugged herself, laughed and twirled around in a frenzy of delight. When had she ever felt so good?

The kitchen phone jingled. She thought about letting the answering machine get it. But what if it was Justin trying to reach her?

"Hello?"

A pause. Then: "Hi."

"Justin?" She leaned back against the counter. "What's wrong?"

"Nothing. I just wanted to let you know I'm taking the rest of the afternoon off and going out to the airfield."

Her forehead wrinkled in dismay, Shelly wrapped the cord around her finger, a cold apprehension touching her. "Why?"

"A . . . loose end I need to tie up."

Her dismay deepened. "What loose end?"

"Something I need to find out about myself."

That sounded ominous. A thousand questions were unspoken, but Justin was obviously not in the mind to explain. She opted for the practical approach. "Will you be home for dinner?"

"I may not be. Don't wait for me. Go ahead and eat."

She swallowed back her disappointment. "Why...can't I come with you?"

"This is something I need to do alone."

The hum of the dial tone echoed in her ear, leaving her to stand there and stare at the kitchen wall. And wonder.

She didn't wonder for long. She grabbed the sack of groceries off the counter, raced to the refrigerator and stuffed it in without unpacking it. Like a streak of light, she ran through the condo and down the steps to her car. Out on the road it occurred to her this was the third time she'd gone racing to Justin. The first two times she'd gone to him to give him her love. This time, she was going to give him a right to the jaw.

IT WAS NEARLY THREE o'clock by the time she bumped over the rough grass to the old hangar at the airfield. The men were standing outside watching the blue Decathlon circle in the air. Hal Henderson, the family friend who liked to tell war stories, stood with his eyes shaded, watching.

"What's he doing up there?"

Thoughtfully, like the gentlemen he was, he cast polite eyes over Shelly. "I'm not sure. But from what I've seen so far, I'd say he was testing his limits. If I'd known he was in that kind of mood, I'd never have helped him roll the plane out."

Two minutes of watching Justin, and Shelly knew Henderson had it exactly right. Justin was watching Justin, and Shelly knew Henderson had it exactly right. Justin was testing his limits, going closer and closer to the edge of disaster. His Cuban eights were too tight. He recovered from his dives an instant later than he should have. His climbs were too high, too fast. As Shell watched with her heart in her throat, it became increasingly clear to her that Justin had taken the first basic rule of aerobatic flying, safety first, and thrown it out the window.

A hot fierce anger burned through her. Who did he think he was, endangering the lives of her unborn children?

When he started on his second outside loop, Shelly whirled around to Henderson. "Is the other plane gassed up?"

"As far as I know. One of the men took it up for a short spin this morning."

"Then help me get it out on the runway."

Five minutes later she was buckling herself in. Seven minutes later she was in the air beside Justin.

When he looked over and saw her, she waggled her wings at him cheerfully, as if they were rehearsing and it was the most natural thing in the world for her to be there. Scowling, he pointed downward in a determined flap of his hand, telling her he wanted her on the ground. She shook her head. He commanded her to get out of the air again, she shook her head again. She kept her plane beside his with supreme confidence and skill, pointing to her chest and then at him, in a whatever you do, I do, gesture.

She didn't mean it, Justin thought, watching her. She wouldn't follow him into a routine she didn't know. She had more sense than that.

He was wrong. She followed him into a Cuban eight. She followed him into a hammerhead dive. She followed him into an inside loop. And now she was following him into an outside loop. He gritted his teeth. If she landed in a heap on the ground, he'd shake her till she was senseless. He'd . . .

He was doing exactly what he'd accused his father of doing. He was acting without a thought of the consequences for those who loved him.

Shaking, he completed the loop, scanned the skies to see if Shelly had come through it safely and heaved his chest in relief when he saw that she had. What in heaven's name had he been thinking of, endangering her like that? Still, he was filled with pride. His woman was something. His equal.

More than his equal. And why shouldn't she be? He'd been spawned by a man who was a coward. Her father was the real hero. The thought hit him like a slap in the face.

Justin eased up on the throttle and let her go into the pocket beside him. Then he pointed at the ground and pointed at himself, telling her he was going down.

Her smile was beautiful to behold.

CHAPTER FOURTEEN

THE GOLDEN LIGHT of the late-afternoon sun blazed behind Justin's back, making him a shadow with a face Shelly couldn't read. When he reached her, he lifted his hand and stroked the hair back from her temple. His fierce need to affirm her existence came through in every glide of his fingertips over her skin. "Don't you ever do that to me again," he said.

"Don't you ever make me do that to you again." His gentle touch melted her anger. How did the man expect her to go on being furious with him when he looked at her like that? Still, she had to make the effort. "You were endangering your life up there. I'm not sure I can forgive you for that. Our children aren't going to like it too well, either."

"We don't have any children." The red-gold strands were all pushed back, but he went on stroking her face.

"Not . . . yet."

His face changed, grew subtly cold. His mouth twisted and he dropped his hand. "Find somebody else to be their father."

"What?"

He grabbed her upper arms as if by touching her he could make her understand. The blaze of need in his eyes held her in thrall. "Find somebody else to love."

She shook her head. He looked as if he wanted to eat her alive and yet he was telling her it was over. None of it made any sense. There must be an explanation, some agony that had driven him up into the sky to fly at the edge of his endurance, but she couldn't think what it was. Obviously he wasn't going to share it with her. Shock tactics were definitely in order. "Well, so much for 'I'll be there when you need me.' That didn't last long, did it?"

Her angry words didn't penetrate. He was caught in a hell of his own making. For the first time she glimpsed the depth of his despair. He pulled her closer, his face dark with fury. But his anger was inner directed, focused on himself. "My whole life is built on a lie. Nothing about me is real."

She stabbed a finger at the sky. "You were real enough up there."

Even while she watched, he began to control his emotions. The man who'd worried about her disappeared. In his place was that coolly dispassionate, totally professional lawyer. If he wasn't careful, she'd give him that right cross after all.

"It was your father who acted like a hero, not mine. The medal should be his."

"What are you talking about?" Shelly placed her hands flat on his chest as if by touching him, she would understand him.

"Our fathers lied. Your father did the heroic deed, my father collected the medal."

"I still don't understand—"

"It was your father who piloted that crippled bomber out of Germany, not mine. Mine was scared out of his mind that he was going to lose his precious life."

"My father piloted the plane?"

"Yes. Mel. Quiet, unassuming Mel. Funny. We should have guessed. I knew my father was adept at telling political lies, but I didn't think he'd gotten such an early start at it.''

Her heart squeezed in pain. She had never heard Justin criticize his father before. Never. Only extreme anguish would drive him to such a harsh judgment. ''Justin, don't.''

He looked down at her slim fingers splayed over his jacket. Those hands were feminine, strong, strong enough to fly a plane with the same skill as he, delicate enough to drive him wild. He wanted those hands on his body. He wanted everything she was, everything she had ever been, everything she would be. But he couldn't have her. Not now. He reached for her hands, folded them gently and released them.

She looked at him, her face as pale as if he'd slapped her.

Something hard twisted in his gut, but he knew what he had to do. And he had to do it now, while he had enough strength left to act the part of a man, even if he wasn't one. ''All bets are off, Red.''

''You can't mean that.''

He let her go, pushing her away a little, as if to ensure the distance between them. ''I do mean it.''

She stepped toward him, total aggressor, total lioness on the prowl. ''You're a coward.''

How steady those eyes. She only realized her mistake after the words were out of her mouth.

''Now, that, Ms Armstrong, is the truest thing you've said today.''

She stood stock-still, absorbing the error. ''You know I didn't mean it that way.''

''Didn't you?''

In desperation she clutched his jacket. ''You can't walk away from me, not like this, not over something that happened forty years ago. Justin, listen to me. You have to forgive your father. He made one mistake, but he's spent a lifetime paying for it."

"He made my life hell. He held himself up as an example to me."

She lifted her head, fighting to keep back the tears, to act as logical and detached as he was. "Yeah, Corbett, you had it pretty tough. Your father expected you to study, practice, work, achieve. To help you, he hired the best instructors, put in a swimming pool, bought you an airplane. Now where are you? You have a strong body, a pilot's license and a law degree. If I were you, I'd give Strom hell for what he's done to you."

"He made me believe he was something he wasn't."

"Don't we all?"

"Don't you understand? My whole life is based on the lie that man lived."

Her eyes locked with his. "That's true."

"Can't dress it up in anything pretty, can you?"

"No."

"I'd like to know what in hell I'm supposed to do."

"Right now, the best thing you can do is forgive him for being human. Can you do that, Justin? Can you forgive him for being an imperfect man who's lived an imperfect life?" Her eyes met his steadily. "If you can't you're not the man I thought you were."

Those expressive eyes captured hers. "That's exactly the problem, isn't it?" The wind blew, the earth turned. But to Shelly, it seemed that the entire universe was contained in Justin's face. "You deserve better, Red."

She stared at him, searching her mind frantically for the words that would penetrate that thick skull of his. And while she stood there searching, he turned and walked away.

WHEN JUSTIN RETURNED to the condo late that night, Shelly's things were gone. He wandered through the rooms, looking for some small sign that she'd been there, her green velvet slippers, her curling iron. There was nothing—except the bag of groceries sitting on the shelf in the refrigerator. He took out the bag, and displaying a streak of masochism he didn't know he had, he began to unload it.

A roll of paper towels. Practical, his Shelly. Not *his* Shelly, damn it. Just...Shelly. A box of spaghetti. A bag of tomatoes. She'd planned to make her own sauce. Resourceful, his—damn!

A bunch of celery. Two onions. If they both ate them it wouldn't matter. Ice cream, soggy now. Chocolate chip, her favorite kind, not his. He opened the box and slowly poured the creamy fluid down the drain.

In the bottom of the bag were the candles. Blue, his favorite color, not hers. Their faint scent taunted him as he carried them out into the dining room and set them into the holders. Pulling a match from his pocket, he lit them. Then he turned off the lights to sit in the dark and watch the flames flicker and dance while he carried out the charade of dinner for two.

He came awake to the faint scent of candle smoke and the sound of the phone ringing. He was still sitting in the chair. The incessant peal of the telephone filled him with a chilly sense of dread. He groped for a light switch. Four o'clock in the morning. His nerves jangling, he went to the phone.

WHEN JUSTIN WALKED into the hospital waiting room on the fourth floor of the cardiac unit a half hour later, Morley met him with a gray face.

"Your father wasn't that bad when we brought him but he seems to be losing ground. He's drifting in and out of unconsciousness."

"Does Paul know?"

"I called him after I called you."

Justin nodded. "Thank you for taking such good care of us."

"If I'd taken better care of your father—"

"Nonsense." It was Justin who should have taken better care of his father. He should have taken better care of everyone. He felt numb, guilty, ashamed.

"I want to see him." He repeated it again to the nurse who shook her head. "Ten minutes only. Family only. One at a time."

Gently, Morley nodded his head. "Go on. He'll be glad to see you."

"I'm not sure of that—"

"I am," Morley said firmly. "You just go along now and stop worrying."

The tubes in Strom's nose, hooked to his arm, seemed an obscene reminder that Strom's destiny was no longer in his hands. Filled with a thousand conflicting emotions—pain, desperation, empty loneliness—Justin approached his father's bed.

He took hold of the hand that had never once clasped his in love, staring at the stubby mature fingers, lightly covered with graying hair, as if he had never seen them before. His throat was full. "It's all right, Dad. Honest. I was a pigheaded fool saying the things I did." He bent over the bed and pressed his forehead to his father's hand, unsure whether he was giving strength, or seeking it. "Please, just forget everything I said and live. Oh, dear God, please live."

Strom heard the sound of forgiveness. He opened his eyes and saw the golden head of his son bent over him. And suddenly it seemed the most important thing in the world for him to do was to show his boy—this man—that he understood and he, too, forgave.

"I...love...you, son. Always have. Always will. Sorry I never told you. Sorry for...so many things. Don't know if I'll have time now...but...meant well. Always meant well. Like to make everything up to you. Just need...time."

Justin made an unintelligible sound and pressed his father's hand to his mouth. "We'll have time, Dad. All the time in the world."

The nurse went in to tell the young man he had to leave. She was used to seeing people, even men, with tears in their eyes. She wasn't used to seeing the same men with tears in their eyes smiling at each other like two idiots. Not only that, her patient's pulse had stabilized and his breathing slowed.

"Evidently your son was just the medicine you needed, Mr. Corbett. He'd better stay around to give you another dose in an hour." Briskly efficient, she nodded to Justin to leave.

Justin gripped his father's hand. "I'll be back, Dad."

Strom gazed at his son, his eyes full. "I know you will, son."

It was hard to let go of his father's hand, hard to turn his back and leave. Still, Strom looked better. The nurse had said he was better. Heartened, Justin gave Strom a determined smile and strode across the room to let himself out.

But outside in the corridor he leaned against the wall, closed his eyes and knew he'd never felt more alone. He needed Shelly. Dear heaven, how he needed her. He was an imperfect man whose life was crumbling into bits, but he'd give everything he had in this world if she'd walk back into his life one more time.

As if by magic he seemed to feel her hand in his. Justin opened his eyes, and she was standing in front of him, her eyes cautious. She was waiting. Waiting for him to make the first move.

He reached for her, wrapping his arms around her in a desperate attempt to take her into his heart, muttering an inarticulate groan of gratitude.

"How is he, Justin?" she managed to ask when he eased his hold on her.

"Better. Ah, lady. I thought you'd left me. You took everything—"

"You needed time to be alone and think. I needed time to cool down."

"How did you know I wouldn't last very long at being noble?"

She gave him a knowing look. "Sometimes loving means knowing when *not* to listen."

"And I thought it was a disadvantage to be loved by a woman who knows me so well." He hugged her tighter. "You even knew how much I needed you just now."

"No, I didn't. Morley did."

"Morley?"

"He had the hospital call me." She leaned away from him, her hand going to his face. "It seems, my indiscreet love, Morley expected me to be there when he called you in the middle of the night and when I wasn't, he...Justin what are you doing?"

He was dragging her along like a demented man—like a Roman with a Sabine woman. He halted abruptly in front of the chair where Morley sat with one shiny shoe crossed over the other.

"We're getting married," said Justin, with the air of a man announcing world peace.

With immutable calm, Morley studied them both over his nose. "High time, I should say."

"High time? High time? Why, you've bedeviled Shelly since the first moment she walked in the door."

Morley raised one dark eyebrow. "How else was I going to get a stubborn Corbett man to see he'd met the one woman who was his match in every way?"

Justin shook his head, amusement dancing in his eyes. "Morley, you're the biggest fraud of us all."

Morley gave him a wise, all-knowing look. "If I had approved of her, she wouldn't have done for you at all, now would she?"

Justin stared at Morley for a long, quiet moment. Then he threw back his head and laughed in glorious relief. To Shelly it was a most beautiful, wonderful sound.

"You're dangerous, my man," said Justin. What an idiot he'd been. He'd been surrounded for years by people who loved him, he just hadn't been bright enough to see it.

Still holding Shelly, Justin reached for Morley and pulled him up into his arms, making a tight circle of love with the two people who understood him best—the man who'd been his surrogate mother and the woman who was to be his wife. And he knew that as soon as both Mel and Strom were well again, the clouds that had darkened his life would roll away, leaving sunshine as far as the eye could see.

EPILOGUE

"JUSTIN, DO SPEAK to your father. If he feeds Janna any more candy, she won't want Christmas dinner."

"You speak to him, love. You have more power over him than I do." Justin leaned back in his chair looking smugly superior, just like a lawyer who'd delivered the perfect rebuttal.

Shelly had long ago learned that frontal assault was the only way to deal with Corbett men. She marched to the chair where Strom sat cozily ensconced and reached for the glass dish of mints and nuts the doting grandfather was gleefully offering to the two-year-old cherub with red hair and green eyes. Before Janna could reach her baby fingers out for another candy, her mother whisked the dish out of her reach.

At Janna's whimper of disappointment, Shelly went down on her haunches to talk to her daughter. Frontal assault worked best on this Corbett woman, too, the first to be born in three generations. "If you have any more candy, you won't be able to eat your dinner and then Morley will be very angry at Mommy. You don't want Morley to be angry at Mommy, do you?"

Soberly, her green eyes dark with concern for her beloved mother, Janna shook her head, her red-gold curls bouncing.

From his place in the chair, Justin smiled at his daughter. "There she is, the third generation of Corbetts to be kept on the straight and narrow path by Morley. Must be some kind of record. What do you think, Mel?''

''Absolutely.'' Mel was standing by the mantel next to the Medal of Honor. He had, with therapy, recovered his speech and mobility, although Shelly teased him by saying they hardly noticed the difference. Mel was still quiet, but no less an important presence. Strom spoiled Janna outrageously, but when she fell down and scratched her knee, it was Mel she ran to for soothing and rocking.

The secret that Mel and Strom had kept for so long was now shared among the four of them, binding them together in a strong family unit. Strom had agreed with Justin that there was nothing to be gained by revealing the truth except unpleasant notoriety for all of them.

After Strom had had the bypass surgery he needed, he'd retired from the House of Representatives—to ease the stress in his life-style, he'd said. Shelly harbored the suspicion that Strom wanted to spend the precious days left to him getting acquainted with his granddaughter... and reacquainted with his son.

Strom's friendship with Mel had grown even stronger. Eased of the terrible burden of secrecy, Strom faced the future with more confidence, while Mel, too, seemed more content since his daughter had learned the truth.

Strom had said nothing when Justin turned down Hanley's offer to become his successor as the district attorney and left public life to enter into private practice. He'd made his peace with Justin that day in the hospital and he was doing everything in his power to hold on to that rapport. Justin was a man to be proud of, doing much better than Strom had thought he could do in the first few years of having his own legal practice. His daughter-in-law was a woman to be proud of, too. Shelly managed to juggle career and motherhood with aplomb. She continued to run the soaring school and maintain her license both as a sailplane instructor and an aerobatic pilot, even while she took excellent care of Janna.

"Shelly, when did you say Paul and Kim were coming?" asked Strom for the fourth time since they'd gathered in the den.

"Sometime after five," Shelly said patiently. "They're stopping every two hours on the road to break up the trip because of Kim's pregnancy. Don't fret, Dad. They'll be here in time for dinner."

"Well, they better be. A man likes to have his family around him at Christmas."

Shelly looked at her husband, sitting there too comfortable and complacent. "On your feet, you lazy lump," she said to him, tugging at his hand. "It's time to pour the wine."

Justin looked up into his wife's face, his own suffused with indulgent love. "Nag. It's only been three years and she's turned into a nag."

"What do you expect a woman to do when she gets dragged into a household of stubborn men with only her small daughter as backup support? Nagging's my best defense."

Justin went to the desk, poured the wine and began passing it around. When he reached her, his eyes gleamed. "Oh, you've learned other interesting defenses along the way," he said in a low voice for her ears alone.

She lifted the glass to her lips, the old heat suffusing her body. He still had the power to bring her to stinging life with a word or a look. "You're incurable," she murmured back to him.

"I certainly hope so. Don't you?" He raised one golden eyebrow, the picture of male satisfaction, his mouth lifting in a smile, his eyes reminding her of the lovemaking they'd enjoyed that afternoon when the grandfathers had taken Janna to the airfield to see the B-17 bomber.

Shelly's cheeks filled with heat. She hoped Strom and her father would attribute her color to the wine.

Strom collected his granddaughter into his lap, arranging her green velvet dress carefully so that it wouldn't wrinkle. Then he raised his glass. "To Christmas at Corbett Hill. May there be many more of them."

"Hear, hear," said Justin, his eyes meeting Shelly's.

She lifted her glass and drank the wine, knowing that it was love that left the sweetness lingering on her tongue.

Harlequin American Romance®

SUMMER.

The sun, the surf, the sand . . .

One relaxing month by the sea was all Zoe, Diana and Gracie ev
expected from their four-week stays at Gull Cottage, the luxuriou
East Hampton mansion. They never thought they'd soon be sha
ing those long summer days—or hot summer nights—with
special man. They never thought that what they found at the beac
would change their lives forever. But as Boris, Gull Cottage's re
ident mynah bird said: "Beware of summer romances. . . ."

Join Zoe, Diana and Gracie for the summer of their lives. Don't mi
the GULL COTTAGE trilogy in American Romance: #301 *Charm*
Circle by Robin Francis (July 1989), #305 *Mother Knows Best*
Barbara Bretton (August 1989) and #309 *Saving Grace* by An
McAllister (September 1989).

GULL COTTAGE—because a month can be the start of forever .

If you missed #301 *Charmed Circle*, #305 *Mother Knows Best* or #309 *Saving Grace* and wo
like to order it, send your name, address, zip or postal code along with a check or mo
order for $2.75 plus 75¢ postage and handling ($1.00 in Canada) for *each book orde*
payable to Harlequin Reader Service, to:

In the U.S.
Harlequin Reader Service
901 Fuhrmann Blvd.
Box 1325
Buffalo, NY 14269-1325

In Canada
Harlequin Reader Service
P.O. Box 609
Fort Erie, Ontario
L2A 5X3

GULLC

Have You Ever Wondered If You Could Write A Harlequin Novel?

Here's great news—Harlequin is offering a series of cassette tapes to help you do just that. Written by Harlequin editors, these tapes give practical advice on how to make your characters—and your story—come alive. There's a tape for each contemporary romance series Harlequin publishes.

Mail order only

All sales final

SWEEPSTAKES RULES & REGULATIONS

NO PURCHASE NECESSARY TO ENTER OR RECEIVE A PRIZE

1 To enter and join the Reader Service, check off the "YES" box on your Sweepstakes Entry Form and return to Harlequin Reader Service. If you do not wish to join the Reader Service but wish to enter the Sweepstakes only, check off the "NO" box on your Sweepstakes Entry Form. Incomplete and/or inaccurate entries are ineligible for that section or sections(s) of prizes. Not responsible for mutilated or unreadable entries or inadvertent printing errors. Mechanically reproduced entries are null and void. Be sure to also qualify for the Bonus Sweepstakes. See rule #3 on how to enter

2. Either way, your unique Sweepstakes number will be compared against the list of winning numbers generated at random by the computer. In the event that all prizes are not claimed, random drawings will be held from all entries received from all presentations to award all unclaimed prizes. All cash prizes are payable in U.S. funds. This is in addition to any free, surprise or mystery gifts that might be offered. The following prizes are offered: *Grand Prize (1) $1,000,000 Annuity; First Prize (1) $35,000; Second Prize (1) $10,000; Third Prize (3) $5,000; Fourth Prize (10) $1,000; Fifth Prize (25) $500; Sixth Prize (5,000) $5.
   * This Sweepstakes contains a Grand Prize offering of a $1,000,000 annuity. Winner may elect to receive $25,000 a year for 40 years without interest; totalling $1,000,000 or $350,000 in one cash payment. Entrants may cancel Reader Service at any time without cost or obligation to buy.

3. Extra Bonus Prize: This presentation offers two extra bonus prizes valued at $30,000 each to be awarded in a random drawing from all entries received. To qualify, scratch off the silver on your Lucky Keys. If the registration numbers match, you are eligible for the prize offering.

4. Versions of this Sweepstakes with different graphics will be offered in other mailings or at retail outlets by Torstar Corp. and its affiliates. This promotion is being conducted under the supervision of Marden-Kane, Inc., an independent judging organization. By entering this Sweepstakes, each entrant accepts and agrees to be bound by these rules and the decisions of the judges, which shall be final and binding. Odds of winning in the random drawing are dependent upon the total number of entries received. Taxes, if any, are the sole responsibility of the winners. Prizes are nontransferable. All entries must be received by March 31, 1990. The drawing will take place on or about April 30, 1990 at the offices of Marden-Kane, Inc., Lake Success, N.Y

5. This offer is open to residents of the U.S., United Kingdom and Canada, 18 years or older, except employees of Torstar Corp., its affiliates, subsidiaries, Marden-Kane and all other agencies and persons connected with conducting this Sweepstakes. All Federal, State and local laws apply. Void wherever prohibited or restricted by law

6. Winners will be notified by mail and may be required to execute an affidavit of eligibility and release, which must be returned within 14 days after notification. Canadian winners will be required to answer a skill-testing question. Winners consent to the use of their name, photograph and/or likeness for advertising and publicity in conjunction with this or similar promotions, without additional compensation.

7 For a list of our most current major prize winners, send a stamped, self-addressed envelope to: Winners List, c/o Marden-Kane, Inc., P.O. Box 701, Sayreville, N.J. 08871

If Sweepstakes entry form is missing, please print your name and address on a 3" × 5" piece of plain paper and send to:

In the U.S.	In Canada
Sweepstakes Entry	Sweepstakes Entry
901 Fuhrmann Blvd.	P.O. Box 609
P.O. Box 1867	Fort Erie, Ontario
Buffalo, NY 14269-1867	L2A 5X3

LTY-H89
© 1988 Harlequin Enterprises Ltd.